Zuriel

Ralph Owens

TEACH Services, Inc.
P U B L I S H I N G

www.TEACHServices.com • (800) 367-1844

Copyright © 2020 Ralph Owens

Copyright © 2020 TEACH Services, Inc.

ISBN-13: 978-1-4796-1128-7 (Paperback)

ISBN-13: 978-1-4796-1129-4 (ePub)

Library of Congress Control Number: 2020906304

Any references to historical events, real people or real places are used fictitiously. Names, characters and places are products of the author's imagination.

TEACH Services, Inc.
PUBLISHING
www.TEACHServices.com • (800) 367-1844

Dedication

To my mom and dad, who started telling me
the rudiments of this story from my earliest years.
Without their tutoring, this book would never have been written.

Table of Contents

Foreword

Dear Reader,

This is your invitation to pop some corn, sit by the fire, put your feet up and lose yourself in a retelling of the greatest drama the universe has ever seen! It is a participatory drama, similar to those who-dun-its where the cast interacts with the audience and appears to be part of the audience.

You will probably finish reading this book in a short time. I'm fortunate. It's been my delight for so many hours. I've enjoyed pondering and dreaming about the scenes of which I've written. I hope they give you as much pleasure as they've given me.

As I wrote, Barney, the cat, would sometimes lie on my lap. His purrer hummed as he contentedly slept while I tried to type-n-click without disturbing him. He loved to talk to me or to anyone who would listen. When I'd tell him what I was doing and what I was writing, he always seemed so interested.

One day, Barney began drinking copious quantities of water—nearly two quarts a day. The kitty-doc diagnosed diabetes and prescribed insulin injections and a specially formulated diet. His kitty-doc taught me how to wield the syringe (my hands shook the first time), what an insulin overdose looks like, and how to tell if he was responding to treatment.

Most of this did not bother Barney, not even the shots, but one thing made him most upset. The kitty-doc instructed me, "Do not leave food out for him all the time. Inject him and feed him at the same time, twelve hours apart. That is the best for a diabetic cat." I chose 7 a.m. and 7 p.m.

So Barney, who was used to grazing whenever he wanted to, suddenly was deprived of his daytime and midnight snacks. I'd get home from work and he'd meet me at the door, talking nonstop. "Meow, meow, meow," he'd say politely as he ran over to his empty dish. I'd answer, "Not now, Barney. Not until 7:00."

"Meow! Meow! MEOW!" He was a bit less polite now! I'd sit down and he'd come climb all over me, his claws digging into my pants and my legs, my arms and my shoulders.

"RREOU! RREOU!"

"Not (ouch!) now, Barney. (Ow!) Sorry, (ouch!) Barney (will you let go!), you have to wait (yeow, that hurts!) until 7:00."

We had plenty of these fragmented conversations. Barney was very … … well … … *persistent* is a kind word. (Any cat "owner" knows what I mean!)

Then, one day, during one of these conversations, I looked at him and said, "Barney, 'my thoughts are not your thoughts and my ways are not your ways.' You just have to trust me."

Those familiar words from Isaiah (55:8, 9) caused a vivid picture to flash through my mind. Yes, I am a superior creature to Barney. I know many things which Barney will never understand.

In like manner, our God is a Superior Being to us and just as Barney never will understand diabetes and insulin, computers or cars, there are things God knows, oh so clearly, that we will never understand. We, too, just have to trust Him.

During my daughter's first year of college, she returned to visit her high school. In talking with her friends, she said, "College is very different from high school." Their response was something like, "School is school. How different could it be?" She said, "I can't describe the difference. You have to experience it. When you are there, you will know what I mean!"

Her words have echoed in my mind as I have thought about Lucifer's rebellion. It seems to me that many of the results of that rebellion were unexplainable to a perfect universe without experiencing them.

One of my pastors asked in a sermon, "Have you ever thought about how handicapped God was as He tried to explain the results of rebellion to the angels? 'If you rebel,' He said, 'you will die,' and the angels all looked at Him and said, 'Huh? Die? What does that mean?'"

How could God have explained wife-beating, child abuse, nuclear war, anthrax, AIDS and death to a universe where no one had ever cried or even seen pain?

Lucifer claimed to have a better way and, simply on the strength of that claim, a third of the angels rebelled along with him. It seems to me that God could not answer the charges against Him and His government in any other way than by permitting Satan to show the sad results of his rebellion through a graphic demonstration.

My pastor's question began my asking, "What do the angels know and when and how did they learn it?" The result is this book. I've picked up other tidbits here and there. I borrowed one scene from a pastor who wove the story of David and Uriah meeting in heaven into a sermon. I had envisioned several similar scenes, but none fit my story line. His fit perfectly.

As I have written this story, I have simply tried to imagine what the various scenes must have been (or will be) like. I do not claim anything other than vivid creativity while expanding on what scripture supplies. The basic story line is fundamentally accurate.

You may disagree with me on the details that I have created. That is fine. They are simply my feeble attempts to describe scenes which none of us has ever seen—a risky job at best! All I ask is that you do not let these minor disagreements prevent you from seeing the awesomeness of our God and the overriding theme of this cosmic drama.

Barney lived a long good life and adjusted (more or less) to the new diet and the strict timing of his meals. Contrary to conventional wisdom, we were able to use diet to manage his diabetes without using insulin.

Before he died, Barney told me that he hoped (Yes, I'm sure that's what I heard him say!) that as you read this story, you will be able to see our God in a new light, one which attracts you to Him. This is my prayer.

The Author

Acknowledgment

Thank you, Maylan Schurch,
For your ever-ready encouragements.
For your constant, cheerful critiques.
For your belief that I could do this.
Without your assurances
And repeated reassurances,
This book would not exist.

Shalem, City of Peace

It's Assembly time! Assemblies aren't the boring things you might imagine. They occur a few times every orbit. Eli Mehlek, Michael, and Lucifer always use them to create delightful times of joy and peace. I can't wait! Sotai and I often fly over together. Sotai is Lucifer's gardener. I'm Zuriel, his mansionkeeper.

As usual, Sotai is working in The Garden. He is a genius gardener. His rosahedrons and parynippers are always perfectly placed and exquisitely trained. The taller shrubs gently stroke the mansion's walls. The shorter plants are casually scattered in front of them. The casualness is a sham. The placements are chosen using Sotai's delicate, careful eye for beauty. The paths through his arbor curve and twist invitingly. He always coaxes extra fragrance from his blooms to perfume the atmosphere. Sometimes it's a subtle aroma. Sometimes it demands attention.

No other mansion's landscaping is quite as gorgeous as Lucifer's. It's appropriate. Lucifer is the Archangel. His position is highest in all of Shalem, except for Deity.

Sotai is bending over his persimples and I catch his eye.

"Hi ya, Zuriel, 'tis a ravishing, radiant, resplendent Rigelday 'tisn't it?" Sotai squeaks out in his odd, charming voice. Two more different angels you'll never find. Sotai is brash and excitable. Me, I'm more reserved and calm. Maybe that's why we get along so well. His high-pitched voice contains some alluring oddities. Perhaps that makes him interesting to talk to!

"Oh, Sotai, how do you ever come up with such phrases as 'ravishing, radiant, resplendent Rigelday' anyway?"

"It's called amazing, amusing alliteration, my friend, with just a twist of the rhyme. You'd do well to learn how to alliterate—yourself."

We chat as Sotai wipes his hands and brushes the dirt off his knees. We fly towards the Assembly Bowl. Shalem shines magnificently below us.

The angelic mansions are strewn as far as I can see. The city is a panorama spreading out to the skyline, its edges many strods away. Beyond, the country beckons. I love visiting the woodland when my work is finished. I also enjoy being in the capital and working for Lucifer.

"Are you ready to sing the new anthem we've been practicing?"

"Aw, easy, breezy, fun, frolic and frivolity! My part is superbly, seriously simple. Didn't even have to practice it more than once."

I laugh at Sotai's alliteration. "It is a fantastic song. The four sections complement each other perfectly. This is the first time we'll sing it in Assembly. Lucifer's directing brings out the music's best. We're ultrafortunate to work in his mansion."

The Assembly carillon peals over Shalem as we join the rest of the angels; it's nearly time to start.

The carillon's chiming spills from the Assembly Bowl throughout Shalem

The choir enjoys this new chorale— the antiphony of the different parts—the calling of the challenge—the echoing of the response. It is a stirring anthem. Lucifer divided us into four troupes located in the four corners of the Assembly Bowl. The anthem rotates through the four groups. Each sings a line, answering the previous line. It's almost as if each troupe is daring the others to surpass their efforts. The trumpet fanfare is starting as we take our places. Sotai's troupe is opposite mine.

* * * *

Listen to the trumpet fanfare—the flourish so magnificent!
Listen to the carillon's resounding—its reverberations so sonorous!
Listen to the lead seraph's challenge— "Awake, O cherub!"
Listen to the lead cherub's answer— "Arise, O seraph!"

The climax fades into stillness. The trumpets quiet. The carillon dampens. The singers' voices hush. All is silent as we wait for Eli-Mehlek's response. Assembly tradition includes Eli-Mehlek's gracious comments about our praises. His cordial responses always thrill us as we learn we pleased Him again.

"Thank you, cherubim. Thank you, seraphim." Eli-Mehlek's voice rumbles from the throne, "That is an excellent piece—a truly delightful work. The four-troupe layout is perfect for that psalm. I appreciate the preparations, the rehearsals, all of which perfected your presentation."

Awake, O Cherub
Arise, O Seraph
To Our God, we will sing
To Eli-Mehlek, we will praise

For He is mighty
For He is strong
For His right arm upholds the heavens
And His left hand restrains the Universe

In His strength, He holds the flower
And in His might, He carries the babe
For His strength is His mercy
And His might is His grace

Our God is merciful
Our God is gracious
Our God is faithful
Our God is Eli-Mehlek

Merciful
Gracious
Faithful
Honorable
Eli-Mehlek is our God

Hear, O Seraph
Give ear, O Cherub
Go, search it in the heavens
Go, seek it in the cosmos
To right column

From left column
No Seraph can see another god
No Cherub can find another deus
None can observe another creator
There is none other like Him

In His strength He holds the flower
And in His might He carries the babe
For His strength is His mercy
And His might is His grace

Our God is merciful
Our God is gracious
Our God is faithful
Our God is Eli-Mehlek

Tell it in the heavens
Speak it past the quasars
Proclaim it among the stars
Voice it through the galaxies

Spread it abroad, you who sail the Univers
Fling it abroad, you who cruise the cosmc

Tell it
Say it
Sing it
Shout it

Shout it
Our God is Eli-Mehlek

We fall on our faces and worship Eli-Mehlek with love and adoration in our hearts. The Assembly starts—gloriously. Lucifer directs the rest of the Assembly from one glorious theme to another even more glorious theme—from one praise to a higher praise to even higher praises.

Through it all, Eli-Mehlek encircles us with His beams of light, bright and glittery, surrounding the angelic hosts, drawing us even closer to Himself. The unity of the Assembly is palpable. All hearts concur in harmony. It is wonderful! I love Assemblies!

* * * *

Lucifer's heart is in turmoil. He is experiencing strange, unknown feelings, feelings arising in the last few orbits. His thoughts are jumbled. Recently, Deity is in executive conclave many times. In his position as Covering Cherub, Lucifer observes much other angels don't see. He's seen Michael going to Eli-Mehlek's throne. He's seen Ruash draw the flaming curtain of mystery around them.

His thoughts are jumbled. *Michael? Why Michael?* To Lucifer, Michael doesn't seem special. He ambles through the streets of Shalem appearing as an ordinary angel. He stops and chats with any angel in sight. Michael sings in the choir, as if he were an ordinary angel, and takes His place in the middle row, towards the right, His voice blending with the others. He is nothing like Eli-Mehlek—with the fire and flame which Lucifer covers—so the other angels are able to endure His glory. The angels don't need shielding from Michael's glory. He doesn't sit on a throne. He appears like an ordinary angel!

> *After the Assembly, all hearts harmonize, except one*

Lucifer's tangled thoughts continue. *So, if Michael is just an ordinary angel, why is He being included behind the curtain of mystery, in executive conclave with Ruash and Eli-Mehlek? Why aren't I, Lucifer, the Archangel—why aren't I included behind the flaming curtain of mystery?* Slowly, thoughtfully, he flies home and sits in his favorite chair—the big ivory chair—his mind quite vexed over this slight to his honor.

* * * *

"Hi, Zuriel! You look ultra happy today," Lucifer greets as I fly in. I'd paused and talked to Jokim, another of my friends.

"Of course, Lucifer. You look exceptionally bright today yourself."

"Well, of course. With your great mansionkeeping, this mansion always compounds my cheer. You constantly make it look so completely charming!"

"Well, t-t-thank you, Lucifer," I stammer.

It is really great working in Lucifer's mansion. He is always most wonderfully kind and gracious, yet today his words startle me. Usually he isn't this profuse with his compliments.

"But all praise goes to Eli-Mehlek," I hasten to add, "I simply use the abilities He gave me."

"Well, yes, of course. However, you're the one who uses those abilities as you exert yourself!"

The quietness lingers for some time. I continue my work as Lucifer sits quietly, thinking. I dust the golden table, my eyes, as usual, admiring the gorgeous jewels with which Eli-Mehlek bedecked Lucifer—rubies, topaz, emeralds, chrysolite, onyx, jasper, sapphires, turquoise, beryl.

"Lucifer's charisma surpasses the attraction of all other angels, either seraph or cherub," I murmur to myself, tearing my eyes away.

I wing my way to the garden and pluck some flowers. The silver chalice, encrusted with diamonds and trimmed with amethyst, is a delightful vase for these blossoms. I arrange them carefully and set the chalice on the royal-blue linen on the table. Lucifer smiles, his thanks apparent on his face.

After what seems like a long time, Lucifer rouses himself, rising, saying, "Well, I'd better fly on over to Gabriel's place. We are already planning the next Assembly."

"Fly swiftly, Lucifer, and Eli-Mehlek go with you."

He departs.

There is something indefinable, something odd about his manner.

It troubles me. Through the window, I watch him soar over the trees, his diamonds glittering in the sunlight. As he vanishes, there is a nebulous question in my heart. Never before have his words been a cause for me to worry. Something isn't normal, yet nothing is identifiably wrong.

I slowly saunter into the garden, feeling the need to talk with Sotai. I often go out and chat with him. Sometimes he comes to visit with me. As Lucifer's two personal assistants, we discuss anything and everything all the time. At times, we help each other with our work.

"Hi, Zuriel. 'Tis a tip-top of the morning 'tisn't it?" Sotai squawks out as he looks up.

"Yes, Sotai, yes it is."

Sotai stops in the middle of transplanting a rosahedron. He has started several in a nursery bed. Now is the time to replant them in between the lilians.

"What's the matter, Zuriel? You don't sound very snappy. Now what could possibly be worrying those azure eyes of yours?"

Only Sotai would recognize that something worries me.

"I'm not certain, Sotai. Something was odd about Lucifer just now. Nothing was wrong—yet something wasn't normal."

"Heh-heh! Lighten up! Laugh a little! Eli-Mehlek is on His throne and all's well with the Universe."

"Yes, of course. With Eli-Mehlek ruling, all is well. But tell me, Sotai, have you ever seen Lucifer just sit for a long time, thinking, never saying a word?"

"Not in an octet of orbits, I haven't … Did he do that just now?"

"Uh-huh, then he just up and flew over to Gabriel's place."

"Well, I'll be plantin' parynippers on Pleiades! That is unusual. I don't know anything about that." He chuckles and the conversation turns to other matters.

Parynippers! Rosahedrons! Persimples! How gorgeous—absolutely resplendent—his garden is. Sotai resumes his transplanting as I step back inside the mansion. Soon I'm immersed in my work and Lucifer's unusual behavior fades from my mind.

Our activities continue quite normally for some time. We are all busy doing our work. Lucifer bustles in and out of the mansion, as he always does—going wherever Eli-Mehlek sends him, doing whatever Eli-Mehlek asks him to do.

* * * *

Sotai looked up, the dirt strewn around. Resheph was gently hovering just over his shoulder, an odd look on his face.

> *Many angels hear rumors insinuating Eli-Mehlek is hiding something and doesn't care about the angel's welfare. Some find the rumors credible. Who is right?*

"Sotai, could we go fly somewhere?"

"Absolutely, positively, unquestionably! What's up?"

Sotai brushed the dirt off his knees and hands.

They ascended rapidly, heading towards the country.

"Sotai, I just need to talk to someone. Have you been hearing these rumors? Do you know they are being spread everywhere? Do you believe them? I am torn inside. Are they reliable?"

"Aw, Resheph, reduce, relieve, relax your mind. Eli-Mehlek is on the throne. All is well in the Universe."

"I know that. But He hides behind the Covering Cherubs. Why do you suppose He does that? Is there something He doesn't want us to see?"

"I don't know. I've never, ever asked any questions like that. Why are you asking? What are you hearing?"

"Perhaps Eli-Mehlek doesn't have our best interests in His heart. Maybe there are some good things He's hiding from us. Maybe that's why He shrouds Himself. I can't imagine what these good things might be, can you?"

"No, I can't either."

They landed on a beautiful knoll covered with rifs and fliods. Sotai's hands still had clusters of dirt clinging to them. Absently, he rubbed them together, scraping the clumps to the ground. The place was charming.

The ground covered with yellow, pink and blue fliods. The rifs towered skyward, majestically pointing toward the stars, their boughs layered nobly upwards. They seated themselves and quietly conversed.

"We really don't know, do we, Sotai?" Resheph analyzed. "Lucifer is a Covering Cherub. I wonder if he would have any answers. You work for him, could you ask him?"

* * * *

Sotai swoops into the mansion, garbling about a remarkable conversation he'd had with Lucifer. His story reminds me of Lucifer's unusual comment and profuse praise to me—the one that flustered me. Lucifer told Sotai that his garden was superbly glorious. Sotai thinks Lucifer's the best governor. They talked for some time. Lucifer seemed quite interested in what Sotai was thinking. He asked Sotai if he'd heard any unusual rumors. He hadn't.

I remember another day when I was sweeping the floor as Lucifer came into the mansion.

"Hi, Zuriel! It is sure wonderful how you do your work."

Suddenly my feathers stood on end. It was the same odd tone of voice Lucifer used before. I tried to deflect the flattery. "Eli-Mehlek indeed gave me wonderful mansion-keeping abilities."

"Eli-Mehlek is glorious, isn't He?"

"Absolutely!" I answered with fervency.

"Zuriel, you get out and visit with other angels, don't you?"

"Yes." I was suddenly cautious, "Sometimes."

"Have you heard any of them asking any unusual questions?"

"No ... What kind of unusual questions?"

"Well, that's just the problem. I really don't know what kinds of questions nor who is asking them. I've heard that they may be asking questions about Eli-Mehlek. Is He fair? Is He just?"

"Who would ask questions like that? The answer is obvious. Of course Eli-Mehlek is fair and just. Why would anyone be questioning that?"

"I'm not at all certain anyone is. But then, that's what I've heard. I'd like to know who it is, so I could set them straight!"

Lucifer glided into the other room and I heard him singing praises to Eli-Mehlek. Deity gave him the most marvelous singing voice, er ... voices, that is. He can sing four parts simultaneously! Not many angels have that ability. His harmonious voices magnify his praises to Eli-Mehlek.

His song soothed my worried heart. But who, I wondered, who could be questioning Eli-Mehlek.

I recount my conversation with Lucifer to Sotai.

"Well, I'll be pickin' persimples in Pargoland. Lucifer told you *that*? I've heard rumors similar to that one. Who was it I heard talking? Maybe it was Gabriel's gardener? I dunno. I never thought about it before I heard the rumors, but maybe the queryin' questioners are quizzin' quite correctly. Perhaps Eli-Mehlek isn't fair." With that, Sotai flies off to get some fresh fertilizer for his garden.

I hover, my mouth agape, my mind awhirl with startlement. Who could be asking these questions? And why? And, unbelievably, it sounds as if even Sotai is wondering if the rumors are accurate!

* * * *

Sotai's garden was disarrayed. Well, not in terrible shape, just little things that were not perfect. He had been talking to many angels. They came and he would fly off with them. Oreb was one of them. Oreb's a fellow gardener like Sotai. The two gardeners chatted about flowers and trees and other good things like that. Finally, Oreb paused for a moment.

"Have you heard any more rumors?"

"Yes, many; what have you heard?"

"One of the rumors is that Michael is being promoted to equality with Eli-Mehlek. That Lucifer is being bypassed in favor of Michael. I'd think Lucifer to be a better confidant than Michael. Lucifer sings so beautifully and shields Shalem from Eli-Mehlek's glory. Perhaps Lucifer is the one who should be promoted."

"I hadn't heard that one before. I hadn't thought about Michael before this ... this ... this spate of rumors we've been hearing. Lucifer is a great boss. He always lets me plant the garden the way I want to do it."

* * * *

Micha coasts into the front yard. He is one of the messenger angels, flying across the vast reaches of the Universe, carrying messages to beings on the planets. He's my chum and frequently flies by just to visit. I often visit his place, too.

"Hi, Zuriel! It's good to see you!"

"Peace, Micha, and Eli-Mehlek be with you. Where do you come from?"

"I've been over to Neptorium. I needed to take a message to the commander."

"That's out on the edge of the Universe, is it not?"

"Yeah, it's a long jaunt. I'm glad to be back."

"Come in. Let's sit and be calm for a while."

We walk into the mansion's great room and find a couple of chairs, chattering all the while. The conversation is robust ... catching up on all the news. It is so good to be with Micha. The update is mostly complete when Micha's nervousness becomes apparent. He stands and looks out the window. His wings tense, his feathers dishevel a bit, his eyes dart back and forth. I wonder what's racing along behind those brown eyes. I wait unobtrusively for him to articulate whatever is stirring within him.

Finally, "Zuriel, you are close to Lucifer, are you not? He talks to you, doesn't he?"

"Yes."

"Has he ever mentioned the rumors? ... About Eli-Mehlek's government?"

"Yes. A few times."

"Does he seem normal while speaking of them?"

"What do you mean?"

"Twice he spoke to me about them. One time, the first, I think, he seemed indefinably different. I'm not certain what I mean. I. I could not even guess what I was feeling. I'm asking you since you see him so often."

"You too, Micha? I wondered if I was dreaming. Twice, I've felt something was wrong. However, like you, I could not understand what I was feeling."

"Whew! I've mentioned this to a few other messenger angels. None of them perceived anything unusual about him. They tell me I'm just imagining things. I've wondered if I'm fantasizing. You feel it, too? I'm not weird?"

"Only twice. Since we don't even know what to call it, let's keep it between us."

"Sure. Sounds good. I'm going to fly. I have things to do. Come on over sometime and we can see if there are any more clues."

Micha's mansion is just a couple of strods across the treetops. I watch him soar up and over to his villa.

In the quiet, my uneasiness deepens. I must find some time to talk to Lucifer. He'll answer Sotai's and Micha's questions. But always Lucifer is busy trying to quell the rumors. I never have much chance to talk to him. He rarely comes back to his mansion. When he does, he seems distracted. Sometimes he tells me what he's found out and how he's set some angel straight ... but always as he speeds in or out of the door. My mind reels with the thoughts the rumors incite. Sotai appears to believe some of the rumors. Me? I can hardly believe my ears. Yet, the more I listen, the more it seems that many angels are finding the rumors credible. Can they all be wrong?

Deity

Sotai flaps in. His babbling even more garbled than normal.

"Oh, hi ya, Zuriel. Guess what?"

"With you, Sotai, it's hard to predict!" I laugh. His feathers are more akimbo than usual. It's almost as if he can't persuade them to lie correctly, even if he wants them to do so which generally doesn't seem to be his desire.

"I'm going over to Resheph's mansion!" He speaks as if it is a huge honor.

Resheph lives on the far side of Shalem, many strods away. His mansion is much smaller than Lucifer's. He doesn't have a mansionkeeper. I don't get over there often. I don't imagine Sotai's visits are too frequent either. *What's this all about?*

"So? Is that enough to cause such a major mental muddle in you?"

"Amazing! An actual alliteration from a normally not-so-zingy Zuriel! It's a serious sit-down seeking to resolve the rumor's rightness. Lucifer is going to be there. Micha and Oreb, too. I dunno who else."

"Sounds interesting."

"Lucifer will help us riffle through these recurring rumors and resolve resultant reasons to believe or to disbelieve. Lucifer stands before Eli-Mehlek. That gives him insights into questions about Deity. Hopefully, I'll finally learn the valid veracity of these various rumors."

He spins in midair and flashes out the door.

* * * *

"Welcome back, Lucifer! It is good to see you!"

"Oh, Zuriel, I've been so busy. All these rumors drifting around. I've been trying to find where they are starting. No one seems to know."

"Does Michael know?"

"I haven't asked Him … Say! That's a good idea, Zuriel. Thank you for reminding me. By the way, I'm having a meeting here this evening."

"Wow, I'll get busy arranging the mansion for visitors."

I whip around the mansion, getting everything ready. Everything must be just right, just perfect! I bring in some of Sotai's rosahedrons and arrange the furniture just so. Lucifer comes in and praises my work just as before. Then Lucifer greets his guests.

"Come in, Gabriel. Welcome. It is good you are here!"

"Here's Oreb! Great to see you. Please sit down."

"Jokim! You've come! Find yourself a chair."

"Resheph, how's that song going? Wonderful!"

Finally all the angels are seated. Lucifer sits down in his chair—calling the meeting to order.

"I think we all hear the rumors going around. We need to talk about the rumors and find out what is causing them. For the first time, there is discord in Shalem. It used to be so peaceful here. I thought if we could get to the bottom of the rumors, we could go to the other angels and show them what we've found, how we should respond to the gossip."

"Yes, Lucifer," Resheph speaks. "There is one persistent rumor I've heard repeated often. This rumor suggests we angels need no law and Eli-Mehlek is unfair to require us to obey His law."

Lucifer jots down the rumor as he slowly replies to no one in particular "I've heard it said that angels are perfect beings just as Eli-Mehlek is perfect. Of course, no angel is like Eli-Mehlek—yet I've heard some say we are perfect. What other rumors have you heard?"

"I hear some say Michael claims to be equal with Eli-Mehlek," Oreb interjects. "Of course, that's not a rumor. What bothers me is they don't seem to know the truth."

Lucifer writes some notes again. "You mean they don't know that Michael is like Eli-Mehlek or they don't really believe that Michael is like Eli-Mehlek? I wonder which is true."

"Well, it seems to be both. Some don't seem to actually know that Michael is equal with Eli-Mehlek. Others don't seem to believe it."

Lucifer makes more notes. "What else?"

"Another rumor is that Deity demands things from us angels without demanding it of Themselves. The rumor says Deity demands humbleness, self-denial and obedience from the angels and are not humble Themselves. They only want submission and obedience in order to exalt Themselves. The self-denial They demand, They do not practice Themselves."

Lucifer's stylus wends its way across the parchment, scribing this rumor in his notes. "So it is said the Deity does not care for we angels, but only for Themselves, correct?"

"Yup, that seems to be the gist of the complaint."

The conversation ebbs and flows. Lucifer takes his notes, ponders them and adds his part to the ideas. Mostly, he seems to echo what the other angels bring up or report another rumor he heard.

At last Gabriel rises to his feet; the others simply sat while they spoke, but Gabriel is different. His speech is very quiet, with frequent pauses. "One of the rumors I hear is that one of us in this room is behind all these rumors. Several angels told me they never even thought of some of these doubts about Eli-Mehlek until one of us planted questions in their minds."

Lucifer's stylus squeaks as he makes more notes. "Who would that be? Could any one of us in this room be suggesting that Eli-Mehlek's government is flawed?" He looks around the room.

Gabriel coughs, looks down and replies "Everyone who told me said it is our Archangel. Just now, Lucifer, I listened carefully to your replies to each of the rumors mentioned. Each reply took the rumor a little farther than it was stated. Each reply added a little more to the rumor than was actually reported. Each reply made the rumor a little more forceful than it was. It almost seems as if you want the rumors to be more detrimental to Eli-Mehlek. Could it be true that you are enhancing these rumors, while claiming to be attempting to thwart them?"

Lucifer's fingers suddenly still. He lays his stylus on the table while answering, "I have the highest regard for Eli-Mehlek. In the time before these rumors started, His government worked very well. I am very concerned about these angels who question Eli-Mehlek's Law. Somehow we need to reconcile them to the rest of us."

Gabriel sits down and the meeting continues. Lucifer resumes note-taking; the discussion focuses on dealing with the rumors.

Jokim had been silent. Finally he speaks, just as quietly as Gabriel, "Lucifer, somehow I need to bring the discussion back to you. I hear rumors that perhaps you feel Eli-Mehlek is unfair to you. I hear other rumors suggesting you are not happy with the position Eli-Mehlek gave you? Yet, you are Eli-Mehlek's Covering Cherub; you are the angel closest to Eli-Mehlek; you know Eli-Mehlek better than any of us. Is it true you are dissatisfied with your position? Is it true you feel that Eli-Mehlek is unfair to you? We need to know where your heart is, Lucifer."

The room is totally still as Lucifer puts down his stylus. "Yes, Jokim, my position is highest, next to Deity. I come and go at Eli-Mehlek's command. I speak with Him constantly. Why would I be dissatisfied? What more could I ever want?"

His answer seems to satisfy Jokim and Gabriel as they relax in their seats. And with that, the meeting breaks up. Lucifer shakes everyone's hand warmly and chats with them as they leave.

My mind reels. I don't know what to think. *Is it possible angels are perfect and need no law? What a heady feeling! Perfect? Like Eli-Mehlek? Is Deity only concerned with exalting Itself? Is it really possible Lucifer is behind all the rumors? So many unanswered questions. I don't know what to believe.* I float around the room, straightening up the furniture. As I pick up the little messes always left after a meeting, I find myself right at Lucifer's chair. His parchment is lying there, just where he left it. I glance down at what he wrote. It is indeed a list of the rumors that had been alluded to and the actions that would be taken. I notice something curious. Beside each rumor is the name of the angel who mentioned the rumor. Beside each angel's name is a mark. Oreb's and Resheph's names have two lines crossing beside them. Gabriel's and Jokim's have a curious little mark with a sharp point at the end aiming right at their names. I wonder what the marks mean. Lucifer comes and picks up the parchment.

I am ashamed to be peeking.

* * * *

I can't concentrate on my work. My mind races with unanswered questions. How can a little mansion-keeping angel find the truth about Eli-Mehlek, the truth about these rumors? I discuss the rumors with other angels. Many of them say they believe the rumors saying Eli-Mehlek isn't really fair. The peace we have known in Shalem was there only because we didn't know any better and, now that we are learning the truth, the peace is gone.

I don't know what to think. I don't know whom to believe. *Is it possible Lucifer is working to spread the rumors instead of trying to stop them? Does Lucifer know something about Eli-Mehlek that we don't know?* I remember the chill from that odd tone Lucifer used with me twice. And then ...

"Hi, Zuriel!" Sotai waggles into the mansion at full speed, squeaking at full pitch. "You won't believe this latest rumor."

"Rumors, rumors, rumors! I'm so tired of rumors!" I sigh, "Okay, what is this latest rumor?"

"Well, I hear Eli-Mehlek is going to make Michael our demanding, demeaning dictator, always telling us what to do. And then, all of our fabulous freedom and luxurious liberty will be gone once Eli-Mehlek elevates Michael to be our demanding dictator. No more raising red rosahedrons on Rigel for me, once Michael takes over. The idea doesn't sound gloriously good to me!"

"It seems to me Michael has always been next to Eli-Mehlek. Is this really something new?"

"Well, the way my reliable rumormonger sees it, Michael is next to Eli-Mehlek and Lucifer is the angelic leader. But no more. Michael is being promoted above Lucifer. This bothers me, Zuriel. This troubles me a lot." Sotai flaps his way out of the mansion with furious ferocity before I can answer.

My heart is pounding. *Michael, beloved Michael! So the rumor says perhaps Eli Mehlek is promoting You. Yet, I don't think anything will really change. You are one with Eli-Mehlek. Eli-Mehlek is supreme. Doesn't that mean You are also supreme?*

* * * *

The messenger angels call every angelic being to an unusual Assembly. Sotai is away, but Micha comes by Lucifer's mansion and we go to the Assembly together.

Assemblies are always special. All hearts are united in love, adoration and praise to Eli-Mehlek. But this one is different. It is not at a scheduled time. Perhaps Sotai is right. What does this mean? Will it mean the end of our freedom?

We angels sit quietly waiting for the Assembly to begin. There is no anthem. We haven't practiced any music. Even Lucifer is sitting, waiting with the rest of us, in lieu of being in front leading the singing. Michael is sitting on a glorious throne, gold and silver, with a gorgeous sapphire forming each of the throne's arms. Eli-Mehlek is sitting on His throne, the one with the crystal river pouring out the front of it and meandering through Shalem.

After we are all seated, Eli-Mehlek speaks. His voice sounds like many waters, tinkling and thundering at the same time. "My beautiful angelic host, welcome!"

"Praise Eli-Mehlek!" we answer in unison, with hearts full of love for Him.

"My heart is full of love for each of you. From Lucifer to Sotai. From Gabriel to Oreb." Eli-Mehlek calls each of us by name. "Zuriel, you will never know how much I love you!"

Our hearts burst wide open and we answer in unison, "How great is Eli-Mehlek!"

"I planned all of you," Eli-Mehlek continues. "I planned your size, your wing color, your duties, where you would sing in the choir. As I planned, I said, 'This is good.' When you were created, I said, 'This is very good.'

"However, there is one here today whom I did not plan. There is one here today, whom I did not create. Michael is Deity just as I am Deity. Michael helped me plan each of you. Michael created each of you, according to My plan. Michael is one with Me."

The angelic audience is totally silent, listening intently to Eli-Mehlek.

"Michael is the only One in the Universe who can totally understand Me. Michael is the only One I take into all My counsels. Michael is the only One who communes with Me. He is My equal.

"Michael has been with Me from the beginning of eternity. When I planned the angels, Michael was with Me. When I planned all of the Sons of Eli-Mehlek, Michael was with Me. When I planned the stars, the nebulae and the planets, Michael was with Me.

"As My equal, Michael is indeed the highest Being in all of Shalem, in all of the Universe. As such, Michael is worthy of all the honor and glory and praise accorded to Me. It is my desire that every angel worship Michael, just as you worship Me."

The angelic Assembly bursts forth in rapturous praise to Michael. Every angel bows in worship of Michael. Every heart explodes with unutterable love for Michael. Spontaneously, the entire Assembly sings an ode of praise to Michael and to Eli-Mehlek.

After the ode finishes, the Assembly quiets down. Eli-Mehlek speaks again, "Go back to your place and to your work. Remember this day. Remember my words. Remember Our love for each of you."

My heart rejoices with all the other angels. Sotai's rumor is wrong. Michael isn't our dictator. Michael is Deity, co-equal with Eli-Mehlek! Perhaps now the rumors will cease. Perhaps now serenity will return to Shalem.

* * * *

Even though I do not suspect such a thing, one heart is tumultuous. One mind is frantically cogitating about what Eli-Mehlek said. One soul is in turmoil, unsure of which alternative to choose. One angel has a decision to make.

Decision Day

Back at the mansion, I am about my work. My heart is bursting with joy unbounded. I can hardly wait for Sotai and Lucifer to come back so we can share our joy. They must be as happy as I am.

As Lucifer enters, I can see he is deep in thought. The look on his face is intense. My joyful song ends abruptly. My happiness evaporates. Lucifer walks into one of the other rooms and shuts the door. It's the one which is mostly his private room. I don't spend much time there, just enough to straighten and sweep. I hear him swishing back and forth from one end of the room to the other. At times, I can hear him talking to himself. It sounds as if he is having a real heart-to-heart discussion with himself.

"I'm the highest angel Eli-Mehlek created. I should be content with that. But I am not! I want to be equal with Michael. But Michael is equal with Eli-Mehlek. That would make me equal with Eli-Mehlek. How can I even dream of such a thing?"

A pause.

Lucifer's internal commotion is obvious. I've never heard or seen tumultuous emotions like this before. Nowhere in Shalem, the City of Peace, has there ever been a conflict such as Lucifer seems to be having. It sounds as if it is tearing him apart inside. I listen more closely. My knees feel weak. My wings shake. I wonder why.

"I don't understand my feelings. I have severe reservations. Should I continue or should I not? I'm the reason Eli-Mehlek needed the special Assembly. The other angels don't suspect me. Well, maybe Gabriel and Jokim might question, but they do not know definitely."

A quiet, yet energetic, swoosh emanates from Lucifer's room.

"I have to decide. Shall I accept my role as Deity gave it to me or shall I define my own role where I am equal with Michael? If I accept Deity's role, I know exactly what will happen. Life will continue as it has been ever since my creation."

A low rustle whispers as Lucifer moseys across his room.

"If I define my own role, I do not know what will happen. It is the great unknown. Will Deity change or will I have to demand my rights?"

I hear more muffled sounds through the door.

"If I remain, I'll have to confess my thoughts and rumormongering to the other angels. I'll have to admit I am the source of all of these rumors. I can't do that!"

On and on Lucifer's conversation with himself continues, rising and falling.

"It would mortify me! The other angels all look at me with respect and love in their eyes. They all do what I suggest to them. I'll have to recant all the rumors I started."

Louder, the tension apparent in Lucifer's voice.

"I'll have to humble myself and I'll lose all respect from seraphim and cherubim, alike. Will the angels still admire me? After I've confessed, will Eli-Mehlek demote me from being the Archangel?"

"I must come back … I cannot come back."

I am stunned. The words "I must come back. I cannot come back" sear themselves into my mind. Does he really believe Eli-Mehlek to be cruel? Does he really believe Deity would disgrace him before the entire Universe? Somehow, that doesn't sound like Michael or Ruash or Eli-Mehlek.

The strange, tormented words continue. "If I come back, I risk shame and embarrassment. If I do not come back, I risk the punishment of Eli-Mehlek. Michael clearly explained it to me a couple of orbits ago. We talked for a long time. He showed me where I was wrong."

Lucifer's voice rises in an odd tone I've never heard before. "Michael dared to tell me, Lucifer, where I was wrong! Me, the most beautiful of the angels. Me, the Archangel. Me, the one who flies to do Eli-Mehlek's bidding. Michael told me I was wrong!"

It is quiet for a while, except for Lucifer's continued perturbation. The energetic flutters of his wings keep my ears tuned to his faintest sounds.

Suddenly, Sotai bursts in the door. He's atwitter, much more than normal. "So, we must choose between Michael and Lucifer!" Sotai garbles so fast that his words run together. "Eli-Mehlek said Michael is His equal, but Lucifer is not."

"Well, Michael is a part of the Deity," I respond quietly, my mind on Lucifer's agitation.

"Yes, but Lucifer is the Archangel. What about that?"

"Yes, Lucifer is honored, but does that make him equal with Michael?"

Sotai's frustrated tone breaks the peace Shalem always had. "I knew you wouldn't understand! I knew you weren't a Lucifer loyalist." Sotai spins in midair and flails out the door.

My heart is troubled as I watch him go. He obviously has very strong emotions running around inside him. I don't know what they are called, but they are not peaceful. His face is contorted and his eyes are bulging out weirdly.

The troubled swishing of Lucifer's wings as he sweeps back and forth comes through the stillness, returning after Sotai vanished.

I hear Lucifer say, "I would rather be the king where Eli-Mehlek isn't than to be even the fourth person in the Kingdom of Eli-Mehlek. I will set *my* throne on high. I will be like Eli-Mehlek. I will *not* confess my wrongs. I can make a better government than Eli-Mehlek. And Michael—bah— He's the cause of this whole problem. If he hadn't scolded me, I wouldn't be so angry. It's not my fault since Eli-Mehlek's law cannot be obeyed anyway. It's Eli-Mehlek's fault as He doesn't follow His own laws. Never again will I worship Eli-Mehlek. Never again will I bow to Michael. I have a better way. Angels are perfect without Deity's law. Angels must be free to do whatever their hearts desire. I must be free to go where I want to go. I'll take whatever consequences Eli-Mehlek gives me. But I'll be like Eli-Mehlek, the highest being in my kingdom."

Lucifer's decision is final. He will not return. The angels must decide between Michael and Lucifer

Shock grips my body. I am stunned. Lucifer will never again worship Michael? Never again will I hear his glorious voices raised in praise to Eli-Mehlek? Never, since the orbit when I was created, have I ever heard such a declaration. What will Eli-Mehlek do? Eli-Mehlek made Lucifer. Will He destroy Lucifer? What does it mean for an angel to be destroyed? Suddenly I am afraid. What does the future hold? I wonder when Michael scolded Lucifer. I've never heard Michael scold any angel. I wonder what it sounds like. But is Lucifer right? Is Eli-Mehlek the cause of Lucifer's unhappiness? Is it really Michael's fault? Is Deity not willing to be humble and submissive as we angels are required to be? I think back to the beginning of the rumors. They started so long ago. I almost can't remember the time before the rumors. Orbits and orbits have come and gone. Eons and ages have passed since the days when Shalem was peaceful and happy.

Lucifer comes out of the other room. He looks tired, but relaxed. I smile at him. Out the door he skims as he smiles back.

I am left with my thoughts. I know something important just happened, but I don't know exactly what it is. Somehow I know things will never be the same again. I wonder if Michael knows of Lucifer's strange talk. I love

Lucifer with all my heart. I love Michael with all my heart. Sotai is my closest friend. What has happened? Why did Michael scold Lucifer? Who is right? Does Lucifer really have a better way?

I go to clean up the other room. There is a large parchment lying there with angels' names written on it. Some names have those mysterious crossed lines beside them. Sotai's does. Others have that single sharp line beside them. Gabriel's does. Some don't have any mark beside them. Mine doesn't.

* * * *

A short time later, Lucifer calls another Assembly. For Lucifer to call an Assembly is not unheard of, but it doesn't happen often. For it to be so soon after Eli-Mehlek's Assembly is also unusual. All of the angelic beings fly into the Assembly Bowl. It is a really sweet place. We angels can sit on the grass as the ground slopes up to the lip of the Bowl. The grass is always kept short by the care-taking angel. There is an extraordinarily beautiful bow arching across the front, with some tall, finely shaped trees standing on each side of the dais.

I sit on the outskirts of the Assembly with a few of my closest friends. Usually Sotai sits with us. Today, I don't see him anywhere. I wonder where he is.

As the Bowl fills, we angels talk in hushed tones, wondering what is going to happen, why this Assembly is happening. Lucifer gracefully flies in and lands on the dais.

The quiet murmurings end.

"Welcome, my fellow angels!" Lucifer's quiet, musical voice carries to the farthest reaches of the Bowl. As I listen, my heart stirs, swelling with love for Lucifer. "I am so glad you are here.

"You've all heard some of these rumors that have been traveling around Shalem. As your Archangel, it has been my privilege to talk with many of you about these rumors. I listened as you told me what is in your heart. But I've never told any of you what to do or what to think. It would be unseemly for me, as the Archangel, to attempt to tell you what to do. Instead, it has been my privilege to help some of you decide what you are going to believe.

"As I listened to the various rumors, it became apparent that someone would need to find the truth. As your Archangel, it seems I should accept that duty and so I have humbly done. Now that I know the truth, I asked you to assemble to receive my report on what I found.

"We angels are created perfect. Because we are perfect, we just instinctively know what we should do. It is part of us. That is why we have perfect freedom. That is why we need no law to restrict us.

"We angels know this intuitively. However, there is One who doesn't know this—One who is intent on taking away our liberty—One who would cause us great pain if He is allowed to rule over us. One who wants to put great restrictions on us."

A buzz crisscrosses the audience. Lucifer pauses 'til the whispering ceases.

"I decided that, in fairness, I would call this Assembly to tell you what I found. It pains me to even say this, but ... this One is ... Michael."

The buzz erupts again. There are many angelic heads shaking back and forth in disbelief. I hear fragments of many stunned conversations. I see many heads wagging sideways.

"No, Lucifer, how could that be?"

"Michael? Are you certain?"

"How can you be sure?"

"Not Michael, He wouldn't do that, would He?"

There are other heads nodding up and down, some thoughtfully and some vigorously.

"So that's the cause of all these rumors."

"I *knew* it. I just *knew* it."

"Not me, He'll never do that to me!"

Lucifer quiets the Assembly as he continues. "As I've listened to you over the last many orbits, I've learned many things. I've learned about a seraph whom Michael scolded. I've heard about a cherub to whom Michael sent another angel to tell him what to do. There are many more examples I've heard as I've listened to you.

"And finally," Lucifer continues calm, majestic, "Michael was promoted at the last Assembly. It seems Michael forgot that I am your Archangel. It seems He influenced Eli-Mehlek into promoting Him above all angels, including both you and me. It appears He is eager to compel your obedience.

"And now because Eli-Mehlek promoted Michael as the supreme ruler over all the angels, it is obvious He doesn't require self-denial from Himself, yet He will enforce His law on us angels. He will take away the freedom we have enjoyed so long. He will use His sovereignty to coerce angelic obedience. I didn't want to believe this intimidation could happen, but Michael came and reproved me. Me! I've never done anything for which I should be reprimanded, but Michael spent a long time talking to me and censuring me."

Lucifer goes on talking for some time—giving us examples of Michael's attempts to destroy our freedom and turn it into bondage. He pauses as Sotai explodes into the air. He's sitting way down in front. His shrill, high-pitched voice hollers, "We can't let Him get away with it! We gotta preserve our famously fabulous freedom." Sotai fairly bobbles up and down in the air as he speaks.

There is nothing calm and majestic about Sotai. But there never has been, either. Irrepressible? Yes. Excitable? Yes. Tumultuous? Yes. Calm and majestic? No! Sotai bobbles down to the grass, landing noisily.

"Sotai is right," Lucifer resumes. "There *is* a better way. There *is* a higher way. There *is* a more glorious way. There *is* a way of total justice. There *is* a way of perfect freedom. There *is* a way of complete liberty." Lucifer's voice is still calm, measured, marvelous, although its intensity is increasing. "I present to you this transcendent way. The way where no angel has an odious law to restrict his freedom. The way where Michael doesn't scold and neither does Lucifer. The way where each angel is treated with the reverence and honor that is due to him. Not the way where the reverence and honor due one is conferred on another, as my reverence and honor were conferred upon Michael."

Again a hubbub breaks out in the Assembly. Never have we attended an Assembly like this one. Cherubs are standing up, talking in tight knots. Seraphim are seated in small circles. Some seem to be agreeing with Lucifer. Others seem totally dismayed by what he is saying. The clamor continues for some time before it finally wanes.

Gabriel rises and flies down to the stage. By his very bearing, he commands our attention. After it is quiet, he begins to speak.

"We have heard some strange things at this Assembly—talk about our liberties being taken away. We have heard some accusations about Michael—that He doesn't demand self-denial from Himself and so would deprive us of all of our freedoms. We hear of a supposedly better, more glorious, more transcendent way.

"But Lucifer, you haven't said anything about Eli-Mehlek. Is Eli-Mehlek not the Sovereign of the Universe? Would Michael do anything without Eli-Mehlek's permission? No! So, in essence, your charges against Michael are also directed at Eli-Mehlek.

"I ask you, Lucifer, are you suggesting Eli-Mehlek is also intent on curtailing our freedom?"

Lucifer is silent a moment. "Not at all, Gabriel. Eli-Mehlek is the Supreme Being of the Universe. But why would He promote Michael above all the angels, including you and me? That is quite arbitrary—is it not? Why couldn't He promote me? Why couldn't He promote you? Or Sotai, here?"

"Lucifer, Eli-Mehlek called that Assembly because some of the rumors questioned Michael's status. You know as well as I that Michael is part of the Deity, the Divine Triune. You know as well as I that Michael created all of us angels. Not only that, He created all the worlds scattered throughout the Universe and populated them with beings. You know that, Lucifer, because you and I and all the rest of the angels watched Him create those worlds and those beings. We all know Michael is *the* Creator. That makes Michael worthy of all the honor and respect due to Eli-Mehlek, for Michael is One with Eli-Mehlek.

Michael is Deity, part of the Holy Triune, the Creator

"It is not arbitrary that Eli-Mehlek "promoted," as you say, Michael. Michael has always been One with Eli-Mehlek. It is Michael's deserved place to have the same love and devotion due to Eli-Mehlek.

"Nor is it any discredit to you that Eli-Mehlek reminded us of Michael's true status. You are indeed the fourth highest being in the Universe. You are definitely our Archangel. Nothing has changed.

"Nothing that is, except inside of you, Lucifer. Where you got these strange ideas, I'll never know. But for you to imagine that the reiteration of Michael's true status shows disrespect for you is simply that—your imagination.

"Oh, Lucifer," Gabriel's pleading voice is soft and full of tenderness, "what's wrong with you? Why can't you be content with the position Eli-Mehlek gave you? What causes this dissatisfaction in your heart? There is no reason for it. Why can't you accept Eli-Mehlek's will for you and be content as our Archangel?"

A trillion pairs of angel eyes focus on Lucifer. Gabriel's plea hangs in the air

Suddenly, Lucifer faces Gabriel snarling, "Slave! Servile, obsequious serf! I offer you perfect, total freedom and you want me to be a slave, a lowly serf. How many of you want to be a groveling, bowing serf?" We angels are stunned into a deep silence.

Gabriel breaks the stillness. His voice is still calm, but he speaks with a conviction that is hard to ignore. "Lucifer, you are revolting against Deity. You are rebelling against the Divine Triune. They created you and Those who create can also destroy. If you persist in this rebellion, Deity can and will punish your defiance. You are created. Michael is the Creator. You cannot win."

Lucifer dismisses Gabriel's comments with sneers and laughs. Gabriel flies off the dais and out of the Assembly Bowl. Many of the angels leave with him. About half stay behind with Lucifer.

I leave, flying home thoughtfully. Many terrifying emotions are running through my body. *There is Sotai. Excitable Sotai. Lucifer's words so stir him that he cannot sit still. There is Lucifer. Is Eli-Mehlek unfair to promote Michael above Lucifer? There is Gabriel. His solemn words echo in my mind. "Those who create can also destroy." What does that mean? Destruction is unheard of in Shalem. We can't even comprehend that word. One thing I know. I love Lucifer with all my heart. I love Sotai, my best friend. I also love Michael. What will happen if Lucifer continues this discontent? Will he be sent away? Where will Eli-Mehlek send him? Will he never come back? Will I have to choose between Lucifer, Sotai and Michael?*

Shalem, the City of Peace is in turmoil. Lucifer is dissatisfied. How will Deity respond?

I shudder at the thought.

* * * *

All of Shalem is in turmoil. It doesn't take long for some of my questions to be answered. Eli-Mehlek calls another Assembly. All angels are to be there—no exceptions. I attend with fear and trembling in my heart. Somehow, it seems as if this is a unique Assembly. Almost as if there is an aura of finality about it. There is no music, no laughter—just solemn quietness. I sit about where I normally sit, perhaps a little closer to the dais so I can get a good view of what is happening. Sotai and Lucifer come in together. They sit on the grass with the rest of the angels. This adds to the peculiarity. Lucifer is normally up in front.

As we quiet, Eli-Mehlek speaks. His great voice sends a thrill through my body. It always does.

"It is good. All of My angels are here. I know all are wondering why I called this Assembly. Yet inside, each of you knows the reason. Some of you are dissatisfied with the order of things here in Shalem. Some of you desire to change things that I ordained. There has been a great deal of talk. Today, let's bring that talk out into the open. Which of you desires change? Who will speak first?" Eli-Mehlek's voice holds no twinge of anything but normality.

The eyes of a trillion angels focus on Lucifer. He rises and begins to speak. His voice also is exceedingly normal. "Yes, Eli-Mehlek, I am dissatisfied."

"About what, Lucifer, would you be dissatisfied?" Eli-Mehlek's response is as gentle as the dew.

"I am Shalem's Archangel, a position that You, Eli-Mehlek, gave me. Yet, it doesn't seem that I am treated as such. At the last Assembly, it sounded as though Michael is above me. A superior Archangel, so to speak. There are many times when Michael has been taken into conference with You—and I haven't been included. It seems to me that since my position is the Archangel, I should be included so I can tell the rest of the angels what the conference is about.

"It seems that You prefer Michael to me. As if I were only a pseudo-Archangel. Would not one in my position of Archangel be the one preferred."

A murmur races through the angelic ranks. Never before have we heard anyone talk to Eli-Mehlek like this. What will Eli-Mehlek do? Some of us fully expect Eli-Mehlek to reach out His arm and crush Lucifer. Others of us don't know what to expect.

"Lucifer," Eli-Mehlek answers, His voice unchanged, "that can never be. Yes, you are Shalem's Archangel. That is the highest position I can give to any created being. However, only Michael is Deity with Me. Only Michael can share My secret purposes. You see, Lucifer, My ways are not your ways and My thoughts are not your thoughts. You are not Deity.

"All of the created inhabitants of Shalem must give Michael implicit obedience, including you. Those who cannot give Michael their wholehearted loyalty cannot live in Shalem."

Lucifer moves to the edge of the Assembly Bowl. Sotai follows. Lucifer speaks. "That is not acceptable, Eli-Mehlek. I now vow that never again will I bow in worship to Michael. Never again will I yield to Michael uncompromising obedience." Lucifer's melodic voice stuns us as it sings out over a trillion pairs of angelic ears, dazing every auricle. "There are those who believe I have a better way. Let those who so believe come up here with me."

"As you wish, Lucifer," Eli-Mehlek rejoins with equanimity. "Michael, why don't you move to the edge of the Assembly Bowl opposite Lucifer? Those angels who believe Michael's way is better may join Him there. Those who haven't made up their minds can remain in the center. Is that fair enough, Lucifer?"

Lucifer appears surprised, but agrees and a trillion angels mill around the Assembly Bowl on their way to one place or the other. Gabriel is the first to join Michael.

I don't know what to do. Michael is standing there, looking calm but pained at this turn of events. Lucifer is looking at his parchment. Suddenly, it dawns on me why Lucifer wrote down all of our names and now I understand what those marks mean. The two lines crossing mean that angel is joining Lucifer. The sharp pointy line means he remains with Michael. Names with no marks show Lucifer doesn't know where they stand.

* * * *

The disorder swirls around me. I cannot contemplate the decisions others are making. After a while, I sense there are only a few of us in the middle. I am so torn I can't even look to see who they are. Tears flow down my face. How can I choose between Michael and Lucifer and Sotai? It is an unbearable decision. I've never cried before—now the tears drip down my face.

Through my misery, I feel a light touch on my arm. "Come on, Zuriel. Don't you want the fullest freedom to do whatever you want?" Sotai speaks tenderly. "Lucifer's way is better. Come on. Join us. You won't be sorry."

"I don't know, Sotai. Why do we have to separate? If I go with you, I'll have to leave all these other friends of mine and I'll reject Michael. Eli-Mehlek said that only those who wish to obey Michael will be able to stay in Shalem. Yet, if I stay with Michael, I'll lose you and Lucifer. How can you do this to me? Why can't Lucifer be content? Why can't you be content?"

"Zuriel, it is a new start. Things haven't been too impeccably peaceful in Shalem recently. That is because Eli-Mehlek's way is fatally flawed. In your heart you know that. Come with us. Lucifer's way *is* better."

Through my misery, I notice other conversations going on in other places. There are some of us in the middle. There are some along the fringes of both sides. Everyone seems to be talking to someone.

"Oh, Sotai, my very best friend, come with me, come back to Michael's side. Somehow what Lucifer is planning just feels wrong. I think you will regret being on Lucifer's side. When I think of the complaints raised by Lucifer, they are really nothing. If you and Lucifer would only obey Michael, I'd be content."

"Ha," Sotai laughs scornfully. "When Lucifer says 'I will never again bow in worship to Michael' he is speaking the words from my own heart.

Never again will I obey Michael."

"Oh, Sotai, how can you say that? Michael is Deity! Where will you go? What will you do? Where will you live? You heard Eli-Mehlek say that those who won't obey cannot remain in Shalem." I'm heartsick about my friend's decision.

"Lucifer has a better plan than Eli-Mehlek. I'm not worried. And besides, Lucifer promised me I'll be one of his trusted advisors. And I'll be plantin' parynippers on Pleiades sooner than you think. When all the other worlds get the idea of how good Lucifer is makin' things, why they'll be signin' up in droves. Eli-Mehlek, Himself, won't be able to stop our winning!"

"Somehow, Sotai, I think you are making a big mistake. I cannot leave Michael and Eli-Mehlek." I rasp out, not certain of my voice. "Go with Lucifer, if you must. I hope I can see you plantin' parynippers on Pleiades some time." And with that, I hug him and stumble towards Michael's side, sobbing uncontrollably.

It is the very hardest decision I've ever made. As I join the crowd on Michael's side, I look behind me. Even through my red, watery eyes, I can see there is no one else in the middle. Sotai and I were the last two deliberators. Some of Michael's angels put their arms around me and dry my tears.

* * * *

I hear Eli-Mehlek's voice, "Lucifer, were these proceeding fair?"

"Yes."

"Michael, was that fair?"

"Yes."

"Is there any angel who thinks that was not fair?"

It is utterly silent.

"Lucifer, you made your decision. You stated you will never again reverence, honor, obey or worship Michael. The angels who joined you chose to follow you instead of Michael.

"Only those who choose to obey Michael implicitly can remain in Shalem. All of you made your decisions knowing these consequences."

Lucifer interrupts. "Look at all these angels who are on my side, nearly half of the angelic host. Will You expel all of these, too? Will You leave such a gaping hole in Shalem?"

Eli-Mehlek answers with the same patience, "The consequences of their choices are known. If they remain with you, they will have to leave Shalem."

I notice Eli-Mehlek's answer surprises Lucifer. Defiant, his answer is ready, "With all these angels on my side, I have nearly as many angels as does Michael. We are ready to battle for our places in Shalem."

"As you wish. However, there is one change I'm making now. No longer is your name Lucifer, the Light Bearer. From now on, you will be called Satan, the Adversary. Now, before we engage in the conflict Satan proposes, there may be some angels whose minds are not firmly decided. There will be a short time during which any angel may change his mind. Afterwards each side will organize for the proposed contest-of-arms."

Some of the angels from Lucifer's—er, Satan's—side come over to talk to some of the angels on Michael's side. And some of Michael's angels advance to Satan's side. Many of Satan's angels, having second thoughts, desire to change their minds. To prevent their defection, Satan tells his angels they've gone too far. Eli-Mehlek cannot take them back; they must stay with him. But the angels from Michael's side assure them— if they repent of their rebellion—Eli-Mehlek and Michael will welcome them back. To some of them, this is a happy message. Many believe the loyal angels and return to Michael's side. They are welcomed eagerly and warmly. As the hubbub settles, my hazed eyes see that Satan is left with only about a third of the angels while Michael has about two-thirds.

* * * *

We organize in divisions, companies, units, platoons. War comes to the City of Peace. It is not an easy conflict. It is most intense. These are our friends, our companions, our colleagues. I am relieved Sotai is on the far side of the combat zone. Eventually the battle is over. Michael and His angels prevail against Satan and his angels. They are expelled. Sotai is gone. Lucifer is gone. They reside no more in Shalem.

Devastation

We are devastated. There is a galactic-sized hole in Shalem. A third of our companions is gone. Our Archangel is gone. My best friend is gone. We participated in a battle we never dreamed would happen. Our emotions are spent. There is no singing, no laughter. We experience emotions we never felt before. The enormity of our loss weighs upon us. Our grief is deep.

My thoughts run wildly rampant. *What is Sotai doing? How does he feel?* My grief bursts out at the oddest times. I still love Lucifer. *Will I ever clean Lucifer's—er, Satan's—mansion again? What will I do now?* I miss Sotai terribly. Shalem's turmoil has subsided. Instead it has settled in my heart. The rumors are mostly ended, but the questions raised still echo in my head. *Has Eli-Mehlek done the right thing? Did He really have to expel Satan and his angels? Is Satan accurate in his accusations?* It seems I have no control over my thoughts or my emotions.

My mind remembers all the events of Decision Day. Eli-Mehlek did everything necessary to be fair at each step. I'm not surprised Michael is equally fair. Michael did not use His omnipotent power to overwhelm Satan. He relied on us angels to win the battle. The fight was angelic power versus angelic power. That's fair.

I could just hear Sotai sputtering, "Yes, that's Michael for you. Always trying to coerce angels, just because He's omnipotent." But since Michael didn't use His divinity, it must be obvious, even to Sotai, the battle was fair and they lost on even terms.

With nothing to do, I glide slowly over to the Palace, Eli-Mehlek's Palace. Dazedly, my eyes roam over the empty streets, the various mansions. I wonder who is still here. I see Michael is talking to Eli-Mehlek. Certainly, they're talking about the next step. Soon Michael comes out and calls for Gabriel. Instantly, Gabriel flies around Shalem, announcing another special Assembly.

It is so quiet at this Assembly. The look on Michael's face shows that His heart is in deep pain. The ache in his voice resonates in our hearts.

"Eli-Mehlek and I have been in conference about our great loss. You lost many of your friends. It is a great sorrow to you as well as to Eli-Mehlek and Ruash and also to me. This is a time of exceedingly great difficulty. There will be many changes in Shalem. We don't want to cause more pain than necessary, so most of these changes will occur gradually, allowing time for each of us to absorb them.

"However, there is one change that must happen immediately. Gabriel is now the Archangel. He will do most of the work that Lucifer used to do. Everyone saw how Gabriel tried to reason with Lucifer. His strong love for Eli-Mehlek and for Lucifer caused him to do his best to win back the Adversary. Gabriel also distinguished himself on Decision Day by his firm stand for Eli-Mehlek. Gabriel is well qualified to be the Archangel and to do Eli-Mehlek's bidding. You can trust his heart. He will not lead you astray.

"The rest of the changes can wait for another time. I will come and talk with each of you individually about how the changes will affect you."

Michal's gentle words intensify my thoughts. I know there will be many changes in my life. I fly to Luci—to Satan's mansion. As I enter, my tears return afresh. The mansion is so empty, so quiet. Not only is Sotai's garden outside, but Lucifer's presence permeates the interior. Where are Sotai and Lucifer? I feel totally alone. I wonder what Eli-Mehlek and Michael plan for me. The tears will not stop.

It isn't even an orbit later when I look up to see Michael standing there with a tender look on His face. He carries a wipe in His hand.

"H-H-Hi, Michael." I stutter through my tears.

"Oh, Zuriel, it hurts doesn't it," He answers, putting His arm around me and dabbing my eyes.

"Oh, yes, Michael. I miss Lucifer and Sotai so much."

"Yes, Zuriel, I know. Lucifer was wonderful, wasn't he?"

"Oh, yes, oh, yes! What am I going to do now, without Lucifer to mansionkeep for?" I cry harder. His arm tightens around my shoulders.

I whisper, "These are strange feelings … . It almost seems like the end of the Universe … . I keep wanting to weep … . So many are gone … . I've never felt this way before."

"I know," was His reply gentle. "None of us ever felt like this before. It was Eli-Mehlek's plan that no one should ever feel this way."

"What is going to happen now? What will happen to Satan and Sotai and all the others?"

"Satan makes some critical charges against Me. He claims his way is better. Some angels—yes, even some who stayed in Shalem with us—wonder if he is right." I blush a little, remembering my own thoughts. "The Sons of Eli-Mehlek on the various cosmic spheres hear the doubts Satan raises about Eli-Mehlek and about Me. They also wonder if Satan could be right. So, Satan must be given time to demonstrate his way. Then all can judge if his way is better or not.

"However, Zuriel, I came to ask you about what you would do now. What would you like to do?"

"Oh, Michael, I'm a mansionkeeper. I desire to be nothing more than what Eli-Mehlek created me to be."

Michael looks at me quietly, almost as if He is reading my very thoughts. "Yes, I see." He is quiet a while longer.

"Zuriel, now that Satan is no longer our Archangel, we need a new one. As you heard, I asked Gabriel to be the new Archangel. He accepted with great fear and trembling, wondering how he can replace Lucifer. But Gabriel's heart is trustworthy. He was one of the first to see what Lucifer was plotting. He fervently tried to change Lucifer's mind, even before you were aware that something odd was happening. He knew most of the Rebels before Decision Day. He attempted to woo them back. You can trust Gabriel. He will not tear the heart out of your soul as Satan did. Sadly, his mansionkeeper left with Satan. Would you desire to be Gabriel's new mansionkeeper?"

Astonished, I throw my arms around Michael. "Oh, Michael, I'd be so honored. Why me? What did I do to deserve this great honor?"

"No, Zuriel, it is not what you did, it is what you are. Your heart is trustworthy. I know how much you love Lucifer and how hard it was for you to walk away from Sotai. You were the last to decide. But your heart kept you in Shalem. Gabriel needs one whom he can trust implicitly. You, too, are trustworthy."

I look at Him startled. "Are you telling me there are still those in Shalem who cannot be trusted?"

"No, all who are here can be trusted. However, there are some here who initially chose to join Satan's rebellion then reversed their decision. That creates doubts in many hearts. Those doubts take time to remove. There are no such doubts about you."

My heart is racing! "I'm honored, Michael! I don't deserve to be the mansionkeeper for the new Archangel, but I accept with thankfulness as well as fear."

"Don't be afraid," Michael's arms wrap around my shoulder as He wipes my eyes again. "Eli-Mehlek will give you everything you need."

We stand there silently for a moment. "Would it be all right if I went to visit Sotai in his new place?"

Michael considers, looking at me carefully. "I believe it will do you good to talk to Sotai. You are very close to him. You may visit him at any time you choose. He will tell you what he sees in Satan's camp. You will see and hear things that will clarify the answers to many of your questions. They are over by Nepherlim."

"Thank you, Michael," I exclaim!

He quietly moves away, "There are others I need to comfort."

"Oh, yes, Michael. Go and give them the same comfort you've given me. You soothe my heart."

With that, Michael leaves and I am alone with my thoughts. Never before did I realize that broken trust takes time to heal. Broken trust never happened ere this. I wonder how many orbits will pass before all doubts are erased from all angelic minds.

It suddenly dawns on me Michael didn't tell me what will happen to Satan, Sotai and the others—just that Satan will have time to demonstrate the principles of his government. Eli-Mehlek is still being fair to Satan. I wonder if Satan is being equally fair to Michael, to Eli-Mehlek. Somehow, I doubt he is.

* * * *

I approach Nepherlim, wondering how Sotai will greet me. Will he be happy to see me or will he be too busy being Luci—Satan's—lieutenant? I see him! My good friend, Sotai! Never before had I been wary of his greeting. We greet each other charily, exchanging hugs. It is so good to see him again! We chatter a bit. It grows silent.

"Sotai, what happened after Decision Day?"

His eyes glaze over; his body stiffens. "We were totally shocked, staggered, stunned. We never dreamed Michael would indeed take up arms against us. But there is no doubt about it, we were beaten, ejected, evicted, expelled from our homes in Shalem. We were so angry, so confused that Michael would dare to cast us out of Shalem. We huddle around in disorganized, dispirited, disappointed chaos. Lucifer—Satan—seems to be dazed and unsure of himself. He watches us bicker and fight. We never acted like this in Shalem. Our disappointment leaves us with turbulent emotions."

I notice that Sotai is different. The alliteration is still there, but the spark is gone.

"Satan shuddered as he gathered a few of us around and told us he was going away to think. He'd be back soon. 'Twas the first time I'd ever seen him uncertain of himself.

"I followed at a distance where I could observe, without being intrusive.

"Satan went towards one of the scintillating, shining star paths with which he was familiar. It wasn't long until Micha went past. Satan called his name. Micha responded with the normal, 'How are you?' and 'It's good to see you' greetings. They were somewhat stiff, formal."

I picture the interaction in my mind.

Sotai continued, "'Would you take a message back to Michael for me?' Satan inquired.

"'Certainly! What is the message?' Micha replied warmly.

"'Tell Him I would like to talk with Him.'

"'Of course. I'm heading that way right now. I'll see Him soon.' With that, Micha was gone."

"What ensued?" I ask quietly.

"Satan swept back and forth. I could tell he was nervous. Michael appeared. He went over to Satan and greeted him. I could tell Michael hadn't changed. His voice was patient and kind. His very patience made me angry. I wanted to prove to the Universe that this was a charade, a sham, a con job. Satan's way is better," Sotai added.

"'I am here, Satan.'

"'Thank You for coming,' Satan's voice was courteous, too. 'I want to talk to You about how I, how all of us, repent. We want you to know that we want to return to Shalem. It doesn't matter if you want to make us slaves. We have repented and are willing to do anything to return.' Satan went on for some time suggesting different punishments for us. He outlined different ways we could work our way back into Shalem. At last, he paused, waiting for Michael to answer.

"Michael's face was alive with emotions I'd never seen before. A great sorrow dominated Him. It took a long moment before the answer. I knew what his response would be: 'No, never, not at any time.'

"'Satan, We all would love to have you and all of your angels back in Shalem with Us. Eli-Mehlek, Ruash, I and every one of the loyal angels miss all of you terribly.

"'However, deep within your soul, you nurtured the rudiments of rebellion. If you returned, that rebellion would not be gone. Those rudiments would grow and bring rebellion back to Shalem. That cannot be. No Rebel can live in Shalem. I'm so very sorry, Satan, but neither you nor your Rebel angels can be allowed to reside in Shalem.'

"If I was angry before, I was livid now. How dare Michael talk to Satan that way? Look at that. He pretends to be kind and then just throws Satan's surrender back in his face. I watched Michael leave for Shalem. After He was gone, Satan burst out with an anger I'd never seen before. With an intense vehemence he said something about, 'We'll see about that.'

"Some of the other angels now followed, looking for Satan. I led the way to where he was. As he saw us coming, he straightened his feathers and stood tall and noble. He carried himself just the same way as in Shalem.

"'Yes, we may have lost this battle, but we will win this war,' he said. 'I have great plans about how to win angels and beings on other spheres to our side. Soon, we will be the victors.'

"A few of us cheered. Others looked dubious. The rest were apathetic. I doubt not that Satan's way is better and his plans will indeed lead us to victory. Eli-Mehlek will learn better than to throw us out of Shalem."

* * * *

I move over to Gabriel's mansion. Before I leave Lucifer's mansion, I walk through each room one last time. I find a copy of the parchment with all of our names on it and those curious little marks beside each name. I study the list. Lucifer was generally right. Most of those with the two crossed lines indeed sided with Satan. Most of those with the single pointy line stayed with Michael. But about me, Lucifer was wrong. There is no mark beside my name. It should have been a single pointy line mark.

I gently close the doors and wander through Sotai's garden. I wonder if he really would be "raisin' rosahedrons on Rigel" soon. Slowly and regretfully, I shut the gate on Sotai's garden and drift over to Gabriel's mansion. He is waiting for me.

"Hi, Zuriel. All settled? Is there anything I can do for you?" Gabriel's smile cheers my heart.

"No, Gabriel. I think I'm all set. Of course, it will take me awhile to get used to you and your mansion. But the room you gave me is very soothing. My heart still weeps. I often have red eyes. But in this room, I can feel as if all is well in Shalem."

"That is good, Zuriel. Eli-Mehlek and Michael have a Plan. They cannot share all of it with us. Parts of it we cannot understand right now. We must wait and watch. By observing, we will find out if Satan's charges are true or not. In the meantime, we must trust Michael and Eli-Mehlek, as we have always done."

"I understand. This business of destruction—I know it means to not exist anymore. Yet I really do not understand it. How could something go away and not exist anymore? I guess that eventually we will absorb its meaning. I wonder how many other unknown ideas Satan's rebellion will reveal."

"I suppose you're spot-on. By the way, Zuriel, I want you to know I asked Michael if you could be my mansionkeeper. I watched the diligent way you kept Lucifer's mansion. Michael agreed and so here you are. I am so very glad you are here. First of all, you stayed with Michael and Eli-Mehlek. I'm elated by that! Far too many angels rebelled and that breaks my heart. Second, your agreeing to mansionkeep for me is such an honor to me and I'm more than pleased that you have come."

With that, Gabriel leaves. There is much for him to do. I slowly waft through Gabriel's mansion. It is so different from Lucifer's. I wonder if I'll ever get used to it. It'll take me some time to decide where to put all of my things. While Gabriel is most wonderfully kind, I still feel as if I am intruding.

Deity's Creation

Several orbits pass. The changes are mostly in place. Goodwill returns to Shalem. Sometimes we sing, though quietly and almost as if it were a prayer. I often think about Sotai and Satan. I wonder what is happening to them. I still miss them.

One morning, Gabriel mentions there will soon be another Assembly. It feels good to think about practicing with the cherubim and the seraphim again. I wonder what Eli-Mehlek will say this time. Perhaps Michael will lead the Assembly. And indeed, after the anthem, Michael does speak.

"This is truly a special Assembly. Eli-Mehlek, Ruash and I have been planning a new sphere and now we are ready to announce it to the angels in Shalem. This orb will be different from every other sphere in the Universe. It is a small planet, little more than an asteroid, without form or shape … just rocks and water. There is nothing living on it. We are going to create a small planet with a hyaline and a welkin, aquians, avians and terrestrials, fructi and vegetali of a style We never made before.

Deity announces the creation of a new sphere. One with new beings and new abilities

"There is a unique part of this new sphere about which Eli-Mehlek and I are especially excited. All life on this sphere will be able to create replicas of themselves. This is something We never created before. To do this replication will require a male and a female. They will multiply and expand to fill the entire sphere."

A buzz reverberates through the Assembly. The flora and fauna on this sphere will create new arborants and animants just like themselves! Eli-Mehlek, Ruash and Michael have exceeded Themselves, having never created anything with the power to produce new life. They always reserved the power to create life to Themselves. Michael pauses as the hum continues. He knows our hearts and waits until we absorb this new idea.

"And lastly, We are going to create a king to rule over this sphere. This regent will be one of the Sons of Eli-Mehlek and will represent this planet when all the Sons of Eli-Mehlek meet together. We will make this new king after Our image and after Our likeness. He and his queen will also have the ability to create other beings just like themselves."

Another buzz vibrates through the angelic ranks. "A being created in the image of Eli-Mehlek? Will wonders never cease?"

"We will begin the creation shortly. Any cherub or seraph who desires can watch as the shaping of this new sphere proceeds. Do any of you have any questions?"

Do we have any questions? Only a zillion or so! Most of them about Satan and the rest of the Rebels.

Jokim arises.

"Michael, I do have a lot of questions. Most of them have to do with Satan. I'll just ask if he will be able to visit this new monarch? Will he be allowed to attempt to entice him to join his rebellion?"

"Thank you, Jokim. That is a vital question. Of course, Satan may visit every realm, star, planet, moon in the cosmos, but he may only stay where he is welcomed by those who choose to rebel with him."

I shudder at the thought.

"Every heart in the Universe, every cherub, every seraph, every Son of Eli-Mehlek has to decide whose side he will choose to join. All of the angels sitting in this Assembly faced that choice on Decision Day. As each angel made his choice, he showed that decision by which side he joined and fought with.

"The new king will also face that same choice. Satan will be allowed to present his case to the new ruler. Gabriel and other loyal angels will warn the new king about Satan and his followers. No one will interfere as the new king opts for Us or for Satan. It must be his decision and his decision alone.

"Eli-Mehlek and I have planned a test for the new king. It is an easy test—not nearly as difficult as Decision Day. As the new king chooses, his actions will show which side he chooses. Everyone in the Universe—Eli-Mehlek, Myself, Satan, the Loyal angels and the Rebel angels as well as the Sons of Eli-Mehlek—all will know the decision the king made."

Jokim thanks Michael and sits.

Eli-Mehlek and Michael always plan things in a good way. I wonder if Satan knows about the plan for this new planet. My mind still roils with lots of questions. Will the new king choose Satan's side or Michael's? What is the test? What will happen if he chooses Satan's side? The Assembly over, I slowly glide back to Gabriel's mansion, deep in thought. Do I want the king to choose Lucifer or Michael? My heart wants him to choose Michael, yet perhaps Satan's accusations against Michael are true. And yet, all along, Michael and Eli-Mehlek have been totally fair to Satan. Perhaps that could be because they know Satan is right. Oooh, I hate these kinds of thoughts. Why can't it be the way it had been before the rumors started? I love Michael and I love Satan and Sotai. I am torn between my love for all the Rebels and the Loyalists.

* * * *

Satan kept us busy. He posted some of us outside the gates of Shalem. Our job was to talk to Michael's angels as they came through the gates. We knew these angels and they knew us. Often, they would stop and chat. We were to tell them how great Satan's freedom was and all the good things happening in Satan's kingdom. Sometimes we'd hear little bits of gossip about what was happening in Shalem.

One day, I heard a wild rumor. Deity was planning a new creation. Hurriedly, I waggled my way back to our abode and rushed up to Satan.

"Satan!" I gasped. "Satan, you'll never guess what I just heard."

"Hi, Sotai," Satan graciously responded. "This must be important; you really hurried to tell me, didn't you?"

I nodded.

"So what did you hear?"

"One of Michael's angels just told me Deity is planning a new creation, a whole new planet, complete with many new forms of life. He babbled something about the king of the planet will be made in Deity's likeness."

"Well, well, well. That is an interesting tidbit. I wonder where this new creation is going to be. Hmmm. Thank you, Sotai, you are a loyal lieutenant. Keep up the good work and I might have to promote you."

"Oh, Satan. I'm just a gardener. What else could I be?" I replied, dreaming of being Satan's second-in-command.

"Well, I haven't figured that out quite yet. But surely there is something an energetic angel, such as yourself, can do to be useful."

"I thank you for the compliment."

I could see Satan was deep in thought. His face flashed between excitement and worry.

"Sotai, go back to Shalem and see if you can find out where this creation is going to be. And when. We might like to watch it. I suspect every angel in Shalem will be watching. We should be watching, too."

"Yes, Satan. I'm on my way!" And away I went, happy as I could be. Satan praised my work and virtually promised me a promotion.

Just after I got back to Shalem, I found out when and where the creation would be. I'd snuck back in, visiting some of my good friends. They were quite voluble talking about the new orb.

Satan applauded my efforts.

* * * *

Shalem is aflutter with excitement. The activity level slowly breaks into my ponderings. Most of the angels are at the outer edge of Shalem ready to watch Michael. How many times had we watched as Michael created what He and Eli-Mehlek planned? But this time, there is a special interest. I look around and see most of my loyal friends. I wonder if Satan and Sotai are watching. I'm in one of my favorite places, a good view but slightly away from the main crowd. I sit and make myself comfortable. To my surprise, I see Gabriel making his way towards me.

"Hi, Zuriel!"

"Hi, Gabriel," I answer. "Would you like to sit down?"

"Thank you, Zuriel. You are most kind." He sits down within easy talking distance. "What do you think about this creation?"

"Well, Gabriel, I'm not certain what to think. In all reality, I'm a little concerned. Jokim's questions are on my mind, too. Since Satan is able to visit the new sovereign, I'm wondering if he will join Satan's rebellion. What will happen if the new king decides to rebel? But if Ruash, Michael and Eli-Mehlek believe it is best to create this new sphere, it must be okay."

"Yes, Zuriel, that is correct. Look! Over there! In that little galaxy … not too far away. See, Ruash is moving."

I follow his pointing finger and, sure enough, Ruash is moving toward a little galaxy where nothing has been created before. It is a unique location to which Ruash makes His way. It contains just a sarsen and some water. It is close to the middle of the galaxy where there is nothing around it. As Michael said, it is devoid of everything. Gabriel and I watch as Ruash brings light to the unusual nebula—glorious light. Ruash moves back and forth above the waters, almost as if anticipating with delight, what is going to be created.

As Ruash rises, we hear Eli-Mehlek's awesome voice behind us. "This is Earth. We chose this place for our new creation. It is without form now.

Ruash brought light to Earth and began its cycle of day and night. This evening and the morning are its first day."

Gabriel stirs as he comments, "Well, that is a big change for Earth. It now has light and dark and days and nights. I wonder how soon Michael will continue the creation?"

We watch as Earth spins slowly around. Michael moves to Earth. He pauses above it, almost as if He is surveying how it will look when He's finished. After Earth's night passes, Michael again moves.

"Oh, Gabriel, see, Michael's moving."

"Yes, Zuriel."

Michael stretches out His hand and, from the tips of His fingers, flows a welkin surrounding Earth. It contains oxygen and nitrogen and a bevy of other elements. He splits the waters. Some He places above the welkin and the rest He leaves below. Earth takes on a gorgeous blue hue.

"Oooh," I breathe.

Gabriel adds, "It's beautiful, isn't it?"

Michael rises again from Earth. He seems to frame it in His hands, almost as if it were a work of art. Eli-Mehlek's voice sounds again. "Michael created what the new king will call the Heavens. And the evening and the morning are the second day."

It isn't long before Earth's second night is over. Michael goes down through the welkin and moves over the entire face of Earth. With His finger, He seems to catch some of the rocks, which follow right where He points. The water rumbles and swishes agitatedly. I began to see it. "Gabriel, look! The rocks are surrounding the water. See how He's gathered all the water into one place?"

"Sure enough, Zuriel. Now watch what is next."

"Oh, yes, Gabriel. I see Michael putting out His hand onto the rocks. He's forming them and arranging them in gentle, rolling berms, hillocks and terraces, smoothing away the roughness. It looks like He's creating the foundation for a park. See, every little nook and cranny is different. It is all so beautiful."

Michael rises from the hills, the lakes and the sea. His pleasure glows from His entire body. He moves back to Earth's surface, lifting His hands as He says, "Let the soil teem with life. Grass, herbs, fruit trees covered with leaves and fruit, orange, red, tawny and emerald fruit, trees covered with needles of verdant green and cunning little hard conic flowers, vines covered with red, purple and green fruit and flowers, big flowers, little flowers, aromatic flowers, sepia, ochre and violet flowers." I gasp with delight! What will Eli-Mehlek and Michael think up next? There are so many different flowers and trees and grasses and herbs—I can't even start to count all the different types. And none are anything like what we have in Shalem.

I am so caught up with the beauty, the absolute gorgeousness of Michael's creation, that Gabriel's voice startles me. "Look at that! Right over there!" My eyes follow his pointing finger. There is a small flower, almost teardrop in shape, deep red, velvety in texture.

"Oooh, I wonder what the new king will call that flower. It's gorgeous."

"I don't know," Gabriel replies, "but it surpasses all other flowers with its beauty."

Again we hear Eli-Mehlek's voice pealing forth. "See. Michael created the Soil and the Seas. The water gathered together will be called Seas by the new king. The land will be called Soil. He created all the plants for Earth. Inside of the fruits are what will be called Seeds. When these Seeds are placed into the ground, another new plant will grow. A plant just like the one from which the Seed came, but yet it will be different also. Michael left much of Earth without plant life. These seeds will be used to cover the entire Earth with plants. The new king and all of the others who will eventually live on Earth will plant these seeds and grow new trees and flowers and herbs as they desire. This is good. This is very good. And the evening and the morning are the third day."

As darkness covers Earth, Gabriel and I look at each other and sigh in ecstasy.

Never have I seen such a display of Michael's power. It is enthralling, totally enthralling! Mere words cannot describe what we witness. I wonder if Sotai is watching Michael's creation.

As the light becomes stronger on the fourth day, Michael does not move back to the surface of Earth, but turns and faces away from Earth. His right hand swings forward as He gently lobs something away from Earth. Suddenly, it explodes into a star. A star that dwarfs Earth, but isn't nearly as big as the very largest of the stars. It is just the right size to cause Earth to orbit around it. Earth is now a planet.

Michael turns from the star and makes another soft toss. This time a small moon is the result, orbiting around Earth. Finally Michael turns and, with His left hand, makes a sweeping motion across the galaxy and suddenly, almost as if flung from His fingers, there are other planets orbiting the star. The fifth planet catches my eye. "Look, Gabriel, look at that huge planet. It's much larger than Earth. It is magnificent!"

"Yes, Zuriel, and look at the sixth! It has some wonderful halos surrounding it. I shall have to go explore those halos sometime. And look, the second planet shines like silver in bright light."

"Ah, look at the fourth one. See how red it is? And the last one is the smallest of them all, just a little ball of ice."

Eli-Mehlek rumbles, "Michael made what the new king will call the Sun and the Moon and the Planets. The Sun will rule over the day and the Moon will rule over the night. This is good. This is very good. And the evening and the morning are the fourth day."

Earth turns its face back towards its sun and Michael moves again. While He passes by, the trees bend their trunks bowing to give Him reverence and the grass blades stand at stiff attention to give Him honor. The seas are beneath His feet as He stops. With bated breath, we listen as He starts to speak. As the words roll from His mouth, the seas begin to roil and churn and the waters are full of life. "Ah, Gabriel," I cry, "What are they?"

"I really don't know. I've not seen anything like them before. Look, at that huge one, why it's bigger than you or me. Watch, it pushes itself with its tail, wide with two halves. See that one over there. It has eight legs. And it propels itself with a jet of ink. There are some tiny creatures, too."

"I see them. Look, they swim straight up and down. And their heads look like something familiar, but what could it be? See those creatures that crawl sideways and have big claws? I wonder what they will be called!"

And before we can even begin to take in all the aquian creatures of the sea, Michael moves on up into the welkin. Again He speaks and suddenly the welkin is full of activity. Creatures with wings are flying through the welkin, big creatures and little creatures. Many of them have feathers in dazzling arrays of colors—fiery scarlet, dazzling blue, sunlight yellow, starlight white. There are some whose wings were soft as gossamer. They flit as they flutter by. Some buzz as they fly, with black and yellow stripes on their bodies and wings which seem too small for them. There are others who spread their wings and soar to the top of the welkin. They glide and float far above Earth, rarely ever flapping their wings.

Eli-Mehlek speaks again saying, "Michael created many new avian creatures. The new king will call the winged creatures Birds and the creatures that live in the water he will call Fish. This is exactly as Ruash, Michael and I planned them. It is so good. Birds! Be fruitful, multiply and expand to fill Earth. Fish! Propagate and reproduce and fill the entire seas. And the evening and the morning are the fifth day."

Gabriel and I just look at each other in amazement. We cannot even talk about what we have seen. It is too thrilling! What else could Eli-Mehlek and Michael plan for Earth?

Earth finishes spinning completely around before Michael moves again. As He goes through the welkin, the avians fly in formation over His head to give Him homage. He moves over the seas and the aquians delightedly convoy Him to the land. I guess at what is coming. There must be some creatures that live on the land!

He begins to speak in His glorious voice. As He speaks, creatures begin to appear on the land. There are big creatures, some with long necks, some with huge bony growths on their heads. One has a long protuberance growing between two of its teeth. There are small creatures, just big enough to be seen, some have long, bushy tails, some have many legs. I laugh, "Gabriel, do you see those? Look at those creatures that swing in the trees by their tails!"

Gabriel chuckles, too, adding, "I see some creatures that walk majestically and I see some that just shuffle along. And look, there are some that hop along, too."

We are still exclaiming over these new creatures when Eli-Mehlek's voice, sounding like liquid power, is heard again. "Michael created the creatures that will live on the land. These creatures the new king will call Animals. This creation is good."

Michael seems to be waiting for something. He moves again. This time, the land creatures kneel in obeisance as He passes. Michael moves into the middle of the delightful Garden He made on the third day. He stands and looks at Eli-Mehlek. A silent communion passes between them. Eli-Mehlek's voice speaks again, reverberating across the Universe. "Michael, it is time to make the new king. Let's call him Adam. Let's give him dominion over the Birds, the Fish, the Animals and the Earth. Let's make him from the dust of the ground. Let's make him in Our image and after Our likeness. Yes, Michael, it is time. Do it!"

Michael kneels down in that enchanting Garden. With His hands, He begins to take handfuls of soil and as He works, we see Adam's form taking shape. We see his legs being formed, his chest, his arms, his neck and finally his head. He lies there, perfect in every way. Eli-Mehlek rises from His throne and joins Ruash and Michael. All of Deity kneels beside the new King as Michael breathes into Adam's lungs. Adam sits up! Never before have I seen such a look on Deity's faces. All Deity is ecstatic. I look over at Gabriel—he has the same look on his face.

Together, Deity and Adam explore Adam's new sphere. Deity calls all of the Birds, the Fish and the Animals to come before Adam and Adam gives them names: Deer, Salmon, Whale, Wasp, Eagle, Bear, Giraffe, Sparrow, Grasshopper, Centipede, Monkey, Cardinal, Bee and all the others.

There are two of each kind of animal. Deity calls them male and female. Yet Adam is alone. Michael comments, "It is not good for Adam to be solitary. He needs a completer! Let's make another like him, but different. One who completes him. One who makes him like Us."

Deity renders Adam comatose. Michael takes one of Adam's ribs and creates another who is like Adam, but different. This time Eli-Mehlek breathes life into the new one. Deity awakes Adam and delightedly Adam says, "Wow! This is Woman. She's beautiful. Oh, wow! Thank you, Michael; thank you, Eli-Mehlek; thank you, Ruash!"

She is beautiful. There is so much I didn't understand about this new sphere. Eli-Mehlek said something about bearing after themselves. I remembered Michael made two of each kind so that the two of them will have progeny like themselves.

Eli-Mehlek's voice resounds again, "It is finished. The creation of the new sphere is complete. It is very good. And the evening and the morning are the sixth day."

It is with an air of contentment that Deity rests on the seventh day and enshrines it as the day when Deity will visit Earth. Adam and the Woman walk and talk with Deity. Deity tells them what they need to know, what is food for them, the work they will do, where they will live. Deity informs them about the tree in the midst of their Garden; the Tree of Knowledge of Good and Evil. If Adam and the Woman eat of that Tree, they will be destroyed. Every week on the seventh day, Deity will come and visit with them, as a memorial of their creation.

Darkness is falling, ending the seventh day of Earth's existence. Adam and the Woman lie down in their Garden and sleep. The rest of the angels and I wing our way back to our dwellings. Gabriel goes to do Eli-Mehlek's bidding, so I am alone in the mansion, reflecting on what I have seen. Every seven days, Adam and the Woman will have their Assembly with Deity. And there is the test. Michael told Jokim there would be a test to see if Adam desired to be loyal to Deity. The test is so simple! Michael made a wealth of luxuriant food for the new King. There will be—can be—no excuse if they eat the fruit of the tree in the center of their Garden. Eli-Mehlek said that, if they ate, they will be destroyed. I wonder what that means. *Destruction* is still a new word in my vocabulary. It sounds like they would disappear, but where will they go? I think again about Sotai and Lucifer. I wonder if they have seen the new orb and what they think about it.

* * * *

Satan was deep in thought. Sotai watched him closely, trying to determine what he was thinking. Sotai loved Satan so much. Finally, Satan made an announcement. He was leaving to do some planning. He'd be back soon.

His angels waited, milling around with nothing to do. A couple of the angels got into a fight about something. Sotai tried to break it up, but couldn't. A couple of the bigger angels pulled them apart, but they were still snapping at each other.

Finally, Satan came back. It seemed he had been gone a long while.

"My friends, I have made some big plans. Since Eli-Mehlek threw us out of Shalem, we need a new home. My plans obtain one for us, simultaneously punishing Eli-Mehlek for our expulsion from Shalem." Some cheers followed that statement. Sotai's was the loudest.

"I have been looking at Earth. It seems pleasant enough, with plenty of room for all of us. Earth will be our new home."

Resheph flared, "And who says Eli-Mehlek won't evict us from Earth? And anywhere else we would go to live?"

Satan answered, "That is a good question, Resheph. Keep on thinking like that and we'll do very well.

"We'll just have to arrange it so that Eli-Mehlek cannot expel us. Remember, I know Eli-Mehlek and how He operates. I have watched Him for ages and eons, longer than any of you, since I am the first created angel. I know how to arrange it so he cannot do anything about it."

"Yeah, just like you figured out how to make Eli-Mehlek keep us in Shalem," Resheph sneered. "Do you expect us to believe you now?"

Satan smiled and answered the sneer. "We have many angels on our side. Getting a full third of Shalem's angels to join our side was a great victory. Many others will be joining us. The prospect of perfect freedom is compelling. We'll have so many on our side that even Eli-Mehlek cannot withstand us. Anyone else with questions?"

Resheph said nothing more, but Sotai could see he was not certain about Satan's answer. A few others asked some questions, such as how and when, to which Satan answered, "That is still being planned."

"Now, I have to finish my plans. I'm leaving for a while. Some of you, like Resheph, seem to be unsure of these plans. Trust me, this is the ideal strategy. It is our best approach. If we fail here, it will be much harder to regain Shalem or any other place in the Universe.

"I need to know if all of you are ready to work with me. While I am gone, you decide whether you want to follow my plans. Resheph, could you moderate the discussion? Thank you, very much."

And he was gone. They looked at each other. A babble broke out. Some didn't want to involve Earth in the rebellion. Others shouted that we had to secure some place to live. Sotai knew what would happen. They would all decide to unite with Satan in his plans. It was indeed the only way. It was obvious; they must work together.

Sotai quietly slipped away and followed Satan. He kinda stayed behind an asteroid, where he wouldn't be seen easily. He saw Satan shudder again as he plotted how to capture Earth. Satan muttered something about, "Even if I succeed, will I have gained anything?"

The rest of the Rebels came and flew to Satan. Resheph spoke for all. "Satan, we decided we will follow you. Whatever plans you make, we will follow. Whatever consequences happen, good or bad, we will bear them with you."

Satan stood tall as he smiled. "You will never regret that decision. It is a wise choice. Now let me tell you my plan. I will go to Earth and convince Adam and the Woman to confederate with us. Since Adam is the king of Earth, when he enlists with us, I will become Earth's king. Eli-Mehlek must respect that.

Satan plots how to capture Earth. His Rebel angels commit to his cause, totally

"I have several options as to how to proceed. If I go to Adam and the Woman and tell them who I am and make a great fuss about how bad Michael is, they will be ready for that and we'll not win.

"If I go as an angel of great power and authority, they will be suspicious and we'll not win.

"But if I go as a beautiful Animal, say a Snake, they will not be prepared for me. I'll be able to surprise them and get them to listen to me. Yes, a Snake, the most beautiful creature on Earth, should work well.

"Get ready to move. We will live on Earth!"

Satan handled Resheph beautifully. Now he was ready to assist, instead of fighting with Satan.

Earth was exquisite. Delightedly, Sotai thought about all those new plants and wondered how they would respond to his touch. Sure, there was a long way to go before the Rebels would be able to relax, but already Sotai could feel the trees responding to his gardener's touch.

More Rebels

Gabriel and Jokim took a trip to Earth. Gabriel told me about it later. Michael asked him to go and tell Adam and the Woman about Satan: how artfully he spread his rumors around Shalem. He told them Satan's complaints about Deity. He told them they would be safer if they stayed together; Satan could only entice them at the Tree of Knowledge of Good and Evil; they would be totally safe if they did not go close to that Tree. Adam and the Woman understood. They promised they would never go near the Tree and also they would stay together.

I hope Satan'll not inveigle Adam and the Woman. I don't want them to rebel. Yet, I still love Satan. And Sotai is still my best friend. Maybe I can talk to him soon.

Gabriel and I fly to Earth. The new creation is so exciting. It is thrilling watching what Michael made. Adam and the Woman are so content. As I watch them, it is almost like watching Sotai in his garden. They have a way of making their delightful Garden even more glorious.

"Look, Gabriel," I call; there is a little alarm in my voice. "Look! The Woman is away from Adam. She rambled away while working in The Garden. See how close she is to the Tree. I'll go warn her."

"No, Zuriel. You cannot warn them. They must be left free to obey or rebel, as they choose. When you were talking to Sotai, did anyone come and interfere with the choice you had to make?"

Deity has devised a simple test of mankind's loyalty. It is so absolutely simple that there is no excuse, should they disobey

"No, Gabriel. You are right. But what if they eat of the fruit? What will happen?"

"I do not know, Zuriel. I trust Deity has a Plan, should that happen, but I do not know what it is."

Just at that instant, Satan comes to the Tree. The Woman does not recognize him, as Satan assumes the form of a Serpent, a beautiful serpent, flying through the air. The Serpent's wings shimmer and twinkle in the sunlight. His long slender body oscillates fluidly behind him. Michael created a wonderful creature in the Serpent. Languorously, he lands in the Tree and with great deliberation, stretches and picks a piece of the fruit. He slowly chews it and, when it is about half gone, he speaks. "What did Michael tell you? Can you eat of every tree in your Garden?"

A Serpent talking to her startles the Woman and she answers, "Well, almost all the trees. Except for the Tree in which you are reposing. Michael told us if we eat of it, or even touch it, we will be destroyed."

I shudder as I hear Satan respond by saying, "You won't be destroyed. I'm eating it and I'm not destroyed. This is a magic Tree, able to give wondrous powers to those who eat of it. How do you think I became able to talk? No, you won't be destroyed. But Michael knows if you eat of the fruit of this Tree, you will be like Eli-Mehlek, knowing good and evil. Here, take some. It's wonderful!" And with that, Satan picks one fruit and hands it to the Woman.

She holds it in her hand and looks at it. It is an exquisite piece of fruit. Holding it has no ill effect. Wonderingly, she moves the fruit to her mouth and takes a bite. She gasps. "It tastes marvelous. I've never tasted anything like this before." And with that, she finishes eating the fruit, all the while chatting with the Serpent.

My eyes can hardly see. They are filled with tears. I haven't felt such anguish since Decision Day.

The Woman reaches out and picks more of the fruit and hurries back to Adam. "Here, have some wonderful fruit. I've never tasted anything quite so delightful." She hands the fruit to Adam. Adam stands there, his somber eyes shifting from the Woman to the fruit. He recognizes the fruit. He knows the Woman rebelled. He remembers what Michael said. Yet he loves the Woman. Even through my tears, I can see there is a battle going on inside of him. In a swift motion, almost as if he is afraid he will change his mind, he takes a big bite of one fruit. Quickly, he gobbles the rest. I weep harder. Great copious tears of grief spill down my face. I hear Gabriel sobbing beside me. We can't watch anymore and turn back towards Shalem.

As word spreads throughout Shalem, so does the grief. There is no singing nor praising Eli-Mehlek. It is so quiet. Not since Decision Day's aftermath has it been this quiet. I ask the same question I hear others asking over and over again. "Now what will happen?" Adam and the

Woman, made in Deity's image, defected to Satan's rebellion. What will Deity do? I half expect Eli-Mehlek to lift His mighty hand and sweep them away, yet He treats Lucifer with fairness and dignity. Will He do less with Adam and the Woman? I don't know. Like Gabriel, I believe Deity has a Plan. Somehow it seems only fair that someone who was tricked like the Woman was tricked should have a second chance. But Lucifer won't have a second chance. Lucifer knows Deity and knows what They are like. His rebellion was different. He wasn't tricked. Round and round my head spins with these thoughts. I don't know what to think.

As my thoughts whirl, I remember Decision Day. I apprehend Adam had the same choice I did. Mine was between Michael and Lucifer and Sotai. Adam's was between Deity and his wife. I understand how difficult his decision had been. I weep aloud, sobbing out my grief.

Shalem grieves as Adam and the Woman join Satan's rebellion. Satan's ranks swell. He has his headquarters. He doesn't know Deity has a Plan for Earth

* * * *

Satan returned, exultant. We gathered around him as he told us what had happened.

"I observed the Woman wandering away from Adam and she was quite near the Tree. So I assumed the form of a Serpent and flew to the Tree. As the Woman came closer, I began to talk to her. She was startled that a Snake could talk and she answered the Snake. She did not recognize me.

"I placed the fruit in her hands and told her, 'See, you aren't destroyed. The fruit is magic fruit. It gives me, a Snake, the ability to speak. It will do great wonders for you, also. Eli-Mehlek doesn't want to share this magic fruit with you and Adam.'

"After the Woman ate, I just laid back and watched. She took the fruit to Adam. Oh, the surrender was total. Adam knew who I was. Adam knew he was rebelling. Adam chose to join our rebellion.

"The most important part of this victory is that now we can eat of the Tree of Life in Adam's—er—my Garden.

"Let us proceed to our new home."

With great joy, we sailed to Earth. It was a most pleasing habitat. We surged over the entire orb, each of us picking the spot we would inhabit. I waited until Satan chose his location and settled right next to him.

* * * *

Grief wraps around all of Shalem. I feel bereft, almost the same as I did after Decision Day. Will Adam and the Woman be expelled from their Garden? Will all contact with them be severed? Will two more whom I love be torn away from me? And what is this thing called *destruction*? What will happen to them?

As the Archangel, Gabriel has much to do. Gabriel's mansion is close to Eli-Mehlek's palace. I slip over to see what Eli-Mehlek, Michael and Ruash will do about Adam and the Woman. Gabriel is busy, but stops to let me know what is happening.

"Michael and Eli-Mehlek are in executive conference with Ruash. They have been in conference ever since Adam ate the fruit."

"Do you know what They are communing about?"

"No, just that we will have an Assembly soon. I am to call all the angels to the Assembly."

At that instant, Michael comes out of the conference. Gabriel flies to His side. They talk briefly. Michael returns to the summit with Eli-Mehlek.

"I must contact all of the messenger angels, Zuriel. That will take some time, but I'll be back."

And with that, Gabriel is off, winging his way across the Universe. It is quiet, somberly quiet, at the palace. Sometimes when Deity is in conference, we can tell They are happy. This time, the sad stillness is all encompassing.

Again Michael comes out of the conference. Gabriel is not back yet. Michael doesn't wait long. He reenters the conference. This is His third time in deep communion with Eli-Mehlek and Ruash. Gabriel returns with a sad air about him. The Assembly Grounds are slowly filling up. None of us angels are anxious to hear what Deity's verdict is. We lost so many angels already. Now this. The Assembly Grounds are full. All the angels are there. The talk is quiet, hushed, somber, sad.

Finally, Michael comes from the conference with Eli-Mehlek. Slowly, He makes His way to the dais. In a voice choking with emotion, He slowly begins to speak.

"This is a sad Assembly. Jokim, do you remember asking about the new king's loyalty? Remember I told you We planned a simple test to determine his loyalty. We planned the test to be so utterly simple there could be no excuse for not obeying Our command. As you are aware, the test was for Adam and the Woman not to eat the fruit of one Tree in their Garden. There was no need to eat of that Tree. There was more than enough other food for them. Gabriel and Jokim warned them about how Satan would urge them to eat its fruit. And that is what happened.

"Satan assumed the form of a Serpent and mesmerized the Woman. He told the Woman she would not be destroyed. She believed Satan, ate, taking the fruit to Adam. He also ate and now they are Rebels along with Satan.

"With the king of Earth joining his rebellion, Satan now claims Earth as his realm and asserts he is Earth's king. Very well, Satan is permitted to live on Earth and to be its king. He claims to have a better form of government. This is his chance to prove it.

"However, all is not lost. Adam and the Woman did not know everything the rebellious angels knew. Also, there will be more people born on Earth as time passes. They must also be given the same choice as to whom they desire to be their Sovereign. With that in mind, before We created Earth, We planned what We would do if even one of Earth's inhabitants rebelled.

"This Plan is what Eli-Mehlek, Ruash and I have been discussing. I will go to Earth and become a human like Adam. Even though it is infinitely difficult and unquestionably risky, Eli-Mehlek agrees. This is the only way any human being can cease being a Rebel. Our Divine Law cannot be changed. The penalty for rebellion against Our Law is destruction. However, the human Rebels will be given another chance to keep Our Law. I, Myself, will take their penalty, destruction, upon Me."

A shocked murmur sweeps through the Assembly. Angels are looking at each other with disbelief. We expected nothing like this. Michael will be destroyed? How can this be?

Michael calmly continues, "I will be born like every human being. I will live like every human being. I will teach the inhabitants of Earth about Eli-Mehlek, about Ruash and about Me. That way, everyone on Earth will be able to know whom they desire to serve, Satan or Deity. While on Earth, Satan will test Me, just as he tested Adam and the Woman. Only My tests will be infinitely harder than Adam's were. Satan will be permitted to do anything he desires to Me. Like every human being, I will be destroyed, but My destruction will be particularly hideous."

Another choked gasp flies through the Assembly. Stunned angels are openly sobbing. *Michael to become a human? To be destroyed? No, that can't be. That means Michael will be … gone.*

Jokim struggles to his feet. He bursts out, "Michael, No! This cannot be. Send me. I'll go."

Gabriel stands up and says, "Or me. I'm the Archangel."

I find myself standing to my feet. I choke out a broken sob, "Michael, send me. I'm just a little mansionkeeper. I won't be missed as You will be missed."

Other angels are also standing and offering to go in Michael's place. We are all aghast at the thought of Michael's destruction.

"No, Jokim. Thank you, Gabriel. Zuriel, you too would be missed. All of your willingness is appreciated, because your offer is based on your love for Me. But no matter how willing you are, an angel's destruction will not satisfy Our Law's penalty. Satan's rebellion—and now Adam's rebellion— is against Deity and Deity must respond. Their rebellion is against Our Law and only Deity can respond to the rebellion against Our Law. Satan rebelled, principally against Me. He said never again would he worship Me. So I must be the One who answers all the questions Satan's rebellion raises.

"There is much about this I cannot tell you today. We cannot reveal many of the details of The Plan today as you are not ready to hear them. In the meantime, You will have to trust Us that this Plan is the only way mankind can be reunited, both with Us and with the rest of the Universe. You will understand more as The Plan and the rebellion unfold. You will see things you've never seen before. They will not be pleasant. You will eventually understand the appalling results of rebellion.

"However, there are many roles for angels. Satan and his followers will attempt to convince all of mankind to join the rebellion. So each human being will be assigned a guardian angel. This guardian angel will go to Earth and stay there as long as their protégé is alive. This guardian angel will insulate his appointed ward from some of the things Satan and his angels will try to do. This will not be easy. Every day on Earth will be like Decision Day. The war, begun here in Shalem, is not over, but continues every day on Earth.

"Some angels will keep a record of everything every human being does and says. We will make some tomes, black ink and styli to write these records. We will keep these records in the archives. At the proper time, these documents will be used to decide which human beings are safe to bring to Shalem and which are not. Now, I suspect there are many questions in your minds."

Jokim rises again, "Michael, this is astonishing. It is too dreadful for words. I'm not certain what to say. But my question is: Will Your destruction allow for the reclamation of any Rebel angels?"

"No, Jokim. I wish it could; unfortunately they are confirmed in their rebellion. It will never change. They know Eli-Mehlek. They know Ruash. They know Me. Nothing We do will alter their rebellion. Adam rebelled, but he and the Woman do not know Eli-Mehlek, Ruash, and Me in as full a manner as do the Rebel angels. With humans, as they get to know Us better, some will cease their rebellion. Sadly, the Rebel angels cannot know Us any better. There is no hope for their reconciliation."

There are a few other questions along the same lines. But mostly, we sit in shocked silence. Michael speaks again.

"This is a sad time. When you weep, know that We weep with you. Many human beings will choose to join Satan's rebellion. But many other human beings will choose to become Loyalists. Both Adam and the Woman will choose loyalty. Many of their children will choose to be on Our side. As Deity, We see not only the beginning but the ending of this sad time. When this rebellion is over, Earth will be populated with these loyal humans, war will cease, rebellion will be destroyed, the Universe will be at peace."

Michael's words lift our spirits. While not gleeful, we believe Michael's words pointing to the outcome and we are able to rejoice at the results portrayed.

Cherubs and seraphs slowly wing their way thoughtfully back to their homes, their work, their friends. My mind is tumbling so busily I can hardly keep one thought from running into another one. *Michael? A human? To be destroyed? Multitudes of humans in Shalem?* How I wish I could talk to Sotai, to Luci—Satan. They would help me organize my thoughts. *Angel guards around the humans? Surely Satan won't hurt Adam or the Woman or any of their children, will he? Not the Lucifer that I know. Surely Michael is mistaken.*

Gabriel comes winging up—a pensive look on his face.

"We certainly did not expect what we heard, did we?"

"No, Gabriel, we did not. It more than shocked me. I wish I could understand what Michael is saying. It seems so unbelievable. So different from anything I've ever experienced before, so different from anything I thought I understood."

"These are some things Eli-Mehlek never planned we would experience. It is difficult to understand."

Gabriel and I talk for a while. Slowly, some of the things Michael said begin to sort themselves out in my mind. Gabriel delivers one more shock on this tumultuous day.

"Zuriel, Michael needs someone for special duty. I suggested you. In The Garden on Earth is a Tree of Life. Those who eat of that Tree will never be destroyed. Satan and his angels desire to eat of that Tree. Michael wants to send two angels to guard the Tree of Life. Will you go and guard the Tree of Life?"

"Me? I'm just a little mansion-keeping angel. I'm not a warrior angel."

"Michael promised you will have everything you need to do this job. All you need to do is to trust Michael. He will make sure you can do what He asks you to do."

"Well," my voice is doubtful, "if Michael thinks I can guard the Tree, I'll guard the Tree."

"Good!" replies Gabriel. "I must warn you it will not be easy. Sotai will be there. He will try to get you to let him by. You must not yield to him. Satan will try to convince you that you must obey him, as you have always done. Sometimes Satan will bully you and sometimes he will talk so sweetly you will think he is the old Lucifer. Do not ever believe him."

"Yes, Gabriel. I see. Satan and Sotai could play on my old loyalties. I will be alert to them."

"There will be trouble on Earth. It will get very ugly at times. You will see things of which now you cannot even dream. I cannot even tell you what it will be like. Michael gave me some hints about what will happen. I am astonished. I cannot see how it could possibly happen. I tell you now, so when it happens, it will not overwhelm you. It will still be frightful, but you will be able to get through it.

"And if ever you do get overwhelmed, Michael will dispatch every angel in Shalem to give you assistance."

"Gabriel?"

"Yes, Zuriel?"

"Who is the other angel who will be with me?"

"Oh, I forgot to tell you, didn't I! It's Jokim."

"Oh, good. That pleases me."

And with that, Gabriel skims over the trees to take Michael's directions to other angels. He flies on to Earth to tell Adam and the Woman even more about The Plan.

I am nervous about this new assignment. I am so glad I'll be able to see Sotai again. I miss him so much. But can I say "no" to Sotai? Can I say "no" to Lucifer? I clean Gabriel's mansion once more. With Jokim, I fly to Earth to guard the Tree of Life.

* * * *

After the initial giddiness and exploration was over, Satan called a meeting. He had news to share and work for us to do.

"Well, did I not tell you we'd get a good place to live? This is a most pleasant substitute for Shalem. Here we can build our kingdom of freedom. Our kingdom without law. As I've always said, 'Angels need no law.'

"Now Adam and the Woman are our newest recruits. Their rebellion proves Eli-Mehlek's law is flawed. So badly flawed that it is totally impossible for anyone to obey it.

"Their rebellion made Michael quite upset. As I was in the Tree observing the results of our victory, I heard Him questioning them about what happened. Adam blamed the Woman; the Woman blamed the Serpent. After all the finger-pointing, Michael told them what would happen. He told them a baby would be born who would become the new King of Earth.

"Gabriel came and gave them many details. What he told them is that the baby will be Michael Himself." There was a gasp, a buzz of chatters as this news was discussed. Satan held up his hand and called for quiet. "We could not conquer Michael in Shalem. But when Michael comes to earth, He will be a human. Humans cannot obey Deity's law. Down here," Satan paused, "down here, we will prevail." We let out a roar of approval. We looked forward to seeing Michael as a human rebel against Eli-Mehlek's law. It took a long time for Satan to regain our attention.

"Now we have to continue recruiting others. We have Adam and the Woman as our two newest recruits, but we need more. So we will have different angels go to different parts of the Universe. There they will talk to the various Sons of Eli-Mehlek and explain to them how our kingdom is better than Eli-Mehlek's.

"Each of you will be assigned different orbs where you can go to recruit. I'll come around and help you on occasion. Since I cannot be everywhere at the same time, often you will have to work by yourselves."

"Any questions? ... Good, now, get to work!"

We milled around, jabbering excitedly. This was going better than we thought just a little while ago. I knew where my assignment was going to be—right at the gates of Shalem. I was a good recruiter. I already brought many angels to the rebellion. Now I would show the loyal angels that they chose the losing side. I thought about Zuriel. *Why had he been so stubborn? It would have been wonderful had he joined us. For a while it seemed he would rebel too, but, on Decision Day, he just would not come. Maybe I could still persuade him.* I cherished that thought.

Sentry Watch

It seems so strange. Jokim and I station ourselves beside the gate to their Garden, carrying the flaming swords Michael provided. I wonder how Adam and the Woman are doing. I can't see them from where we stand. I wonder how long it will take for Sotai or Satan to appear. I hope I'll be able to say "no" to them. "No" was something I never said to Lucifer and my heart still yearns for Sotai.

The scene outside The Garden is quite different from that inside. Outside, things don't look quite finished. I can tell the plants have not been dressed. No one loves them or cares for them. The Garden is different. Adam and the Woman love it and care for it. That love and care show.

Not too far away is a small pile of stones. It was obviously built by someone, but what its use can be, I cannot imagine. There is a small heap of black and gray powder on top of it, which I don't recognize.

Jokim and I stand there all day. Towards evening, the sky is beginning to darken, the sun is moving closer to the edge of Earth. Adam and the Woman come out of the trees on the far side of the glen. Adam is carrying a small, white, fuzzy animal. In her hand, the Woman carries what appears to be a little sword. There is a look of sadness, mixing with horror, on their faces.

I look at Jokim with questions in my eyes. He shrugs an answer. He doesn't understand either.

"I don't want to see this," snaps the Woman.

"Do you think I want to do it?" asks Adam, somewhat sharply. "But Michael promises if we constantly obey and continue to choose not to rebel, that someday we will be welcomed back into our Garden."

"Yes, from what He told us, this is our part. But He also told us we must be redeemed. That's a funny word. I don't know if I understand what it means."

"What I think I understand it means is that Deity will somehow be able to treat us as though we never rebelled." Adam stands there stroking the head of the animal with slow caresses. It snuggles trustingly in Adam's arms, looking into Adam's face, contentment oozing from its eyes.

"Do you understand why we must destroy this lamb?"

"I think somehow it is an example of how we will be salvaged. I think it means Michael must be destroyed, just as this lamb must be destroyed, to accomplish that recovery."

They stop by the stone pile and kneel as they talk to Eli-Mehlek, to Michael and to Ruash. They talk for a long time.

> *The lamb's destruction reminds them the result of rebellion is destruction. They live because another will accept destruction for them*

Adam's tears spill from his eyes as he picks up that little lamb and holds it in his arms. "Scamp," he calls it. "Scamp, I'm so sorry I have to do this. You have to take the punishment for my rebellion. This is happening to you, because I chose to rebel. This is the consequence of my decision. I rebelled and now you have to bear my punishment. I am supposed to be destroyed for my rebellion. Instead, you will be destroyed, so we can live. Oh, Michael, how can I do this to You? I didn't know I was choosing to kill You."

With tears streaming down his face, Adam takes the little sword and plunges it deeply into the side of that lamb. He lays the lamb upon the stone pile. Its head droops over the edge of the stones. Its eyes stare unmovingly. Its tail falls over the other side and Scamp lies motionless.

With a whoosh, fire falls from the sky and that little lamb burns. It doesn't take long, just a few moments and all that is left is more of that gray and black powder.

Jokim and I watch, unable to turn from the scene. Neither of us has ever seen destruction before. That lamb, which Michael created on the sixth day of creation week … gone, destroyed, nonexistent. Is this what destruction is all about? My heart aches for the lamb, for Adam who must destroy it, for the Woman who watches. I puzzle over Adam's words, "I think it means Michael must be destroyed, just as this lamb was destroyed." Will Michael be gone, just as that lamb is gone? Is that what it takes to redeem man? That sounds similar to what Michael said. I convulse with wonder.

* * * *

Resheph and Sotai watched as Adam slaughtered that Scamp. They have not seen anything destroyed before now. It startled them a little. Satan was just a little way off. He was watching intently. Deep in thought, he was obviously trying to understand what he'd seen. It was so mysterious. What was it Adam said? "Scamp, you must be destroyed, so I can live."

Sotai thought confusedly, *I don't understand. Oh, well, Satan can figure it out. He's the smartest being in the whole Universe. He's the only one who found the flaws in Eli-Mehlek's government. He'll figure it out.*

* * * *

Guarding the Tree of Life is generally easy. Jokim and I have a lot of time to talk. Every so often, I see Satan flying by. Sotai is often close behind. All the rest of Satan's angels are in and around Earth. Satan sets up a throne for himself and sometimes he sits upon it. But mostly, he is busy trying to get other Sons of Eli-Mehlek to rebel against Michael. He flies off to this sphere or that star and is gone a long time. Then he comes back with a choleric look on his face, his failure obvious. One day, I look across the landscape and there is Sotai flapping towards me.

"Hi ya, Zuriel, 'tis a tiptop morning, isn't it?" he squawks.

"That is it," I answer with a chuckle. "And how are you?"

We start talking and chatter about so many things. Sotai is telling me all the neat new things he's found on Earth. "It's a honey of a home. Much better than silly Shalem. Nobody here bully-bosses us around. We can do anything we want to do."

As we are talking, he casually reaches up to pick a fruit from the Tree. I don't realize what he is doing, until Jokim's glittering sword flashes between Sotai and the Tree.

"Yeow," Sotai sputters as he snatches his hand back. "Hey ya, Jokim, be careful with that flaming firebrand. You almost hurt marvelous me." He rubs his hand and looks at it carefully.

"You be careful, Sotai. Michael told me not to let anyone eat the fruit of this Tree. Not you, not Satan, not Adam, not the Woman, no one. Not even Zuriel here. As Michael's servant, I cannot let you eat. If you insist on trying and lose your hand, it is your fault. You know what I have to do."

Sotai's face contorts with anger. "I'll eat of this Tree yet," he snarls. "Just you wait. Supersmart Satan and I will figure out a way to get past you two imbecilic idiots. You two aren't as smart as you think you are."

With that, he spins in midair and zooms across the sky. Jokim and I stand there, watching him go. His anger shocks us more than his attempt to eat the fruit.

Gabriel's words come back to me, "He will try to get you to let him by. Do not yield to him." I nearly let him get by. It is so much fun to talk to him. We haven't chatted much since Decision Day. I am so glad Jokim is here to be alert, when I'm not. I thank Jokim fervently. What would happen should Sotai succeed? I wonder if Eli-Mehlek would throw me out of Shalem, just like the other Rebels. I never feel Michael is angry with me. Yet, if I made a mistake and Sotai had been able to eat the fruit, would Michael, would Eli-Mehlek, would Gabriel be angry with me? The thought scares me just a little, well, quite a bit. I am just so glad Jokim was there.

* * * *

Angrily, Sotai flew back to headquarters. Resheph was there. Sotai sputtered about Jokim and Zuriel.

"I almost had it. I almost had it. I distracted that seriously simple Zuriel. He and I were talking, just like old times. I reached behind Zuriel and almost had my hands on that fabulously fantastic fruit."

"Great! What happened?"

"Jokim is really good with that super sharp sword. Rigel, oh, Rigel, if I hadn't been fabulously fast, I would have lost my limb," Sotai squawked angrily. "Maybe you can come along next time and distract Jokim."

"Good idea. Hmmm, there's only the two of them, aren't there? How about we get a dozen or so others and some of us will get the fruit. I'll take on Jokim, you take on Zuriel—the others can eat all they want."

They laid their plans, recruited the others and flew back to the Tree of Life. Zuriel and Jokim were there.

* * * *

"Don't even think about it, Sotai. You might have tricked me before, but not this time." I speak in a quiet, even voice.

"Hey ya, Zuriel, don't be so acerbically aggressive. I'm not trying to get to that fruit. I learned my lesson last time. We just came by for a little chatting. So how are things over here?"

It is all quiet for a moment. Gabriel flashes into view.

"Hi, Gabriel. How are you?" I sing out. "Good to see you."

Gabriel and a whole platoon of angels land right beside Jokim and me. "Well, I'm fine, Zuriel."

"How's the mansion? I haven't been able to clean it for a while"

"Oh, it's doing fine. I dust it every so often."

* * * *

Resheph and Sotai looked at each other. Their plan was spoiled. They could never, in a gazillion orbits, distract all Michael's angels. Angrily, they flapped away, leaving Zuriel and Gabriel talking about … mansionkeeping. Sotai growled, "Wait 'till I get him alone. I'll get Zuriel, sooner or later."

Resheph and Sotai jabbered for a long time. They didn't like being embarrassed like that. But they couldn't figure out a way to get some of that fruit. Maybe Satan would have an idea.

Progeny

I sense great excitement on Earth. Jokim feels it, too. The Woman looks quite different. She is happy, radiantly happy. Adam's delight is obvious. Their coming baby excites them and me, too. I've never seen a baby before! But neither has anyone else, anywhere else in the entire Universe!

"Adam!" she quietly calls.

"Yes, dear," he answers.

"It's time."

And with that, Adam hurries to her side. He leads her away and gently lays her on the bed. Soft cries and low moans can be heard. Adam is talking quietly to her. There is a mighty outcry, followed by quietness.

Adam bursts from the bower and in his hands is a tiny human being. Holding it up towards Shalem and with a mighty whoop and a loud roar he calls out, "Look Michael! Look, Eli-Mehlek! Look Ruash! My son! See my son! Eve has created a man, just as Michael did." He looks over towards us. "See Zuriel? Jokim, can you see? I have a son. Look at my son. His name is Cain. And the Woman's name is Eve, because she is the mother of all living people."

Adam is so thrilled! Such a tiny little person! Adam can easily hold him in his hands. But he is complete—two eyes, two ears, ten fingers, ten toes, not much hair, no teeth. I can't take my eyes off him. Somehow, I understand that Cain will grow to be as large as Adam and Eve, but it will take time. Right now, Cain can't walk or talk or do any of the things humans do. But he'll learn how to walk and how to talk and how to do all the other things a human can do.

Another son is born, Abel. And soon there are lots of other babies being born. Some are female, like Eve and some are male, like Adam. I watch them as they grow taller. Soon they are nearly as tall as Adam and Eve. Oh, it is wonderful, this idea of babies. Adam and Eve's are not alone. All the animals have babies, too. Cubs and kittens, kids and lambs, eaglets and auklets; I see little robins and fox pups. Even the aquians produce offspring! Even so, there is something special about Adam and Eve's babies. Perhaps that's because they remind me of Deity.

As the children grow, they come and talk to us and ask us why we are there. We tell them about Shalem and Decision Day and Satan and the Creation of their Earth and the day Adam and Eve joined the rebellion. We remind them why they can't eat of the Tree of Life.

Some of the children go away thoughtfully and come back to ask us if they are Rebels, too and is there any way for them to quit being Rebels. The first really thoughtful one is Abel. I tell him to talk to Adam about why he needs to kill the lamb and watch it burn.

Others of the children go away angry. I hear Cain muttering something about how awful it was of Eli-Mehlek to expel Mom and Dad out of their Garden just because of a piece of fruit. Cain doesn't want to know about the redeeming and the lamb and the sacrifice.

> *Michael stipulated a lamb. Cain brings garden produce. He never understands Michael's refusal to acknowledge his gift*

As the children grow older, Cain becomes a gardener and Abel a shepherd. When they are grown, disaster happens. Right there at the altar in front of The Garden. Cain walks up with his arms full of fruit and vegetables. He places them right there on the altar. He kneels down and talks to Deity, just like Adam does. But nothing happens. There is no fire from Shalem. While Cain is waiting, Abel comes up with a lamb he raised since birth.

"It's no good, Abel. Eli-Mehlek doesn't want our offerings." Cain growls, "Look, my offering just sits there. No fire from Shalem burns it up."

"Well, that's true, Cain. Don't I see fruits and vegetables? I thought Michael asked for a lamb?"

Cain snaps, "A lamb, some fruit, some veggies. It's all the same. What difference does it make anyway? You grow sheep. I grow veggies. Why won't Eli-Mehlek accept the fruit I've grown as easily as He accepts that lamb you've grown? I don't have a lamb. I'm not a shepherd. I'll bring what I have and Eli-Mehlek can accept it or not."

And with that, Cain turns to leave, but pausing, watches Abel prepare his offering. He lays the lamb on the altar and uses Adam's small sword to destroy the lamb. He kneels in front of the altar to talk to Deity. As he prays, fire devours Abel's offering.

The look on Cain's face is livid hatred. He walks over to Abel and snarls, "So, you think you are so good, huh? Eli-Mehlek accepts your offering, but not mine? Well, I'll tell you, my offering is just as good as yours."

Abel answers quietly, "But Cain, your offering isn't what Eli-Mehlek desires."

"You dunce, I'll teach you not to sass your older brother." With that, Cain begins beating Abel. Seeing Adam's small sword lying there on the ground, Cain picks it up and stabs Abel, destroying him.

Jokim and I are shocked! *How can anyone destroy another? Is this a part of Satan's government? Is this what his government leads to? I'll ask Sotai the next time I see him. Or maybe I'll catch Satan as he flies by and ask him.*

I hear that Eli-Mehlek talked with Cain and a punishment was given to him.

He never came back to the altar.

* * * *

As orbit after orbit go by, things on Earth are never peaceful as they are in Shalem. Adam and Eve have another son, Seth, who becomes the leader of the Loyalists even as Cain becomes the leader of the Rebels. We angels watch what is happening on Earth and some angels volunteer for protection duty. Their assignment is a single person and they defend that person from some of the mischief which seems to happen so frequently. This mischief never seems to happen in Shalem. We never can see quite what happens, yet some of the Rebel angels are always close by as the mischief occurs. My suspicion is somehow the Archrebel is instigating the mischief just to make Eli-Mehlek look bad. Yet, I wonder if maybe Satan is right and Deity is at fault. Perhaps, he's seen something that Eli-Mehlek is attempting to hide.

My heart is torn by how much I love Lucifer. *Can Lucifer be wrong? Yet, if he is right, Eli-Mehlek must be wrong.* Obviously, I have faith in Eli-Mehlek or I would have gone with Satan. Oh, how my head hurts as these thoughts keep churning around.

Occasionally, one of these guardian angels comes by and talks with Jokim and me.

"Hi, Zuriel," said Azgad . He is one of these guardian angels.

"Oh, hi Azgad," I reply. "How is your human Adah doing?"

"Not too well. She seems to be a Rebel."

"Oh, that's too bad. Is there any chance she'll repent?"

"I don't know. Michael reminds me to always hope for the best and work to help her choose Deity."

"I'm sure He does."

"I think Sotai must be assigned to her."

My ears perk up. "Sotai?"

"Yes. I don't understand what's happened to him. One minute, he'll be the old charming Sotai—the next instant, he'll be furiously angry. Some of the things he says about Michael can't be true, but as he says them, they sound true. When he is charming, that's when he says the worst things."

"Like what?"

Sotai asks Adam and Eve, "If Deity is loving, why did They let Abel be destroyed? He was your son … They let him be destroyed. They don't love you."

"I also wonder about that. I know Michael loves each person on Earth. Yet why does He let such bad things happen to them? We know Eli-Mehlek could stop all the bad things, if He desired. And we know He desires to. So why doesn't He?"

"I don't know, Zuriel. But one of the things I've been thinking about is how boundless Eli-Mehlek's thoughts are. I think He has some Plan about this that we don't yet understand. You know, we never knew what destruction was until Adam rebelled and the lamb was destroyed. Then Abel was destroyed. Now we understand what destruction means. How could Eli-Mehlek ever describe destruction to us? I wouldn't have understood, would you?"

"No … I don't think so. I knew it meant "ceasing-to-exist," but now I understand it because I've seen it."

"Right! You know, I'm thinking there may be a lot of other concepts Eli-Mehlek, in His infinity, understands which we do not yet understand. I think it is probable that Eli-Mehlek lets these bad things happen, just like He let Abel be destroyed, to demonstrate something we do not yet understand."

"You know, Azgad, I have a fascinating thought. Do you suppose it is not Eli-Mehlek who has the hidden flaws, but Satan? Perhaps Eli-Mehlek is letting Satan show the Universe what is in his heart? You know Eli-Mehlek is always more than fair with Satan, beginning with Decision Day."

"That's true, Zuriel. And I know Sotai has really changed. I don't know that I'd trust him anymore. I've seen too much of how he works.

Don't forget he is Satan's closest disciple. If what Sotai has become is the result of Satan's better way, I'll pass. It does make you wonder if Satan himself is more like Sotai—perhaps he is the one with the hidden flaws. Well, I've got to go. Adah needs me."

With that, Azgad is gone, winging his way back to Adah, his human. I am left with my thoughts. *Sotai not trustworthy? Satan flawed? I don't know about that. I lived with Lucifer for orbits and orbits. I think I know him better than anyone else. Surely I'd know if he has hidden flaws, wouldn't I? Yet, I've seen enough of Sotai to believe <u>he's</u> really changed …. But Satan is still the same kind, gracious angel he's always been, isn't he?*

* * * *

There are now many human beings on Earth, perhaps billions. Every day, some choose to rebel, some choose to be loyal. Michael is right. Every day is like a miniature Decision Day. One day, I notice a young person offering his sacrifice at The Garden gate. Jokim says his name is Enoch and his father is Jared, of the line of loyal humans.

I often see him talking to Adam and hear Adam telling him about the rebellion and Deity's wonderful Plan for reconciling humans to Deity. It seems Enoch desires to know Michael more and more, especially since his son, Methuselah, was born. As he seeks Michael, angels and even Michael occasionally visit him, teaching him much other humans do not know. Afterward, he goes and tells Earthlings what he has been taught.

He often seeks out the Rebels and tells them where their rebellion will take them. Gently, but firmly, he rebukes their wickedness. After periods of preaching and teaching, Enoch retires to pray and visit with Michael.

"Jokim?"

"Yes, Zuriel?"

"Enoch is a special human being, isn't he?"

"Yes. He is steadfastly loyal and true to Michael."

"Sometimes I think Michael has a special plan for Enoch. I think Michael visits with Enoch more than with any other human. That makes Enoch such a powerfully persuasive person. He gently reminds people of the difference between Michael's way and Satan's way. Some listen and some don't."

"Yes, that is true. It seems to me that, after his son was born, Enoch became closer to Michael than he had been before. Somehow he seems to understand the implicit obedience that Michael asks of His loyal beings. Perhaps he sees in his son a picture of how he needs to obey Michael."

"I like that idea. Did you hear the Rebels mocking Enoch the other day?"

"Yes, it was sad. If they mock Enoch that way, they would mock Michael, Himself."

"Yes, that is true. How old is Methuselah now?"

"More than 300 years old."

"Look, something is happening! Right over there."

Sure enough, Enoch is walking with Michael. Enoch's face is glowing with a radiance unseen on Earth for many an orbit. They walk up a small hill nearby, talking constantly. They keep right on walking, up through the welkin, across the Universe, right into Shalem.

Oh, Jokim and I want to be there! There is a great feast in Shalem, welcoming Enoch. There haven't been very many feasts in Shalem for a long time. The war occupies our minds totally.

As we guard the Tree, I ponder the events of the day. Does Michael love Enoch more than other humans? Surely not. He loves all the angels the same way. Perhaps it is to make a tangible promise to both angels and humans that those humans who are loyal to Deity will indeed be welcome in Shalem.

Saturation

The rebellion on Earth continues to become greater and more extensive. I wonder what Deity will do. Only a few humans, just a handful really, desire to be loyal. The Rebels' actions are wantonly flagitious. Surely, Michael can't let things continue as they are. I wonder when Eli-Mehlek will act. Eli-Mehlek is fair in all of His dealings with the Rebels. Somehow it seems unfair for Eli-Mehlek to summarily destroy the Rebels. Still, something has to happen.

Satan intrudes on my thoughts. "Hi, Zuriel, you look troubled."

"I am. There are so few humans who want to side with Deity and they have a difficult life. It was never this way before your rebellion. Look at the destruction of both life and property, the debauchery, the anger, the hate, the sadness, the pain. It was never this way anywhere in the Universe before your mutiny."

"Ahhh, Zuriel, you are so observant and so exactly truthful. I observe the same things and I also wonder if my government causes all these evils.

Most humans are Rebels. Evil is pervasive. Something must happen

"What I notice is that it isn't my government at all. Deity's laws are actually the cause of this misery. The problem is not my way, but that Michael doesn't actually let me run my government my way. He and Eli-Mehlek are constantly interfering with the rightness of my cause.

"As you can see, it is impossible for a human to keep Eli-Mehlek's law. As you are aware, all on Earth have broken Deity's law.

"Soon, all will see how bad Deity's laws are and how good my laws are. It will be obvious how impossible Their laws are and how easy my laws are.

"And Zuriel, if Deity destroys all of these Rebels, They will prove They are not the loving Creators they claim to be. Rather, They will prove Eli-Mehlek Himself is a vicious destroyer. Even though His laws are impossible to keep, when the human fails, poof—Eli-Mehlek destroys him."

Satan flies gracefully up over The Garden; Jokim flies beside him, his sword flicking one of the fruits out of Satan's hand. Satan had distracted me and grabbed a fruit on his way by. Jokim always covers for my mistakes.

As I think about Satan's words, questions plague my mind. *Have I chosen the wrong side? Should I have chosen Satan's side on Decision Day?* I don't think so, but I can't help but ask the question.

Gabriel comes flashing by. I wonder where he is going. Soon he comes back and pauses to talk.

"Hi, Zuriel, Jokim. How are things here?"

"Well, it's pretty quiet here. Not many humans come by to worship anymore," I answer.

"Yes, that is true. There are not many loyal humans anymore. Michael sent me to talk to one of them whose name is Noah."

"Oh? What message did you have for him?" Jokim asks.

"Deity set a limit. He said, 'Ruash will not always plead with humanity.' There will be a Decision Day on Earth. One hundred twenty years from now, a flood will destroy Earth."

"A flood?" Both Jokim and I stare at Gabriel, not comprehending, "What's that?"

"A flood is when the waters rise up over the ground and cover everything. Michael says all Rebel humans will be destroyed in the water."

"What will happen to the loyal humans?"

"That's what I talked to Noah about. He's going to build a boat, a kind of house that floats on the water. This boat is to be huge, big enough to take a pair of each of the animals and as many humans as desire to be loyal. I gave the plans to Noah. He's getting ready to build right now. I think he will build it somewhere close by here. Michael wants the humans to return to this spot—maybe building such an immense vessel will attract them. Noah is going to preach about evil, why they should repent, the flood is coming—things like that."

"Oooh. I wonder how many will listen to him. Isn't Noah fairly old? Nearly five hundred years, I think and he doesn't have any children yet."

"It may well be few will listen and enter the boat, but Michael doesn't want to exclude anyone, except by his own choice. Noah will be loyal and true and will warn them. If they do not listen, is there more Michael can do?"

"No, I guess not."

Gabriel flies back to Shalem. Jokim and I talk about the flood for some time. We wonder what will happen to The Garden, the Tree of Life. Will the flood destroy them? If the flood entirely covers Earth, what will happen to Satan and Sotai and all the other Rebel angels. Does destruction await them also? Is Satan correct when he says that destroying man will prove Michael does not love man? I have heard enough to know what Satan will say about the flood— "It's all Michael's fault."

Noah preaches faithfully, but few listen. At first a strange disquiet bothers a few. They listen carefully. Yet as the days and years go by, they decide Noah is a foolish old crackpot whom they can ignore. Noah begins to build, right there beside the gate into The Garden. Jokim and I watch his progress with interest.

Three sons are born to Noah, triplets. They and a few hired workers help with the construction. The boat is immense. As Gabriel said, it must be big enough for the animals and any people who choose to enter the refuge.

It's made from gopher wood, which is very tough. It's hard work to cut the timbers to the desired shape. The boat is round, without being round on the bottom. One long timber, carefully pieced together, runs the entire length of the boat, almost like the spine of a human. The sides rise and finally the top is built. There is an enormous open door in the side—acting as a ramp leading up from the ground.

At last, the boat is finished. Noah fills the craft with provender for both man and animal. There are supplies enough for all the animals as well as any humans who would board the boat.

One last time, Noah delivers the warning. "It will rain. There will be a flood. Everyone who is not in the boat will be destroyed."

The crowd laughs and ridicules Noah as he speaks. Suddenly, the ridicule dies as everyone is speechless. Gabriel is leading animals into the boat. Two by two, the unclean animals enter the ark. The crowd can't see Gabriel and to them it appears as if the animals are coming in on their own. With pale faces, the onlookers watch the parade. The clean animals come in groups of seven. Gabriel leads them to their designated cages, boxes, pens, until all are safely aboard, shutting those doors and gates behind them. Finally, he flies to where Noah is still warning the listeners.

"Noah," Gabriel says, "it is time. Come into the boat. Bring your wife, your sons and their wives. In seven days, the rains will fall."

"My friends," Noah cries, "my friends, come into the boat. Come in now! The rains will come. You will perish! Please, won't you choose safety? Today is the day to decide. Come now!"

No one moves. Some start to laugh again. One shouts, "Noah, I'm getting married! I'm not about to get into that big crate."

Another hoots, "Noah, tonight I've planned a big party. If I were to go into that boat, my guests would never quit laughing."

So, with great sadness, Noah ceases speaking and goes to his home. Shortly, he comes back with his seven family members. Slowly they climb the ramp into the boat. They had already moved their belongings into the boat and all they carry with them are some small, last-minute things.

As they enter, Gabriel lifts the ramp up and shuts the door. They are sealed inside; they are safe.

For seven days, the people outside hoot and holler about "that old fool, Noah. Thinks it's going to rain." The jeering continues. The wedding takes place. The gala is a huge success. The entire populace is in such a good mood.

On the morning of the eighth day, Gabriel flashes back to Earth.

"Zuriel, Jokim, you have done good work for Eli-Mehlek. He is well pleased with you. Now, Eli-Mehlek will take the Tree of Life and The Garden to Shalem and you will not have to guard it any longer. However, the fury of the storm will be unmatched, and you need to shield the vessel to prevent its demolition. Eli-Mehlek knows He can trust you with this assignment and asks that you shield the boat and its contents."

With that, he leaves. As he departs, we feel water drops on our faces as the water above the welkin begins to fall, slowly at first, then with greater and greater volume. The rage of the storm increases. The ground fissures and fractures. Great geysers spout through gaping holes. Gigantic rocks become projectiles, arcing high above the ground, only to crash to earth, smashing anything they hit. Uprooted trees shoot through the sky like arrows. It seems as if everything is flying in every direction. We are constantly dodging the zooming debris.

The doomed people crowd around the boat, yelling—then pleading, begging, to be let in. With the rumbling of the elements, Noah can't even hear their pleas and isn't able to open the door, could he hear them. Some are so desperate they attempt to chop their way into the ark. They find the gopher wood walls too tough and thick and the storm too violent for them to break in.

Others pray to Eli-Mehlek, begging Him to save them. It is too late. They should have prayed eight days earlier but they scorned that chance. And now that was gone.

The forest creatures race about looking for safety. Their roars mingle with the general noise of the gale, giving an eerie feeling to the storm.

Jokim and I hover over the boat, keeping it from capsizing and repelling all the hazards. The work absorbs most of our attention. The raging winds and waves threaten to destroy the craft every moment.

Out of the corner of my eye, I notice Satan and Sotai flying through the storm. They spot Jokim and me and struggle over to where we are. The look of fury on Satan's face is so different from his normally suave demeanor.

"This is a fine way for a loving Deity to behave." The sarcasm is heavy in his voice. "Eli-Mehlek is not the loving God He claims to be. Michael wishes for all mankind to be destroyed. Michael is totally unjust and unloving."

"Zuriel, you are an idiot, an imbecilic idiot." Sotai chimes in, his squeaky voice trembling with rage. "How can you believe Eli-Mehlek loves everyone, when He drowns nearly every person on Earth? Where is the justice in that? You tell me! And I hear Eli-Mehlek is supposedly merciful, too. Some mercy this is."

Satan takes up where Sotai left off. "Eli-Mehlek wants my destruction, too! Jokim, He'd really like me to be destroyed. Then He can continue to delude all you Loyalists—without me there to show where you are deceived. How can you serve a harsh dictator like that?"

Jokim and I are too busy with our work to answer him, so we reply nothing. Finally Satan and Sotai fly away, Sotai muttering imprecations under his breath.

Forty days and nights we diligently guard the boat. Finally, after all the waters above the welkin have fallen and all the waters in the underground sea are depleted, the tumult eases. The waters still churn under the boat, but the all-encompassing fury of the storm abates. For the first time during the storm, we can take a moment to think, to reflect upon what happened, to wonder what is to come next.

As we recall what happened during the storm, we realize sometimes things were happening so fast that we couldn't keep up with it all. We became completely exhausted. And we thank Eli-Mehlek for what He has done for us and praise Him for accomplishing what we could not do ourselves. Truly it is only by a miracle of Eli-Mehlek that the boat was preserved.

I remember that look of hatred on Satan's face. I shudder as I think about it. When he is angry, Satan is so different from the Lucifer that I served. When I ask him about it, he comments, "If Eli-Mehlek didn't treat me so badly, I wouldn't get so angry." But perhaps, it is the other way around. Perhaps it is Satan who is so angry and that causes Eli-Mehlek to treat him in such a manner.

I wonder if maybe Satan brought all of this trouble on himself. Some, perhaps most, of his subjects are nothing about which he should brag. I'll ask Sotai about that next time I see him. But it seems to me Sotai is always rodomont about Satan's cause, even when it doesn't seem appropriate. So will questioning him do any good?

* * * *

The forty days of violence are over. But our job isn't. Waves, higher than the boat, surge over Earth on the boundless waters. Tsunamis charge back and forth. Geysers erupt and eddies roil. Those in the boat are still in danger.

Even the ground itself continues to move. After the geysers empty the underground sea, the resultant cavern collapses and immense sheets of Earth's crust slide into the hole, colliding with each other and tossing up gigantic piles of broken rock. Such jagged mountain crags were not on Earth before the flood. Jokim and I chatter about the differences from before the flood.

The sunshine is much harsher since the water atop the welkin fell. Previously, the water helped to keep the glare of the sun away from Earth.

The devastation is so total that even Earth itself is thrown out of whack. Now, instead of spinning vertically, it tilts to one side. On both the top and bottom of Earth, a strange blue-white substance forms. It floats in the water and is very cold. If you warm it, it turns into water. Neither Jokim nor I have ever seen anything like that before.

Finally, we guide the boat to a quiet place. There, surrounded by a few of those jagged rocks, it floats gently on the water. Occasionally, the rocks shift. Other vertices are already visible as the water retrocedes, but this particular place seems to be an ideal spot for the boat to settle as the water ebbs.

More rocks show every day. Where the land had been gentle rolling hills, now there are mountains, ridges and chains of peaks. Many of them are much higher than any of the hills before the violent water reworked the landscape.

The flood tide slowly subsides. It takes nearly a year for the water to ebb back to something like normal. I wonder what Noah and his family will do for food after they come out of the boat. There are no trees and no gardens, either. The ground is mostly bare and muddy.

Eventually, Noah exits the boat. I hope this time humanity learned its lesson about obeying Eli-Mehlek, but I have grave reservations.

There, look at that! It's a huge, multicolored arch stretching across the sky. It is gorgeous! Actually two or three of these arcs nestle inside of each other. Their brilliant hues are vibrantly luxurious and illusory at the same time. It looks as if you could reach out and touch it, yet at the same time you can see right through it. It is similar to the arch over Eli-Mehlek's throne, but I've never seen anything like it on Earth. I hear Michael's voice.

"Noah!"

"Yes, Michael."

"Noah, look at that arch in the sky! Isn't it beautiful?"

"Yes, Michael. It is dazzling! What is it?"

"It is My bow. It will come when there are clouds in the sky, just as there are clouds right now. After the storm and the flood, you might be afraid when you see clouds in the sky."

"Yes, Michael. The last time we saw clouds ..."

"I know, Noah. Not only you, but the animals will be frightened, too. So I am making a promise to you and to Myself. Never again will I destroy Earth with water. This promise is not only for you, but also for all of your posterity forever.

Look! It's gorgeous! Arching across the sky, luxurious, illusory, transparent! It's a promise!

"This arch is the sign of this promise. When the clouds come storming overhead and the winds blow violently, I will see this arch and remember my promise I have made. When you and your children see the rainbow, remember My promise, my everlasting promise."

Noah and all of his family fall on their knees in worship of Michael. They praise Him for the promise He made. Even more, they thank Him for remembering their fears when they see a cloud.

Michael. Gentle Michael. I remember He came to wipe my tears after Decision Day. I remember He begged Eli-Mehlek to allow Him to pay the penalty for rebellious man, even when it was so difficult for Eli-Mehlek to agree to Michael's destruction. And this time, here is Michael again treating Noah with tenderness because of his fears.

My heart leaps with love for Michael. How can Satan believe Michael is unfair?

Gabriel coasts to a stop beside Jokim and me. Our job on Earth is done. There might be another task later on, but for now, we are to go back to Shalem.

Quietly, we wing our way across the Universe to Eli-Mehlek's royal city. I return to Gabriel's mansion and to my room. It is so pleasant to be back. I am still a mansionkeeper at heart.

Assembly is soon. I can hardly wait to go! It's been so many orbits since I was able to attend Assembly. I clean Gabriel's mansion from top to bottom and soar over to Assembly. It is glorious!

Trenchant Test

Satan called a meeting of all Rebel angels. They gathered around—squabbling over the best places, those closest to Satan. The pushing and shoving continued until he spoke. Then all quieted.

"We have made some really great progress here on Earth. Most of the human beings joined our side. Every day it becomes more obvious that Deity's law cannot be obeyed. But there is one eminent Loyalist we have not been able to convert. That is Job," he paused, "and I've been thinking about him." Satan laughed his beautiful laugh. "His vast wealth and scores of servants and all his children exist because Eli-Mehlek is protecting him. If Eli-Mehlek terminated His protection plan, Job'd join us faster than a meteorite incinerates."

Heads nodded and voices said, "Hear, hear." "Yeah, that's right."

"So, I'm going back to Shalem."

Bedlam broke out. "Sure, Eli-Mehlek is going to welcome you, isn't He?" some sneered.

Others hooted, "You can't sneak in. All of them know you."

"Oh, I know Eli-Mehlek will let me in … as the king of Earth. All the kings of the various orbs, spheres and planets meet with Eli-Mehlek—don't they? I represent Earth. He'll have to let me in."

"So, what?" came another derisive snicker.

Satan is puzzled. Job has not succumbed to his blandishments. What can he do?

"So, I'm going to demand that Eli-Mehlek let His Job-Protection Plan lapse and give me access to Job. I crave for the entire Universe to see how his loyalty fades as his wealth subsides."

The demons cheered at the prospect of Job joining the Rebel side—our side!

There were a few other human Loyalists who caused Rebel grumbling before Satan was off, streaking across the cosmos toward Shalem.

Job was one of the last hominoid-holdouts, denying Satan the entire sphere as his domain. We'll never be able to show the Universe how good Satan's government is, until Earth is totally loyal to Satan. All this trouble is simply because of Eli-Mehlek's flawed law. Once Loyalists are eliminated, the promise of no law will become reality. Sotai fluttered in anticipation.

* * * *

It is time for Assembly. I am in my place. Suddenly a buzz shoots through the angelic crowd. A trillion angel eyes look up to see what's happening. There is Satan, demanding admittance!

A few angels stand at the edge of the Assembly Bowl—blocking Satan's path, swords drawn. Gabriel is one of them. Satan halts, demanding entry, but neither Gabriel nor the other angels move.

"Let me in!" Satan snaps.

"No," is the firm answer. "You don't belong here anymore. This is Michael's kingdom, not yours. Yours is on Earth."

"Yes," Satan arrogates, "but as you said, I am the rightful king of Earth. I see all of the other kings of the other spheres are here. I also have my rights, you know."

Michael enters the Assembly. He looks over at Satan. "And from where do you come?"

Satan stands tall and haughty and proud. "From walking around in my kingdom."

Michael calmly answers, "Oh. Right. Have you seen My servant Job?"

"Yes," he replies. "And I can assure you there is a reason Job serves You."

"What would that reason be?" questions Michael, a serene tone pervading His voice.

"Your Job-Protection Plan. He serves You only because You've made him rich. If You don't keep guard around him, he'll rebel against You, just like everyone else." Satan sounds so convincing.

"Okay," answers Michael. "Let's see if you are correct or not."

Satan is nonplused. "What do you mean?"

"Well, you just claimed that if We didn't protect him, he'd rebel. So, We will let the so-called Job-Protection Plan lapse. Everything he possesses is within your power. You may do with it as you wish. The one restriction is you may not touch Job, himself. Fair enough?"

Michael's words trap Satan, turning the tables on him. He can hardly say "no" without looking like he doesn't really believe what he's saying. Yet will Job really rebel? Besides, Michael also said clearly whatever happens to Job cannot be charged against Michael. Satan recognizes the trap, the big risk, considers it and decides proceeding is a better gamble than capitulating and leaving Job to Michael.

"Okay! I can do whatever I want with anything he owns? Is that right?"

"Yes. Gabriel, please inform Job's guardian angels." Gabriel nods and flies off to Earth.

"Everybody, watch! See Job rebel!" With great bravado, Satan soars out of Shalem, following Gabriel back to Earth.

We continue with our Assembly. It's no longer a routine Assembly. Satan's challenge intriguingly alarms us. Michael makes a few announcements and leaves us discussing Job's upcoming trial. The look on Satan's face gives us the impression it will be a vicious test.

Michael permitted Satan to do what he wants with Job's riches. Well, obviously, Satan wants to destroy them. I understand Satan's plans. By his accusation that Job serves Michael only because Michael protects Job, it is obvious the only way to test that accusation is to remove the protection and let the wealth vanish.

Without warning, rich, prosperous Job is bereft of all of his wealth. Everything is gone in a trice. Stolen, captured, killed, destroyed— everything is gone, even his children.

Job's face turns ashen as he hears the ghastly news. One servant after another comes dashing up to tell him what is happening. When he hears his children are destroyed, he staggers into his tent and, with tears streaming down his cheeks, worships Michael. "Michael gives and Michael takes away. Glorious is the name of Michael."

Our emotions are mixed. We weep along with Job, his sorrow totally enveloping. We also cheer, as Job did not rebel! I hear some of the kings of the other spheres say they also cried and cheered.

* * * *

At the next Assembly, Satan returns. This time, no one attempts to prevent his entrance.

Michael again meets Satan calmly. "From where are you coming?"

Again Satan haughtily answers, "From walking around in my kingdom."

"Ah, yes. Have you noticed My servant Job? He didn't rebel, did he?"

Satan blanches. "Sure, You still reward Job for serving You. Yes, You protect his body. Let me touch his skin—then he'll rebel, too." Satan chuckles his beautiful laugh, a revealing touch of nervousness noticeable.

"Okay, we will test Job one more time. You may do with him as you desire, only you may not destroy him. Fair enough?"

This time Satan spouts no parting braggadocio. We wait to see what horrible torture Satan devises for Job. It doesn't take long. One day, boils cover Job's body—angry, pus-filled boils, painful and throbbing. Job's wife and his few remaining servants do what they can to ease Job's pain, but nothing helps.

Job's wife screams at him, bitter tears gushing from eyelashes to dimples to chin. "Is this what you get for being loyal to Michael? We are pauperized. Our children are destroyed. And now … and now … the … the unimaginable agony of these boils. Michael obviously doesn't appreciate your loyalty. If He did, you wouldn't be suffering like this. So why don't you rebel and be destroyed? There's nothing else to do."

We hold our breath, awaiting Job's answer.

"Do we only serve Michael when life is good? Did we not love our children, even when they erred? Can we not serve Michael even when life is bad? See, Michael gives and Michael takes away. I extol the name of Michael!"

With these words, we whoop with delight. Cheer upon cheer echoes and reechoes throughout Shalem. We praise Michael, even when those miserable friends of Job's come to accuse him of mutiny. Their accusations lance Job's heart as each of them denunciates Job's character. Yet Job does not rebel against Michael, even in his heart.

It is a joyous, happy time in Shalem as Job passes this most bitter, trenchant test. As the ordeal finally ends, Michael goes and talks to Job and his friends, giving them a thought-provoking nature discourse.

Satan's claim that Job serves Deity because Deity protects or bribes him is totally disproved. It was a severe test Satan devised, but Michael knows Job's heart. Michael knows Satan's accusations against Job are wrong! Job vindicates Michael's trust in him before the watching Universe. From Betelgeuse to Rigel, all the Sons of Eli-Mehlek roar with exultation. Job proves to be a true Loyalist. Satan's discomfiture rankles his soul; his trouncing is bile in his mouth.

I wonder how many more times Satan will charge a person as he indicted Job. I suspect sometimes Michael will win and Satan will retreat furiously—but other times Satan will win and Michael's desolation will be palpable. Satan continues to live up to his name, "The Adversary," accusing everyone of serving Michael for reasons other than love.

I wonder about The Plan. Michael said the tests He would endure would be very severe. Incredulously, I question, "What else could Satan devise as a test? What else could be worse than what Job has been through?" I shudder as I contemplate.

Skeptical, yet Obedient

I'm wondering if Michael has lost His mind. Never before has He ever demanded something so incomprehensible. In fact, He forbade His people to do such a thing. Now He demands it from one of Earth's Loyalists.

My mind races around in circles, struggling to understand. Gabriel is not available. He's off somewhere in the Universe, so I can't ask him any questions right now.

I ponder how human society is so dispiriting. How Deity cleansed Earth and gave it a new start—yet Earthling's rebellious actions remain unchanged. How their evil actions persist unabated. How they continue choosing Satan's side far more than Michael's side.

Right now, they are disbelieving Michael's promise. Leadership is worrying about what to do if another flood comes. They don't need to worry, Michael's promises are kept. But they have doubts. Their decision is to build a colossal tower, tall enough to reach above the waters of any future flood. Satan encourages their rebellious lack of trust.

Michael watches sadly. He must act. He does—with a unique response! He confuses their language! They can no longer communicate well enough to continue functioning and building.

The tower construction is halted. The builders scatter across Earth; their one language is transformed into several distinct vernaculars, each totally inscrutable to outsiders. The various language groups drift to various spots on Earth's crumpled, broken surface.

Their behavior remains unmodified. Loyal Earthlings become scarcer. It seems that no one on Earth is loyal to Deity anymore. It makes me wonder *Is Satan right? Did I choose the wrong side? What will Deity do now?* I don't have long to wait.

After Job's trenchant test, Michael talked to me. I mentioned that I still love Satan. I worried about him during the storm. I tell Michael, "He flew by, spewing hatred towards you, Michael. I didn't know what to do. I wish he wouldn't hate You so much. Every time I talk to him, more questions come to mind. Sometimes I think I have more questions than You have answers!"

Michael chuckles with me. "It is good to have those questions. If you followed either Satan or Me without question, you would be a mental cripple. I'll tell you what I would like you to do. Would you be willing to be an observer?"

"An observer? I don't understand."

"I have several other angel watchers already. You would fly around Earth, witnessing things that happen, examining events to determine exactly what happened and why—scrutinizing the behavior of angels, demons and earthlings. You'll see much that will help you to answer your questions."

"Uh, okay. When do I start?"

"Right now! There are going to be triplet boys born to Terah, in the city of Ur. One of them will be called Abram. Watch him closely."

* * * *

Ur is a beautiful town. Terah is one of its leading inhabitants—quite wealthy, more than most. Terah's wife—feeling somewhat lethargic in her ninth pregnant month—walks slowly and ponderously. With triplets coming, it is good she hasn't any other children!

The guardian angels for Abram, Nahor and Haran are there, waiting for the birth. They are constantly there for the next few orbits as the triplets grow and develop into young men.

Michael visits Abram one night and gives him some definite instructions. "Depart! Abandon your country, your relatives and your father's house. I have a better place to show you. There, I will make of you a great nation. From there, I will exalt them that exalt you and I will trouble them that trouble you. From your descendants, all Earth will be elevated."

I listen to Michael's promise—it cheers my heart. Deity knows what They are doing. "All Earth will be elevated." Earth certainly needs some elevation. Things are in a miserable condition.

The next day, Abram begins to prepare for travel. Canaan is in his thoughts, though Michael hasn't specified the destination. It takes some time to organize Abram's considerable wealth for the trek to wherever Michael leads. Abram's nephew, Lot, also prepares for the travel. He will go with Abram. They can't travel swiftly, what with the swarms of sheep, donkeys, camels, cattle. Slowly, Canaan draws closer. When the caravan is well within Canaan, Michael visits Abram again saying, "This is it! This is the land I promised you. This land I give to you and your descendants. It is yours."

Abram puzzles. How can his progeny inherit this land? He has no children. Sarai is no longer able to bear children. Besides, Abram is seventy-five and Sarai is sixty-five. How can such old people have children?

I watch Abram and Sarai dialoguing, wrestling between Michael's promise and the obvious obstacle of their ages. This discussion lasts for nearly twenty-five years. How can such an aged couple conceive heirs? But Michael promises. Again. And again. Over and over.

The last time the promise reiterates is when Abram is ninety-nine. Michael reappears to Abram and reintroduces Himself. I watch as Abram falls on his face in worship. Michael changes their names to Abraham ("father of a host") and Sarah ("queen") as He repromises they will have a child. Abraham laughs, thinking, *Sure, I'm 100 and Sarah is 90. A child? Really? He must be joking.*

Michael imperturbably declares, "Sarah, your wife, in about a year, will indeed have a son. Call him Isaac. I will attend him and his descendants after him."

> *Descendants? Progeny? Really? We have no children. We are well past child-bearing age. Such utter nonsense!*

I also am surprised. It seems impossible for Abraham and Sarah to have a child.

* * * *

By now, Earth's time is normal to me. Scarcely a month later, Michael and Gabriel fetch me for a stroll. We saunter along the road in front of Abraham's tent. The sun is sizzling. He is sitting under the awning on a rug. We tread the dust, not looking at Abraham, simply walking on by.

Abraham bounds to his feet, advancing toward us, bowing low in front of us. "If it is acceptable to you, I'll get some water to clean the dust from your feet. There's a tree here; you can rest in its shade. I'll retrieve some provisions to satiate your hunger. After refreshments, you're welcome to travel on."

Michael responds, "That sounds acceptable."

The cookout complete, Michael inquires about Sarah. "In the tent," is the reply.

"Sarah will have a son."

Sarah, listening, snickers, "I'm years past childbearing. Abraham is older than I. It's not going to happen."

"Why did Sarah laugh, saying, 'It's not going to happen?' Is anything impossible for Deity? No, Sarah will have a son."

"I didn't laugh," Sarah blushes and protests.

"Yes, you did laugh!" Michael chuckles.

Michael, Gabriel and I stand, preparing to leave. Abraham escorts us back to the Sodom road. The city is beautiful; verdant foliage abundant everywhere; marble houses shine in the evening sun; palm trees wave their bushy crowns in a zephyr breeze. It looks so peaceful, the corruption invisible from this distance.

Michael looks at Gabriel and me. "Abraham will become an immense nation. He needs to know what I intend to do. The rumors about the rebellions of Sodom and Gomorrah are so significant and the claims about their depravity are so persistent, I have come to examine the cities to see if these allegations are accurate."

Gabriel and I continue along the road towards Sodom. Michael and Abraham are standing together as we leave. Abraham knows the charges are true. Earlier, his nephew Lot, moved into Sodom, his family, too. His children, excluding two, married Sodomites. Abraham visited Lot and realized the perversions of the inhabitants.

I hear Abraham petitioning Michael on Sodom's behalf. "What if some upright people reside there? Fifty, forty, thirty, twenty or even ten?" Michael promises He won't obliterate Sodom if just ten honorable people are found there.

We approach Sodom in the golden light just before dark. Lot is sitting on a bench at the gate, Sodom's life swirling around him. He watches us approach and promptly invites us to his home for the night.

"Oh, no, we won't bother you. We'll just sleep in the town square."

Lot's eyes bear a look of terror. "No, no, my lords. Please honor me with your presence."

We follow him to his palatial residence. A feast is prepared. Lot provides bed rolls. Before we can lie down, the night explodes with noise. The men of Sodom surround the house. Raucous voices demand that Lot produce his guests. Lot steps outside to calm the crowd.

We watch from the inside and then it's time to act. We reach out, grab Lot's hand and heave him back into the house. The rabble persist their noisy assault on the house. Before the door shatters, we blind their eyes. They can't locate the door and eventually give up.

Early morn finds Lot still dawdling. We grab his hand, his wife's hand and the hands of the two daughters still at home and pull them out the door, through the gate and down the road. "Rush or the coming conflagration will engulf you! Flee and don't look back! See those hills? Get there quickly, or you will vanish along with Sodom."

We go back to Sodom. The solemn work begins. We send fire, brimstone, burning sulfur and molten rock upon Sodom's evil. The warning was given. They choose to ignore it; their destruction is their own culpability. Those who chose rebellion are destroyed along with the rebellion.

* * * *

Isaac is born despite Abraham's and Sarah's laughter. He is now a young adult. I watch one night as Michael again visits Abraham. Shock fills me as Michael tells Abraham to take Isaac, the miraculous son of his old age, to the land of Moriah and offer him for a sacrifice. If I am shocked, Abraham is devastated. His son? Isaac? How can Isaac be the father of many nations if he is slaughtered? Why is Michael asking this?

He distresses the rest of the night. Just before dawn I hear him say, "If Isaac is sacrificed for Michael, Michael can raise him up from ashes and restore him to me. I must obey."

Quietly, he rouses two servants and Isaac, telling them they are going to sacrifice. They gather the wood, the knife, the fire, leaving before Sarah awakens. Abraham can't bear to tell Sarah or Isaac what Michael commands. Silently, they tread the three days to Moriah. Abraham—confused, morose, troubled. Isaac—trusting his father.

I watch, confusion troubling me. Michael decrees that child sacrifices should not be done—yet here He is ordering Abraham to do that very thing. What is Michael thinking?

On the peak, Abraham builds an altar of stone. He arranges the wood on the altar. He speaks, his voice gentle and breaking, "Isaac, Michael commanded me to sacrifice you on this altar."

A thrill of terror surges through Isaac. He stares at his father. He is young; Abraham is old. Surely, he could flee. His character refuses that easy option. If Michael commands, he, Isaac, will obey. Abraham ties Isaac securely. Isaac lies on the wood. Gabriel arrives, standing beside the altar, invisible. Abraham prays over his sacrifice—horrors, his son! He lifts the knife. He plunges it downward. Gabriel seizes Abraham's arm, arresting it instantly. Michael speaks, "Abraham! Stop! Do not harm the lad! Now I—and the watching Universe—know that you will obey Me.

You didn't refuse Me your son, your only son."

With utter relief, Abraham shakily lays the knife down and unties Isaac's hands and feet. Isaac steps down from the altar. Their eyes drift across to a bush in which a ram is tangled. Freeing the ovine, they place it on the altar—a substitute for Isaac.

My heart calms down, but my mind is atwizzle with assorted thoughts. *Michael has been testing Abraham. I remember how Abraham tried to help Michael by having Ishmael. But this ordeal, Abraham endures with magnificent submission and obedience.*

Other thoughts roam my brain. *Michael told us He would become the substitute for rebellious humans, just as that ram replaced Isaac on the altar. He described how He would give His life to restore humanity and His destruction would be particularly offensive.*

And as Isaac is Abraham's only son of promise, so Michael is Eli-Mehlek's only Son. Now Abraham is possibly the only human who can understand how difficult it is for Eli-Mehlek to permit his Son to be the surety for mankind.

Abraham and Isaac walk down the hill, join the servants, return home. Their return is much more jovial. Sarah greets them effusively. Life goes on.

Deific Pageant

At Satan's urging, Pharaoh enslaves The People. The People are Abraham's offspring. They requested refuge in Egypt from a drought in the land Michael had promised Abraham. Pharaoh granted them the territory called Goshen. The People have become so numerous, a new Pharaoh, under Satan's guidance, sees them as a scheme for his enrichment.

The People's knowledge of Michael faded. Their slave masters compel them to work seven days a week, causing them to lose their understanding of Deity's rest day. Their memory of Michael's promises to Abraham is gone.

* * * *

"Look at that! I've got The People right where I want them!" Satan bragged loudly. "They are ignorant slaves. They've forgotten all they ever knew about Deity. I'm proving Deity's law cannot be kept by anyone—even those favored by Michael. Soon, I'll have everyone on Earth on my side. Pharaoh does everything I want him to do. I'll suggest killing all the male children of The People."

It's Freedom Time. Michael and Satan confront each other

Sotai, Oreb, Resheph, everyone cheered.

"We'll win this war in the long run. Even Deity cannot withstand the truth. Soon the entire Universe will see the flaws in Deity's character."

Satan flew off to Pharaoh's palace, urging him to increase the harshness on The People.

* * * *

Michael visits Earth. Gabriel and I escort Him as He seeks out an eighty-year-old shepherd. Locating him at the foot of the mountain, Michael selects a nearby small desert shrub—releasing a small amount of light from His Glory Shroud. The warm glow makes the shrub appear to be aflame.

"Look at that! That bush is on fire. But it doesn't burn up! Hmmm. How odd!" Moses ambles over to see why the bush keeps burning. As he approaches, Michael speaks.

"Moses, wait there; take off your shoes. I am the Deity of Abraham, Isaac, Jacob. I see the struggles of The People. I understand their sorrows. I recognize their woes. I have come down to deliver them. I am going to take them to a land where there is an abundance of good things—back to Canaan, the land I promised Abraham."

Moses shrouds his face, terrified.

"I want you to go to the king, to Pharaoh. I want you to lead The People from Egypt to Canaan. Pharaoh will resist. Yet I will bring them out. I want you speak for Me."

"Who, me? Who am I that You should send me?"

"I will be with you. I will bring The People to this mountain. Tell them that 'I AM' sent you."

Moses hesitates and falters and dithers and equivocates. He really doesn't want to accede to Michael's request. I can tell Michael grows exasperated. "I will also send Aaron, your brother, to accompany you."

We know what Michael is planning. He revealed it to us as we winged to Earth. It is time to release The People from slavery. It is time for them to take their place among the nations of Earth. It is time for Deity to visibly demonstrate Their power. It is time for The People to occupy their promised home. This will be interesting as Pharaoh will balk, not wanting to lose the opulence the slaves provide.

* * * *

Moses outlines to his father-in-law the duties with which Michael charged him and Jethro releases him to obey. He sets out for Egypt. I watch with concern. Aaron, his brother, meets him along the way.

The People listen coolly. Their disbelief is palpable. I wonder "What's wrong with them?"

Pharaoh listens with even less warmth. I can't believe his arrogance. "Who is Michael? I don't know Michael and I will not let The People go!" he roars. Moses and Aaron perform all the wonders that Deity provided. Pharaoh doesn't care. His magicians duplicate them all. Pharaoh doesn't see Satan's devils providing the magic. Michael increases the pressure by abusing one of Pharaoh's gods, turning the Nile River to blood. Pharaoh pretends to capitulate, yet, when the river is restored, he reverses his decision. Satan encourages his stubbornness, cheering each defiance.

Eight more times, Michael strikes at Pharaoh's gods. Eight more times, Pharaoh feigns yielding. Eight more times, Satan struggles to defeat Michael and is thwarted in each and every strategy he adopts. Egypt is obliterated—its fields gone, its trees destroyed, its air reeking with frog-pile stench, its cattle slaughtered, its horses killed, its sheep slain, its buildings hail-shattered, its gods humiliated. Michael spares The People's houses in Goshen. They aren't touched by the scourges Michael sent. However, all the wealth The People created for their enslavers is destroyed. I cannot remember any time when any place in the Universe is so devastated. Yet Pharaoh refuses to yield and his anger is magnificent.

"Get out of my palace! Do not return! If ever I see your face again, I will execute you." The roar is heard all through the palace.

Moses simply replies, "As you wish. You will never see my face again."

Moses and Gabriel exit the palace. Pharaoh and Satan remain behind, smoldering, stubborn, seething.

* * * *

That night, Gabriel visits Egypt, sent by Michael. The eldest Egyptian child, of any age, is destroyed. An enormous turmoil seizes Egypt. Every house in Egypt is grieving. Pharaoh is anguished. The palace is full of bodies of eldest children.

At last Pharaoh yields, calling Moses and Aaron to him. I guess he's forgotten his threat to see them no more. "Get out! Go! Take your wives and your children and your flocks and herds as you repeatedly specified. Remove yourselves from Egypt—before we are all destroyed."

The People are free! The Egyptians frenzy as The People depart. They bring out vast quantities of wealth and shove it at the freed slaves. It is appropriate. Their wealth was derived from The People's labor. Well over a million people march south from Goshen, Ahead is a vast wilderness. I tremble for their future. Provisions will be scarce. Water will be prized. I trust Michael has a plan.

* * * *

Mountains rise on both sides of the camp. The ocean waves greet them ahead. A dust cloud is rapidly approaching behind them. Unbelievably, Pharaoh again rescinds his permission and commands his army to recover his slave labor force.

The People panic, trapped between the mountains, the ocean, Pharaoh's army. They surround Moses with screams and curses. "The graves of Egypt are better than this. Why have you brought us into the desert to be destroyed?"

"Michael is our salvation. Wait and watch! See what He will do. You will never see these Egyptians again!"

Michael calls Gabriel, "Go back to Shalem and get a phalanx of angels. Bring them here. Don't dally."

Soon angels fill the air. A foggy cloud covers the Egyptian army. Michael arrays about half of the angels across the water. The other half rings their comrades—preventing interference from Satan's minions. On command, the inner circle pushes the water away, opening a muddy channel between the two dikes made with angel hands. The outer circle is fully occupied, preventing harassment by Satan's Legions. The People, their oxen, sheep, cattle, belongings all enter the gap, marching to the opposite shore. Dawn sees the last weary lamb being led up the slope by its small master.

Michael lifts the fog and the Egyptians realize The People have escaped. The channel is still open and Pharaoh foolishly charges after The People. They get to the middle of the pathway. The muddy ground becomes like quicksand. The chariot wheels stick. The entire army is befuddled, knowing not what to do. They begin cursing as The People move beyond their reach. Michael issues the order and the angels release their hold on the water, which instantly collapses. The soldier's armor weighs them on the ocean floor. Soon, nothing is left of the powerful enemy. The entire army—Pharaoh, his soldiers, his chariots, his horses, his banners, his bravado—all drown. Only a little debris washes up on the shores. Satan watches, irately, totally confounded, totally defeated.

Octogenarian Miriam seizes her tambourine and leads the women's song of praise to Michael. "The horse and his rider are cast into the sea." The praises continue for days. Word drifts across the plains, the deserts, the mountains, the forests, telling what Michael did to the Egyptians. All humanity is learning that Michael is omnipotent!

* * * *

Satan skulks around The People as they cross the desert. Sotai dithers agitatedly, seeking any possible means of disrupting Michael's plans. Michael provides a shield from the inhospitable daytime heat. Gabriel confronts Satan whenever his interference is excessive. Michael directs Moses to have The People set up a more permanent camp. After three months of travel, they rest awhile.

The encampment is enormous, sitting at the foot of the harsh mountain. Tents innumerable are pitched in a haphazard manner. There is no order, no streets, no center. People squabble over a hands-breadth of land. Michael looks with pain and pity upon The People. After so long in slavery, they are ignorant, unclean, undisciplined, uncouth. They barely remember Deity. They barely remember the promises made to Abraham, Isaac, Jacob. They barely remember the promise of a Savior.

It is time to transform The People's thinking. It is time to remind The People of Deity's promises to Abraham. It is time to give the Universe a new demonstration of Deity's Plan for Earth. It is time to present to the Universe another view of Deity's will. Michael speaks to Moses from the mountain; Moses ascends the peak.

"Tell The People 'Your eyes have seen how I rescued you from Egypt. You witnessed the destruction left behind. You observed how I brought you here as if on eagle's wings.'

"'I promise that—should you always obey Me—you will be My special people. I will make you a nation of priests for the entire world.'"

I know Michael's plans. The People, Abraham's descendants, are to live in the crossroads of the world. People will come to them to learn what makes them flourish. They will spread the knowledge of the goodness of Deity throughout the entire planet. Michael will make them known to all peoples of all ages, using them to demonstrate that rebellion is undesirable and loyalty is far better for all.

Moses conveys Michael's message. The People respond, "That sounds good. We'll do it." Moses scales the mountain and reports their answer.

"Have The People get ready. Have them wash their clothes. Build some fences around this crag, to protect man and mammal. On the third day, I'm going to talk to The People."

At no other time has Michael spoken to a large group of people. My surprise is that He will now. I ponder how He's never compelled another nation in the way He coerced Egypt to release The People. Perhaps, Michael is changing the way He's dealing with rebellion. Perhaps He's becoming stricter?

* * * *

Michael's voice thunders over the valley— "I AM the one who carried you away from Egyptian slavery!" I shiver. Michael's voice is insistent, adamant, resolute. I fear for what He might say. "Here are the rules I require you to obey."

Michael articulates His ten rules. He writes them on two stone slabs. I am amazed! I have known these statutes for every orbit since Michael created me and I never realized they could be written down so concisely. My astonished ears tingle with surprise as Michael expresses them so precisely. My reaction is so strong I almost forget to observe The People's response.

They are terrified! They retreat a long far away from the mountain. They call to Moses, "We are going to be destroyed—the thunder and lightning and trumpet heralding and mountain smoking. We tremble with fear! You teach us. We will listen. But we're afraid of Michael—we might be destroyed."

> *Michael said, "Speak." Moses struck. Michael is sad. Punishment ensues*

Moses soothes them, "Do not be frightened. Michael's impressing you with His Divinity. When you understand Deity, you will not rebel." The People remain knotted in groups at the far edge of the basin while Moses strides into the black screening cloud buffering Michael, beyond the protective fence, up into the mountain. The People watch. Finally, they quietly drift away to their tents.

Eventually, Michael returns to Shalem. Moses returns from the mountain. The People pack their tents, ready to continue their march to the land Michael promised them.

* * * *

Early in the wilderness trek, Michael instructed Moses to provide water for The People by striking a rock. It seems this is a reminder that Michael will be struck and destroyed for humanity's salvation.

Now, at Meribah Kadesh, Michael instructs Moses to speak to a rock to provide water for The People. They are malcontent. Satan senses another opening. Moses is frustrated, nay angry. Satan riles him up even more. Moses goes to the rock; turns to The People; calls them Rebels; asking, "Must Aaron and I bring water from this rock?" With that, he hits the rock. Water cascades lavishly enough for everyone, men, women, children and all the beasts.

Michael's face is long and there is sadness written all over it. He speaks to Moses and Aaron. "You were not faithful to Me. You will both be destroyed without going into Canaan. Another will lead The People into the land I promised."

As The People near Canaan, Michael again speaks to Moses, "Take Aaron and his son to the top of Mount Hor. Transfer all of the priestly robes to Eleazar. He will replace Aaron as High Priest. Bury Aaron there."

The People mourn for Aaron for thirty days.

Sometime later, as The People near Jericho, Michael whispers in Moses' ear, "Go climb Mount Nebo. You will be buried atop the mountain, for both you and Aaron rebelled against Me at Meribah Kadesh. I will show you the land from the mountaintop, but you will not enter the land I am giving to The People."

Moses gives a last, long discourse to The People. He reminds them of all Michael did for them, since before He led them out of Egypt. The plagues, the sea path, the water, the ten rules, the cloud cover by day and the glow by night, the forty years in the wilderness. Moses reminds them of all of it.

The recitation takes several days. As his address nears its end, Moses blesses each tribe and tells them what their future will be.

Moses turns, walks away from The People and climbs Mount Nebo, alone. He stands on the crest. Michael shows him all of the land of Canaan. Rich, verdant, luxurious, productive green fields and stunning orchards. Moses' keen eyes devour the scene.

Michael speaks, "This is the land I've promised to Abraham, Isaac, Jacob."

"Thank You, Michael, for permitting me to see this land. I appreciate what You've done for me." Moses lies down, closing his eyes for the last time. Michael, Gabriel and I bury him on top of Mount Nebo. No one on Earth knows where his grave is.

The People mourn for Moses for thirty days.

* * * *

Orbits later, Gabriel seeks for me. He reports some exciting news! "We're going to get Moses."

"B-b-b-but Moses is destroyed."

"Come along!"

We zoom to Earth—Michael, Gabriel and I. We know where we are going. We remember the precise spot. To no one's surprise, Satan confronts us. I can tell he is concerned. The destroyed are his. Michael is invading his territory.

Brashly, Satan boasts, "Even Moses, the man who talked with You face to face, even he could not obey Deity's law." He rudely states, "Moses took to himself the glory due only to Deity—the very rebellious act for which I am exiled from Shalem. By his rebellion, Moses is under my jurisdiction." Boldly, Satan reiterates all of his original charges against Deity and restates his grievances about Deity's unfairness to him.

Michael looks squarely at Satan. I wonder if He will say anything about Satan's cruelty, falsehoods, temptations. There is so much retort that Michael can use. Michael continues to face Satan. Finally, Satan finishes his accusations and the bombast reduces to a trickle.

Michael speaks, "Eli-Mehlek will reprimand you, Satan. Moses, we are here! Welcome back to life!" I am shocked! Moses, long destroyed, long decomposed, reappears!

"Hi, Michael!"

"Welcome back, Moses. We've awaited this day for some time. I am taking you to a place even better than Canaan. Its name is Shalem. You will love it there." He grasps Moses' wrist and shoots through the welkin, across the cosmos, through the Pleiades of Orion, via the star ways and past the gates, into Shalem. Gabriel and I tag along. The sentries use their spears to create an archway for us. The trumpeteers' fanfare arrests the attention. Spectators—angels—Sons of Eli-Mehlek—line the broad thoroughfare as we conti nue, right to the throne where Eli-Mehlek sits. Eli-Mehlek moves slightly, creating a space for Moses to sit beside Him on His throne.

> *My mouth drops open. Michael speaks, as though Moses is alive. B-b-but he's destroyed! What's happening?*

The Assembly Bowl fills quickly. Trillions of angelic eyes want to see the revitalized Moses, sitting on Eli-Mehlek's throne. Trillions of angelic voices sing of Michael and Moses. Trillions of angelic minds are learning that destruction does not have to be permanent.

I watch the joyful Assembly, thinking of Earth's Canaan, comparing it with Shalem. Perhaps Moses was denied Canaan, but Shalem is infinitely better than Canaan.

Looking at Moses, I realize destruction doesn't have to be permanent. Michael demonstrated to the Universe that destruction is reversible! This is exciting. We will someday see some of our human friends alive again. Whoa! Destruction is not eternal!

When Michael first talked to us about redeeming humans, we were slightly worried. What if those humans were Rebels? Would we even want them in Shalem? Since Satan's expulsion, Shalem is so peaceful again. But Moses! Moses is so close to Michael and has allowed Deity to modify his behavior dramatically. We are totally comfortable with Moses. Now we're excited to see which other humans can also be recreated and transported to Shalem.

Mehlek

Saul proved to be a disaster. Even though Michael selected him to be king over The People, even though Michael gave him stunning victories over the enemy nations, even though Michael stabilized his kingdom, Saul turned Rebel.

* * * *

Satan was ecstatic. "We've got him!" He gesticulated broadly. "He's the leader of The People. He'll be a great help to our side."

Sotai fluttered with exhilaration. "With him leading The People, he'll bring them our way. He'll make them all Rebels!"

Satan nodded sagely.

"I wonder who I can get to be his successor. Jonathan is the logical one, but he's loyal to Deity. I don't want him."

* * * *

Samuel, Michael's seer, conveys the official word. "You defied Michael, thus He chooses Himself a loyal man to be king over The People." The fire smolders in Saul's eyes. *A rival to Jonathan? Bring him on! I'll uproot this upstart.* Saul's reaction shows the depth of his rebellion.

A veteran warrior against a teenage tyro? Who's kidding whom? Gabriel, what ARE you doing?

Samuel delivers the incredible news to a stunned shepherd still in his youth. But Michael sees his loyalty. Brave. With the heart of a tiger, armed only with the simple weapons of his occupation, he dispatched both a lion and a bear. He's handsome with stunning eyes, plays the harp as a maestro and sings so beautifully he could join Shalem's choir. Young as David is, Michael is about to introduce him to The People.

Saul declares war against the Philistines. Without Michael to assist, the war is going badly. Forty days, the huge Philistine champion taunts them. Forty days, Satan encourages his defiance. Forty nights, the army of The People lies in its beds trembling. Forty nights, Sotai allures the Philistine hero with appeals to his ego. He is gigantic, fearsome, terrible, undefeatable. No one in The People's army dares face him.

David saunters into The People's camp, ostensibly on an errand from his father. Gabriel directs David to challenge the behemoth. David wastes no time proposing to engage the egotist. Saul reluctantly sanctions his request. In his simple shepherd's robe, armed with only a leather sling and a shepherd's rod, David faces the enraged titan.

The challenge he makes is heard by all the forces on both sides of the valley.

"You compete using bronze and steel. I compete in the name of Michael, the Deus of The People's armies. It is He whom you have defied. Today, He will consign you into my hand and I will destroy you. I will cut off your head. I will give your body and the Philistine corpses to the wild birds and animals.

"Everyone will know there is a Deus in the midst of The People. All people of the earth will know Michael does not rescue by bronze and steel. This battle belongs to Michael. He will deliver you to me."

I shiver with anticipation as I watch David race to the attack. He seems puny contrasted with the giant. The haughty champion thrusts his helmet back on his head. There's no need for protection from this nonthreat. Roaring, he ponderously totters towards David. David's nimbleness, his fleetness, utterly outwits the titan.

Utilizing the same weapon he used to kill both lion and bear, he boldly attacks. A round sarsen propelled from his leather sling rockets through the air. It smashes the titan's forehead, precisely at the spot his helmet just vacated. The champion drops to the ground. Both armies gasp in astonishment! David unwaveringly continues forward, still running, snatches the titan's gigantic blade from its scabbard, severs the enormous head.

The People's army, inspired by David, attacks the stunned, retreating Philistine army, chasing them 300 furlongs to the very gates of their cities. I fly along—reveling in the victory!

It is a stunning victory for Michael's army. Within a day, David's name is on everyone's lips. His oration to the giant reverberates throughout The People's towns. Michael's name is again spoken and reverenced.

* * * *

Praise-craving Saul seeks to obtain some of the magnificence of David's triumph. He compels David to remain with him at the palace. Saul's eldest son, Jonathan, recognizes Michael gave David the hearts of all The People. He correctly understands he, the heir to the throne, is not Michael's choice to be The People's next king. He intuits Michael's choice of David to replace his father as the king and Jonathan's loyalty to Michael allows him to accept Michael's verdict, even though he yearns to be the king.

Gabriel coaches Jonathan, Jonathan quietly coaches the shepherd in the ways of the palace, teaching him the polish of the palace refinements, the discernment necessary for exchanges with other nations, the wisdom needed to rule The People

* * * *

Jonathan is very isolated. As the crown prince, he is unable to trust anyone's purported friendship. Most associates are seeking what they can obtain from him. They flatter and grovel, seeking his largesse. Even his brothers remain remote. When he is king, he can execute them at any time for any reason. There is no one who is his friend.

In the palace, David is also lonely. He is an outsider, embraced by the king because of his victory and because of his music. Saul loves the music. It quiets his temper. David, knowing his life would be forfeit should his appointment as future king become known, can let no one into the intimacy of friendship.

Gradually, apprehensively, these two lonely people increase their confidence in each other. David's unassuming ways and deference to both Saul's and Jonathan's positions allays Jonathan's fears. Jonathan's discreet manner of tutoring David, of coaching him in kingly behavior, builds trust in David.

One day, Jonathan reveals his knowledge of David's selection as Saul's successor. David is terrified. The man whose position he must take knows his appointment to take it. Jonathan quietly reminds David of his loyalty to Michael. "That loyalty is above even my loyalty to my father, the king."

Jonathan requests David to make a pledge of friendship with him. David agrees. The pledge is created and sealed. As tokens of the oath, Jonathan gives David his complete garb, including his royal robe and his weapons, saying, "You will be king over The People and I will be your subordinate."

In their mutual loneliness, dictated by their unique positions, fueled by their mutual meekness, the pledge is fulfilled. Their friendship is the instigation of legend, the inspiration for song, the inauguration of an eternal closeness rarely seen on Earth.

* * * *

Saul perceives David's appointment and isn't pleased. *Jonathan is my heir. Jonathan will be king after me.* His anger intensifies. At first, David's popularity shelters him. Eventually, Saul succumbs to Satan's manipulations and openly attempts to destroy David. He sends soldiers to David's house with orders to destroy him.

With his wife's help, David flees from Gibeah, departing so rapidly he leaves his weaponry behind. He conceals his whereabouts in a few cities; discerns that some, for hope of reward, will gladly inform Saul of his location. His presence also endangers the occupants; Saul's fury will stop at nothing—even the execution of innocent inhabitants—to achieve David's destruction. With nothing else to do, David secretes himself in the wilderness, a dense woodland south of Gibeah. There is a plethora of caves dotting the region. One of the largest is Adullam, where David camps.

All troubled, indebted, malcontents gather around him, about 400 men in all. During this time, he learns the principles of leading men. They are a fractious group. He welcomes them all, puts them to work hunting, earning cash, building the camp. It takes considerable food to feed his troop. They are actually quite comfortable.

David's command grows to nearly 600 men in his squad.

During this time, David continually seeks Michael's directions. Many times, Michael gives David specific instructions. "Go here. Do that. I will give the enemy into your hand." Very few people are as closely coached by Michael as is David. Few people have as many successes as David.

* * * *

Samuel counsels David until the day old age destroys him. Often his advice is of a practical nature similar to Jonathan's training. Occasionally, he makes predictions about things that would happen in David's life.

One of these is a prediction that Michael would give David's enemies to him to do with them as he sees best. While in the wilderness, David shares that prediction with his brigade. "Michael places an incredible burden on my conscience when he tells me that." His men nod in agreement. They understand slightly. I wonder about these decisions David will make.

While David is hiding in En Gedi , Saul brings 3,000 men of the army searching for David. David's men secrete themselves in a cave. It is a sizeable cave, with enough room to encompass David's entire team, all 600 of them.

In surprise, the men all watch as Saul appears in the cave's opening, walks in a few steps, squats down, relieves himself.

The men surrounding David whisper urgently, "Now! It's now! He's in your hand. Michael places him under your power, as He promised He would do. You are free to kill him. Here's your dagger. Go! Now! You'll never have this chance again. Hurry!"

David rises, knife in hand, approaching Saul, who is oblivious. I hold my breath. David grasps Saul's robe, cutting off the fringe so gently Saul feels naught, retreats, holding the scrap of cloth in his hand. His men protest as Saul escapes. I relax.

"He is Michael's appointed and my king. Michael prohibits me from slaughtering His appointed one."

His men sigh with infuriation.

"Remember, Michael gave the decision to me. This is my decision."

David turns away and exits the cave. Saul is only a few steps away. "Honored sovereign," David exclaims, falling on his knees, face to the ground, "why do you call me your antagonist? Because others sully my character? Just now, Michael permitted you to come within my power and I didn't injure you. See this piece of your robe?" David flattens himself on the ground. "Certain people told me to assassinate you. I could not slaughter my king, Michael's appointed one. I prefer to demonstrate my mercy to you. I cut off the fringe of your robe instead. I am not your enemy. I have done nothing hostile to you. I will never harm you. I give judgment to Michael, who will decide between us. He will judge between you and me, not I."

David's appeal is so powerful. I watch Saul's face to see if there is a response. Many emotions flicker across his face. He gasps several times. His breathing seems challenged. His emotions spill out. "David, my son! Your innocence is true. Mine is not. Your treatment of me is superior to my behavior towards you. I pray Michael will recompense you with good. Today, I recognize you will be king over The People. I beg of you not to obliterate my descendants."

Saul goes home.

Sometime later, Satan urges Saul, "Go, apprehend David. He will supplant Jonathan as The People's next king." Saul puts David's mercy out of his memory. The reminder that David will supersede Jonathan as king rankles his pride. He is still resolute. Jonathan *must* succeed him as king. Saul arms another 3,000 soldiers and marches to the wilderness.

Messengers appraise David of Saul's advance. His scouts verify the intelligence. David's band treks over ridge and gulch to a peak overlooking Saul's camp, Saul is in the camp's center, with soldiers sleeping around him, a human buffer to shield the king. David decides to infiltrate Saul's camp.

David's nephew Abishai enthusiastically accompanies him. The night's stillness is unbroken by their footsteps. Michael uses some divine anesthetic. Not a soldier stirs. They steal silently to center camp. Saul lies before them. He quietly snores, his armaments surround him.

Abishai whispers, "Again! Michael places your enemy within your power. I can use his spear to spike him to the ground. Just once. It will not take twice."

"Don't slay him! Can one butcher Michael's appointed king and not be rebellious? Michael will destroy him, or he will be destroyed in war. Do not ask me to assassinate Michael's appointed. I will not do so.

"See his spear and water skin. Take them and retreat."

I am not surprised. David's mercy towards Saul is legendary. He and Abishai return to camp, carrying Saul's spear and water skin.

Early in the morning, David stands atop a peak, a valley between him and Saul's camp. His voice carries clearly into the camp. "Soldiers of Saul, where are you? Why didn't you protect your king?"

"Who's awakening the king?" Abner Saul's general snarls.

"General, you're Saul's best warrior, so why did you not protect the king last night. Look around. Do you see his spear and water skin? This is not good. Your negligence cries for your execution."

"Is that you, David?" Saul's voice quavers over the canyon.

"Yes, it is I, my honored sovereign. Why is my sovereign pursuing his slave? How have I offended you? I could have destroyed you in your sleep, yet I did not."

"I have rebelled against Michael's will—again. I have been foolish and erred terribly. Come home. I will not damage you, because you preserved my life last night."

David whispers, "I don't trust him! That's exactly what he said last time. I can no longer rely on his promises." Abishai nods in agreement.

"Here is the king's spear. Send a soldier to fetch it," he calls. "Michael rewards everyone's fidelity and honesty. He will protect me."

"I pray you will be successful in all you do." Saul's tone is sad. He recognizes his evil ways cause David's subtle condemnation of him.

The breach in their relationship is permanent.

Saul goes home depressed.

David flees, equally depressed.

A vivid picture appears in my mind. In Assembly, Satan was given permission to do whatever he desired to Job. Pain and misery followed. That picture contrasts with David's actions. He also had been given permission to do whatever he wanted to his enemies. Honor and mercy followed.

* * * *

I watch the Philistines attack The People. Their assaulting pagan army is huge, obliterating most of The People's army. Saul and Jonathan are both destroyed. I mourn along with David and all The People. I remember Saul as he was before he rebelled. My thoughts go to Satan. I also remember him before he rebelled. *Has he changed as Saul has? It is possible, I guess.*

After the mourning is over, David inquires where he should settle. Michael answers, "In Hebron." David leads his army to Hebron and settles there. His men build houses, invest in sheep, horses, cattle. Their lives return to normal.

David, on the other hand, is not allowed a life of normality—instead his life becomes quite abnormal! The leaders of Judah assemble to coronate him as the king of Judah. He is astonished at their request. He's just a little shepherd boy, isn't he? He struggles as he learns the duties of a king are quite different from those of a commander of a small band of troops. Often he yearns for the normality of the sheep pasture.

After eight years ruling Judah, David has established his court and learned how to enforce law and order. Watching his approach to governance, the rest of The People crown David king over all The People. His men, augmented with additional troops from The People, aided by Michael's directions, rout all the nations around. David becomes emperor over all Canaan.

* * * *

Uriah and Bathsheba build their home abutting the palace. It is a nice home, with a knee-deep reservoir out back—perfect for Bathsheba to soak in. While Uriah is away fighting, Bathsheba utilizes the reservoir frequently. It keeps her skin soft.

Bathsheba is Ahithophel's granddaughter. Ahithophel's a long-time, highly valued Davidic counselor. All her life, grampa took her to the palace. An exquisite young girl, her access to the entire palace was unfettered. Old men, young men, boys and girls hasten to do her bidding. While not truly a member of the court, Bathsheba is almost treated as if she were a daughter of David.

She and Uriah have known each other since Bathsheba jounced on grampa's knees. Now she is of marrying age. Her beauty has matured into a delicate vision of splendor. With Ahithophel as David's wiliest counselor and Uriah one of David's elite warriors, Uriah and Bathsheba have known each other for years. Recently, Bathsheba's winsome smile, radiantly inky hair, enchanting movements and vivid dark eyes have made Uriah aware of a component of his life that is missing. He hesitates. He pauses. Finally, he sends a messenger to Ahithophel, requesting an appointment.

Ahithophel is gratified by Uriah's offer. Uriah and he will give his great-grandsons an excellent genealogy. Uriah will take good care of his granddaughter. Uriah takes Bathsheba as his wife.

After the compulsory newlywed one-year hiatus from battle, Uriah goes with Joab to fight against the Ammonites. The Ammonites all flee to their city and secrete themselves behind its gates.

David's warrior skills are no longer essential as his army is victorious without his presence. Consequently, David stays in Jerusalem. General Joab sends him daily updates on the war's progress. David reads them with interest and realizes he is restless for the frontlines. He feels old, abandoned, bored. After the midday rest, he restlessly rambles around the palace—attempting to recover his old zest for life. His languor is an opening for Satan's intrusion.

His rovings find him on the palace roof, gazing longingly over the distant vista, humming a melancholy melody. His ennui deepens. His jaded eyes drift down towards the city. Just below the palace walls, he spies a woman immersing herself in a bath. She is beyond gorgeous. His eyes mesmerized, he watches, wondering who this splendid is. Satan urges, "You're the king. You can do it!" He turns behind to the page who always attends him. "Who is this woman?" His spirits lift. Satan smirks.

"I don't recognize her."

"Find out. I want to know."

"Yes, my liege."

A few minutes lapse. The page returns with word that she is Bathsheba, the granddaughter of Ahithophel and wife of Uriah.

"Bring her here. I want to talk with her." The boredom exits.

"Yes, my liege."

He strides back to his living quarters. There is purpose to life. He is the king. His will is always obeyed. She enters. He plies her with food and drink. He dazzles her with his kingliness. He feels young again. His blood pulses. The old thrill of wooing and winning a woman seizes him. Satan urges, "Yes, yes, yes." David takes her hand—leading her to his bedchamber.

The king's business keeps David busy. Lawsuits, weapons, supplies for the army, food stocks for the palace require David's attention. A rolled, sealed papyrus arrives. David opens it. "I'm pregnant. Bathsheba." David's world falls apart. He closes court, returns to his living quarters, his mind racing, his thoughts twisting rapidly through his head.

He calls for a scribe. Joab is instructed to send Uriah for some detached duty with the king. David presumes Uriah will sleep at home. That will explain the pregnancy.

Uriah arrives in haste, but doesn't behave as David expects. He will not accept privileges the other soldiers can't have. David's mind races again. He writes a second note, "Joab: Place Uriah where the nastiest fighting is occurring, withdraw from him, allowing the Ammonites to destroy him." He gives the memo to Uriah to take to Joab, who obeys the order. Bathsheba mourns Uriah. Afterwards, David sends for Bathsheba. She becomes his wife.

David feels great. His infidelity is hidden. His murder of Uriah is charged to the Ammonites. His stunning new wife sways his passions simply by espying her. No one need know his rebellion. After all, he is the king, isn't he? He forgets we angels know. He disremembers Michael knows. Satan and the demons rejoice, "We've got him now. This is better than Saul's defection!" We angels mourn for David's lost integrity. A displeased Michael sends Nathan, the seer, to David.

Nathan tells David about a rich man who stole from a poor man. David is incensed. "The rich man should be destroyed!"

"You are that rich man," Nathan denounces. Without stopping, he continues, "Michael says 'I chose you to be king. I preserved you from Saul's anger. I gave you Saul's house. I gave you both the Southern Kingdom and the Northern Kingdom. If that isn't enough, I would give you more.'

"'Why have you rebelled by doing things I abhor? You murdered Uriah, one of your faithful, trustworthy warriors, using the Ammonites as your weapon. You stole his wife.'

"'Because of your rebellion, I can no longer protect you as I guarded you previously. Trouble will stalk you, beleaguer you, harass you, vex you.

These troubles will come from within your own house. You acted covertly. I will punish you in public.'"

As Nathan speaks, David's face blanches. His conscience awakens. His guilt appears before him in its greatness. He shrinks inside his royal robes. Horror fills his soul. Heartbroken, he confesses, "I rebelled against Michael."

Nathan continues, "Certainly. Michael pardons your rebellion. You will not be destroyed. However, because of your contempt for Michael, Bathsheba's son will not live." Within a week, the babe perishes.

* * * *

The predicted troubles come quickly. David's son forcibly violates his daughter. Her brother destroys the guilty one. David's eldest son attempts a palace coup and is destroyed. An evil man tries to become king and is beheaded by the townspeople. There is a three-year famine.

Every time a new disturbance materializes, David recognizes it as another punishment from Michael and he mourns his rebellion anew. Bathsheba's splendor is a continual reminder. She bears another son. Solomon is a thoughtful child. He revels in stories about Michael. He yearns to see His power as shown when the stone slabs were given to Moses. He longs to hear Michael's voice.

David isn't surprised when Gabriel arrives with word that—of all of his many sons—Solomon is Michael's choice to succeed David as king. He promises to obey and also promises Bathsheba her son will be the next king.

One last trouble comes to David. He is now old, feeble, shaky. Adonijah, one of Solomon's older brothers, attempts to induce The People to make him king. He presumes David is too weak to countermand his actions.

Nathan perceives the cause of the clamor, as some of The People are beguiled. Immediately, he acquaints Bathsheba with the threat and instructs her to inform David. While she is addressing the king, he will enter and confirm the situation.

David immediately abdicates and crowns Solomon as king. Adonijah's followers abandon him in panic. Solomon sits on David's throne.

David writes one last poem.

Ruash spoke, using me
His thought my tongue uttered
Michael spoke; He spoke to me
Who rules impartially

Who rendered Godly verdicts
My house is sanctioned by Michael
He made an eternal pledge to me
He eternally provides for me
He completes and finishes all I crave.

I watch the recording angel close his journal about David's life. His final notation: "David did all that Michael required his entire lifetime, excluding Uriah, the Hittite."

As the celebration surrounding Solomon's recoronation resounds across The People's land, I return to Shalem, thinking some deep thoughts. *Saul's rebellion seems so minor compared to David's misuse of Bathsheba and Uriah. Yet Deity forgave David his great rebellion while not forgiving Saul's.* As I ponder the difference, an idea emerges.

Perhaps it is not the magnitude of the rebellion that concerns Deity, but the size of the Rebel's repentance. Rarely have I heard such heart-rending penitence from any human, much less a king. My mind remembers David's words. Saul never broke his heart as David did. Listen!

O, have mercy on me
Wipe away my rebellion
Wash away my wrongdoing
Cleanse me of my depravity
I am aware of my debauchery
I am conscious of my evil
Against You, and You only, have I rebelled
I have done what is evil against You
Your confrontation is just
Your condemnation is appropriate

Deluge me with water and I will be clean
Launder me and I will be untainted
Present the ecstasy of being forgiven
Hide Your face from my rebellion
Obliterate my guilt
Craft a pure heart for me
Refurbish my tenacious spirit
Do not discard me
Do not take Ruash from me
Cause me to feel the elation of deliverance
Nurture my desire to obey

I will impart Your hesed to Rebels
Transgressors will turn to You
Liberate me from the guilt of murder
My God who delivers me
My tongue will surge with joy
Because of Your release
Give me words
So my mouth will praise You

The surrender God covets is an abased spirit
A humble and repentant heart You will not reject.

Roeh

Satan gathered his followers around, reporting their progress. He holds a long list of successes to tout. His angels listened avidly.

"Rebellious Ahab is king now. He's our man! I've gotten The People to split into two countries, the Northern and the Southern. The Northern People have continuously rebelled against Michael—ever since they rebelled against Rehoboam, splitting from the Southern People. Their first king, Jereboam, made two golden calves and instructed the Northern People not to go to Jerusalem to worship, but to worship those golden calves.

"Listen, our plans are going even better now! It has been about 100 years since I engineered the split. As I mentioned, our man Ahab is the Northern king now. He is married to Jezebel. Her father is Ethbaal , king of Zidon and the high priest of Baal . (Isn't that wonderful!) A strong-willed woman, she intimidates Ahab and all the Northern People and drives them to worship our Baal, her father's god!

"She tells them Baal is the source of the abundant water they enjoy and the sunlight in which they revel. Their rebellion against Michael has reached epidemic proportions. He is nearly forgotten by all. I am profoundly happy! Things couldn't be going better!"

His demons cheered, clapping and yelling excitedly. They were greatly energized by Satan's upbeat report. They could taste victory! It seemed so close.

* * * *

Yes, Michael is nearly forgotten, yet not totally. There is a man who remembers the great things Michael has done for The People. His soul mourns. His indignation rouses. "How, Michael, can these People be brought back to you?" The Gilead Mountains see his longing for them to cease their rebellion before they are destroyed totally. His home town,

Tishbe, watches his yearning for them to turn their worship back to Michael before Michael's aroused justice obliterates them.

Day after day, month after month, this roeh —Elijah—begs, "Michael, send your judgments upon them, if that is what it takes. Remove the dew and the rain. Baal doesn't supply them, You do. Please Michael, do something."

Michael's compassion yearns after these People also. Tenderly, He sends them reproof. They do not listen. Gently, He appeals to them. They do not change. Sternly, He warns them. They continue in their rebellion.

Now, while Satan is gloating, it is time to act. Michael answers Elijah's prayers. "Go to Ahab and tell him there will be a drought starting now."

Elijah immediately leaves for Samaria, traveling day and night. Arriving at Ahab's palace, he boldly passes the guards. He seems unseen as they remain at their posts. Without invitation or announcement, he stands facing the king—his bearing imposing, his clothing coarse, his belt leather. Ahab, speechless at the interruption, focuses on the intruder.

Without preamble or apology, Elijah announces, "As Michael lives, whose agent I am, there will be no dew or rain until I consent." Ahab sits frozen—listening to Michael's decree, his astonishment obvious. Ere he recovers, Elijah turns and exits, leaving the entire court gaping at the verdict.

Gabriel whispers in Elijah's ear, "Go east to the rivulet called Cherith. You will be safe there, drinking from the streamlet. And I'll send the ravens to sustain you."

In the palace, Ahab is furious; Jezebel is livid. Satan rages. The king's squads search for Elijah. The Queen curses Elijah. Baal's priests execrate Elijah. Jezebel defies Michael. Ahab's dispatched messengers demand to know if Elijah is in any foreign country. Baal's priests demand rain—from Baal. Elijah vanishes. Jezebel whips up the hatred of The People towards Elijah. Farm fields parch. Trees shrivel. The People riot. Rivers dwindle. Cattle dehydrate. Baal's priests implore, "Baal, bring the rain!" Prophets of the Groves shriek, "Elijah is an imposter." Jezebel scorns the belief that the drought is Michael's judgment on her kingdom. Elijah remains unfound. Courtiers tell of Elijah's intrusion and decree. Word spreads throughout the land; this is a judgment from Michael! The drought is all The People can talk about. That and the theory that angels whisked Elijah away.

The rill called Cherith fails. Gabriel tells Elijah, "Up in Zidon, in Zarapheth, there is a widow. Go there. She is indigent. I will provide for her, her son, you."

The widow seeks two sticks—just two sticks—but they are hard to find in the drought. Two sticks to bake her last bit of flour. Starvation awaits. The drought consumes all of her resources.

"Please, may I have a drink of water?" the stranger asks. The widow rises and turns toward her home. "And would you please bring me a piece of bread, also?"

She looks at him in shock, recognition upon her face. "Oh, as Michael your Master rules, I don't have any bread. All I have is a smidgen of flour in a canister and a drop of oil in a jug. I'm seeking two sticks to cook our last morsel. Then my son and I will eat our last meal before we starve."

"Don't be anxious. Continue with your cooking, but bake me some bread first. Afterwards, bake some bread for you and your son. Michael promises your canister of flour will not empty and the jug of oil will not diminish as long as the drought lasts." His tone is gentle.

It is a struggle—giving away her last food is hard. Her generous heart desires sharing, but her son needs the food. Yet that promise! Can she believe? He says it is Michael's promise. He says Michael sent the drought. Baal's priests haven't done much good. She decides to trust Michael, bringing Elijah the first baking.

As Michael promised, her flour and oil last until the rain returns.

* * * *

Ahab, urged by Jezebel, continues to seek Elijah. Michael is bringing the promised penalty for worshipping other gods. The drought is severe. Elijah begs Michael to bring The People's worship back to Him. Daily, his petitions are heard in Shalem. As the drought worsens, he sees suffering and privation everywhere. His heart is tender towards The People. Their agony is his agony. Their pain is his pain. He leaves the timing to Michael.

Three years pass and more. Jezebel and Baal's priests are totally impotent to break the drought. Satan's reports are less upbeat—his followers' cheers are fainter. Finally, Michael sends Gabriel with directions for Elijah. "It's time. Go talk to Ahab. I am ready to break the drought."

Approaching Obadiah, the manager of the king's house, Elijah instructs him, "Go, tell Ahab I'm here."

Terrified, Obadiah blurts, "Do you want to destroy me? While I'm gone, an angel will spirit you somewhere and Ahab will angrily destroy me."

"I swear by Michael's life, today I will meet with Ahab."

In terrorized astonishment, Ahab receives Obadiah's message. He's been seeking Elijah continuously in order to destroy him. Elijah would not lightly meet with him. Is Elijah about to pronounce another curse upon The People? With dread in his heart, he and his bodyguard meet Michael's messenger.

Stammering, he asks, "Are you the cause of this drought?"

"Not I. You and all Israel abandoned Michael and worship Baal. Now go, gather all The People to Mount Carmel, including all the prophets of Baal." His bearing is authoritative, not to be defied. The king frantically complies with his directive.

* * * *

Walking along the hillside, Elijah's eyes drift across the scene. I glide along with him, looking where he looks. Mount Carmel is desolate. Before the drought, it was a luscious place. Now it is withered and sear. The woodlots containing the shrines to Baal are leafless. The ground is grassless and barren. The shrines stand in vivid contrast to the old altar dedicated to Michael with its stones jumbled, rocks weedy.

> *Another Decision Day. It is time to make a decision. If Michael is our God, follow Him. If Baal is our god follow him.*

The People arrive, singly and in large groups. The priests of Baal march in formation, imposingly magnificent. Satan and his angels march with the priests of Baal. The king arrives in regal splendor, his throne positioned with the priests behind it. There is fear and apprehension in the air. The priests remember the word of the roeh, stating the beginning of the drought; their gods have not been able to overturn his pronouncement.

Another Decision Day. It is time to make a decision. If Michael is our God, follow Him. If Baal is our god follow him

All look at Elijah with hatred and fear in their hearts. All blame him for the drought and its related distress. Unafraid, unabashed, Elijah stands in front of The People, the sole representative of Michael. (Well, not really! Gabriel and I are there. Also a legion of loyal angels support him.)

"It is time to make a decision. If Michael is your God, follow Him. If Baal is your god, follow him." Elijah's voice can be heard at the crowd's periphery. No one dares to answer Elijah's challenge. No one dares to speak for Baal. They listen intently. No one dares turn away from Elijah.

"I am the only one here representing Michael. Baal retains 450 priests. Let those priests furnish two bulls, keeping one and giving me one. Let them prepare theirs for sacrifice and place it on their altar without fire. I will place mine on Michael's altar. Let them call on Baal. I will do likewise, calling on Michael. Whichever god responds with consuming fire is the true God."

The People consider. The proposition is simple. They answer, "A reasonable idea."

Elijah tells Baal's priests, "There are many of you; you can go first."

Baal's priests put on a valiant front. Inwardly, they are panicked. Elijah chose a test they cannot falsify. They begin their incantations, dancing around their big magnificent altar. All morning they continue. They attempt fraud with their own fire, but Elijah is watching. At noon, Elijah twits them, "Shout louder! Maybe he's asleep." The sun travels on, getting lower in the sky. Baal is not responding. Satan attempts to send fire. We angels prevent him. That would not be from Baal. Sotai sneaks by, nearing the altar. I spot him. He retreats. After several hours, Baal's priests are hoarse, bloody, exhausted. Despairing, they collapse in defeat.

At Michael's evening worship time, Elijah stands. "Come close to me." All eyes are on him as they fearfully creep nearer. They recognize the significance of his timing.

Quietly, he selects twelve stones from Michael's altar. The People recognize this represents one stone for each tribe. He uses the stones to build a small altar. He digs a trough around the altar. He slaughters Michael's bull, placing the wood on the altar and the bull on the wood. He calls for four pithoi of water to be brought. He directs them to pour it over the altar, slowly, so the water has time to drench the wood. Twice more the dousing is repeated. The people watch, their eyes riveted on Elijah, on the altar, on the water overflowing the trough. It is too wet, Elijah cannot cheat.

Elijah again stands, his bearing magnificent. He repeats the history of their apostasy. He reiterates how their rebellion awakens Michael's anger. He invites them to humble themselves and begin to worship Michael. Only thus can the drought be broken.

In stark contrast to Baal's priests' shrieks and dances, Elijah engages in no histrionics. He bows, offering a simple prayer, "Michael, show The People that You are the God of Abraham, Isaac, Jacob. Show them that I am Your representative and have done these things at Your command. Remind them that You are God alone. Gather their hearts to You." No drama, just a simple prayer.

A stir fills Satan's ranks. We turn to see its cause. Michael has come near.

Michael is listening to Elijah's prayer. Michael responds. He points at the altar. A flash of fire, brighter than lightening, speeds across the sky, arching downwards to the little altar—consuming the bull, the wood, the stones, the water in the trough! All that is left is a small, charred spot on the ground.

The People fall face down on the earth, crying, "Michael, He is God. Michael, He is God." Baal's priests also fall facedown, not because they worship Michael, but from terror. With unrepentant hearts, they remain priests of Baal.

Elijah commands the people to seize Baal's priests, "Be certain all are captured." The People take them down to the dry wadi and destroy them, all 450.

Satan is furious! Sotai is in a rage, storming around! I wonder what happened to my friend. Satan flees, along with his minions.

* * * *

The rains come. Elijah leads Ahab's chariot back to Jezreel. He finds a sheltered nook and falls asleep. It's been a long day and a long run back to Jezreel. He's tired.

While in deepest sleep, a messenger arouses Elijah with a warning from Jezebel. "I'm planning to destroy you, like you did to Baal's prophets."

Elijah is groggy, slow to waken, benumbed with weariness. Startled, fearful, he exits the city, bolts for safety. He races into Beersheba, in the Southern Kingdom, continuing a day's journey into the wilderness.

He lies down under a tree. He prays that he might be destroyed. "I am no better than my fathers." He sleeps.

Gabriel lets him sleep a long time, then gently taps Elijah's shoulder. "I baked a cake and filled a jug with water." He wakens, sees the food, eats.

Again, he sleeps.

Gabriel reawakens him. "Eat some more. The rest of the journey is long and difficult."

Elijah continues on to Mount Horeb and finds a cave in which to hide. We left him alone, some forty days, to think, to brood, to recover.

I am troubled. If Elijah had stayed and withstood Jezebel, Michael would have gained even greater honor. However, Elijah is a human, with human weaknesses. He panicked while tired. All Shalem watches with patient tenderness.

Finally, Michael bids Gabriel to go talk to Elijah. Gabriel quietly queries, "Why are you here, Elijah?"

"I have been very protective of Michael's name. Yet The People break down His altars, forget their promises, destroy His prophets. I'm the last one and they want to destroy me, too."

Gabriel directs him to prepare.	Michael is coming.
A mighty hurricane blows.	Michael is not there.
A massive earthquake rumbles.	Michael is not there.
A colossal fire burns intensely.	Michael is not there.
A gentle whisper sounds.	Michael is there!

"Why are you here, Elijah?" Michael gently reproves His seer.

Elijah's discouragement resurfaces. "I am very zealous for You, Michael. The People break their pledge to You, destroy Your places of worship, massacre Your servants. I'm the only one left and The People want to destroy me."

Elijah's work is complete. It's time for his reward and some reward it is!

I listen carefully. Elijah's words are partially true. How will Michael answer him?

"I have others who will help you in your work. Anoint Hazael as king of Syria. Anoint Jehu to replace Ahab. Anoint Elisha to be your assistant. The evil that eludes Hazael will be handled by Jehu, the evil that escapes Jehu will be scrubbed by Elisha.

"And besides you, I have 7,000 of The People who are Loyalists. They will assist also."

Chastened and encouraged, Elijah leaves the cave to obey Michael's instructions.

* * * *

Shalem is always charming. When it is festooned for a party, it passes simple beauty and reaches exquisiteness! We are adorning the streets, the mansions, the trees, the gates, the flowers, the arches, the Assembly Bowl. Deity provides an exceptional rainbow and covers the sky with a cloud formation unlike any I've seen before.

> *Elijah's work is complete. It's time for his reward and some reward it is!*

Gabriel and I fly to Earth carrying an astonishing message to Elijah, Elisha and the schools they established. Michael is bringing Elijah to Shalem! Elijah bore the burden of standing between The Rebel People and an angry Michael. Michael's anger is not like human anger. Human anger is almost always anger at other people. Michael's anger is always at the rebellion. Elijah shared in Michael's work of attempting to woo The Rebel People to terminate their rebellion.

Now, Elijah is to share with Michael Shalem's rewards. Our excitement is palpable. First Enoch, then Moses, now Elijah! Deity is demonstrating that Loyal humans are accepted in Shalem. Enoch is a delight, having walked right into our hearts. Moses is a thrill, having been destroyed, but not permanently. Elijah is electrifying, having stood boldly in front of hostile people, princes, priests. We can scarcely wait for his arrival.

Gabriel alerts Elijah of his well-earned honor. He warns Elisha of his upcoming succession. He informs the students in the School of the Roehs at Jericho. Worried, the students whisper to Elisha, "Do you know Michael is taking Elijah today?"

"Yes," he whispers back. "Shhh! Don't tell anyone!"

After Elisha encourages the students, the two seers stride purposefully toward Jordan. Elijah continues directly into the current, hitting the water with his cloak. The Jordan parts. They cross on the exposed riverbed. Elijah asks Elisha to wait there. It is a test. Elisha declines. He passes the test.

"What can I give you before I leave?"

"I want twice as much of your character."

"That is a hard thing to give. I don't know … If you see me depart, your request is granted."

They continue. Without warning, a chariot emerges between them. Direct from Shalem, it gleams with the fiery intense radiance of Eli-Mehlek. The horses glisten as if they are on fire. Michael is the charioteer. He holds out His hand to Elijah, "Welcome aboard." Elijah steps in. They swoop upward. Elijah loosens his cloak, drops it over the side. It flutters to earth.

Elisha, realizing the enormity of his calling and the vacuous lack of Elijah's guidance, tears his robe in half, crying, "Abi! Abi! I see Michael's chariot and His horsemen!" He seizes Elijah's cloak and clutches it in his hand. With tears flowing down his face, he stumbles back to the Jordan. He strikes the river with Elijah's cloak, calling on Elijah's Deus. The river divides, exposing a pathway for his passage.

He is alone.

He has Elijah's cloak, Elijah's instructions, Elijah's Deus.

He is not alone.

Shalem's party begins! It lasts a long time.

Deific Allies

Often Michael needs to discipline. Back when Michael brought The People out of Egypt, the nations occupying Canaan were evicted or exterminated. The city of Sodom was annihilated, its residents destroyed. Noah's flood terminated billions of people. Now I see Michael's disciplines are happening again.

Babylon is attacking The Southern People. The Northern People, even after Elijah and Elisha's reforms, continued in their rebellion. Michael chastised them with the armies of evil nations. Finally, The Northern People ceased to exist as a nation. The Southern People seem to be sucked into the same destructive vortex. Michael sends messenger after messenger, warning of increasing chastening. Finally, He decrees Jerusalem will be destroyed; the luxurious temple Solomon built will be torn down; the Southern People will be captured, chained, carted away for seventy years.

* * * *

"We have The People on our side. We conquered their hearts. We made Michael so angry at The People He is giving King Chad a free hand in their destruction. Pretty soon, we'll have Michael destroying the entire planet again," Satan exulted.

"That didn't do Michael much good last time, did it?" Sotai's shrill giggle screeched loudly. "Earthlings came our way in droves after that."

"Right! Michael's law cannot be kept. It is impossible. So, all people rebel against it."

"And if Michael redestroys the world, we'll retout His malevolence from Alexandria to Arcturus, from Bethlehem to Betelgeuse."

"Heh, heh, sounds glorious. Now, I need to go help Chad. It looks as if he has some leanings toward Michael."

"I'll go with you. I can get some of his underlings to do some really good things for us."

"We'll get Chad to destroy Jerusalem. We'll have him steal all the gold from the temple. We'll get him to capture all of the people and take them to Babylon."

"I'll wrangle the king into rebelling against Chad. That'll rouse Chad's anger—he'll destroy even more of The People."

"Great, great! That's excellent!" Satan grinned one of his gloriously evil grins!

* * * *

With dismay, I see all of the smaller towns and villages are crushed, their people captured. My heart breaks as Jerusalem is surrounded by Chad's armies. In a few days, its walls will be breached, its wealth stolen, its surviving people chained, forced to march across the sandy distance to Babylon.

I am distressed. I go to visit Michael. He greets me sadly. We talk for some time. He understands my sorrow. I see the anguish on His face. I'd never before seen how deep His agony is. We cry together. Michael wipes my eyes and points to four young men in Chad's caravan. "Watch them," He smiles through his sadness, "You will see things you've not seen before! They will be My allies in Babylon. They will help Us incredibly."

The caravan plods through the dust and sand of the wasteland. I glide along. Daniel, Hananiah, Azariah, and Mishael are cousins, descended from David and Solomon. Their parents raised them to follow Michael. Sotai is busy encouraging the captors in their brutality.

Chad orders the prisoners' dispersal. "Find all young men, handsome, of royal extraction, blemishless, intelligent, well educated. Put them in my school to teach them Babylon's language, lore, literature. Feed them the best food, such as is served on my own table. In three years, they can join my elites."

I hold my breath as the command is executed. The foursome impresses the selectors and they matriculate into Chad's institute of higher learning.

Their initial loyalty test comes the first night. Their evening repast is a gorgeous delight, featuring luxurious indulgences. There are abundant wines—beautiful burgundies, laced with intoxicants. Roast pig on a silver salver dominates the serving table. Opulent confections spread out enticingly. It's an alluring change from the sparse rations supplied during the compulsory march across the sere, sandy wasteland. The prisoners' senses are seduced. The four cousins confer.

"We can't eat this stuff."

"Look at the swine. It's unclean."

"I'm so hungry, I'm tempted. Let's go back to our rooms."

"What will we do?"

"Daniel, why don't you ask the melzar for some simple food?"

"Let's pray first. Michael can help soften the melzar's heart."

I look over at the melzar. He's hot and sweaty as he lugs the last tray of food from the kitchen to the dining hall. He's tired and grouchy, with the sweat running down his neck. Daniel approaches and takes the tray from his grasp.

"Hi, melzar. Let me help you a little." They walk along together. "You look as if you are all done in. Can we sit for a minute?" Daniel sets the tray on a table.

The melzar plops down on a stool. "Don't mind if I do. What's on your mind?"

"Well, melzar, as you know, I am a Jew, captured at Jerusalem. In our religion, there is much our God commands us not to eat. My cousins and I won't defile ourselves with these foods Michael forbids. We would rather eat simple food—vegetables and fruit, with water to drink."

Sotai is there urging, "No, melzar, no. The king will remove your head!"

The melzar pales, "You don't know what you are asking. If I accede to your request and you become malnourished, I'll lose my head. I'd like to help you boys, but I do like my head even more!"

"We'd rather you retain your head, too! We're not here to cause you any difficulties, yet we cannot eat the king's food. This is an enigma. Let me think about it … . Say, how about this? Could we try a ten-day test of our simple food … . See what happens. After the ten days, you can compare us to the rest of the students eating the royal bounty. That will allow you to judge for yourself."

Jokim murmurs in the melzar's ear, "It's only ten days. Give it a chance. You'll make the assessment at the end."

"Ten days? Hmmm, that's not too long. It's short enough that it shouldn't do too much damage. You should recover soon. I'm curious to see the results! The test is on!"

Ten days of continuous prayer and their humble diet showcase the benefits of Eli-Mehlek's simple food. The difference between them and the other young men is astonishingly clear. They are noticeably healthier than those dining on the royal delicacies, convincing the melzar of the wisdom of their dietary regimen.

At the end of three years, Chad assesses the trainees. None is found to be as wise as Daniel, Hananiah, Azariah, Mishael. They are even wiser than the experienced counselors already advising Chad. The king instantly takes them into his service.

Michael implants His allies in the king's court. Satan is very displeased. Michael has big plans for His allies embedded in the court of the king. I watch eagerly, fascinated by the possibilities.

* * * *

Chad is sometimes an unruly bully, being unreasonably demanding of his courtiers, his subjects, his family. This morning, he is even worse. His face glowers. His eyes smolder. His voice rumbles with pique. He commands all of his advisors, his counselors, his magi to appear instantly.

> *Chad attempts to bully his magi into doing something impossible.*
> *Their destruction is ordered. Michael saves His allies.*

It is only the onset of dawn, but they arrive with evidence of haste. Clothes not quite perfect. Hair slightly disarranged. Rubbing their eyes. Breathlessly, they await his wishes.

Chad attempts to bully his magi into doing something impossible. Their destruction is ordered. Michael saves His allies

"I have had an important dream. Tell me what it is and what it means." They gape at Chad in astonishment, his blunt demand flabbergasts them.

Satan's face is a study in intensity. How can he ascertain the dream? If he knew the dream, he could let his allies, the advisors and counselors, in on the mystery. He can't. His fury surfaces.

"Of course." They bow to the king. "Tell us the dream and we will tell you the interpretation."

Satan rages, "Make it hard on them!"

"You heard me. Tell me the dream and what it means. I'll reward you beyond belief. On the other hand, failure will cause you to be slaughtered and your possessions destroyed." He stares at them furiously, seeing the consternation visible on all faces.

"O king, tell us the dream and we'll be glad to give you the interpretation."

Satan pushes the king. "Go, go! They're filibustering"

"You're stalling. If you don't tell me the dream, you're frauds. By telling me the dream, I'll trust your interpretation also."

"With all respect, no king ever requires this. There is no man on earth who can recount the king's dream. Only the gods—and they aren't here today."

Sotai is agitated, fluttering excitedly. He sees the ambush, yet cannot prevent disaster!

"Frauds! You claim to know what the gods think. Now I see you're all impostors. I can't believe I've trusted your hoaxes. Guards—take these swindlers out and destroy them. Include all the fakes that are not here. Don't forget the charlatans in training. Let none escape. Include their families also."

The cousins are in their rooms. Chief executioner Arioch comes to apprehend them for their destruction. Daniel requests, and is granted, an audience with the king. "Please, sir, give us some time and I will declare to you what you desire to know."

Sotai and Satan sag in despair. The trap is set. There is nothing they can do.

All night the four cousins' prayers continue, prayers for Michael's glory, not for their own safety. Michael hears their prayers and gives Daniel the answer to the king's demand. In the morning, Daniel goes to the king, telling him, "Michael is the God of gods—and only He can make known the dream and its meaning to the king."

Chad listens in awe. Satan listens intently, as Daniel recounts the dream exactly as Chad remembers it—a humanoid sculpture made of various metals, each representing a discrete demesne. The head made of arum symbolizes Babylon. Chad is amazed at the unraveling of its meaning, impressed that Michael would share the future with him. "Your God is a God of gods, one who divulges secrets and mysteries." He falls on his face and venerates Daniel, who gently, humbly points him to Michael as the One due his adoration.

Gabriel whispers, "Promote him. A man like Daniel can be trusted with power and control and influence."

"Bring all the gifts I promised. Daniel earned them. In addition, Daniel shall be the head of state and chief over all of my counselors and sages."

Satan's swagger returns; now he knows what Chad saw; now he can concoct his version of the interpretation; now he can give his allies answers for Chad.

Michael continues working on Chad's heart.

* * * *

While Chad is prominent in his dream, his kingdom is only a part of the vision. His vanity rankles at the umbrage. Satan, seeing an opportunity, works on his egotism, encouraging his irritation. "Hey, Chad, look at that! You're only the head. Sure it's arum, but it's only the head. You should be the entire statue, not just a small portion of it. Your kingdom will endure forever! No other kingdom will take its place."

So, a few orbits later, Chad decides to make a copy of his dream's image, except it is pure arum. He erects it just outside Babylon on the plain. He calls his entire administration to inaugurate it as a symbol that Babylon is immortal.

Satan is pleased. Sotai ecstatic, quivering with glee.

> We need not be suave. Our God has the power to deliver us. Even if He chooses not to intervene, we will not worship your idol.

The entire plain is saturated with Chad's officials. Daniel quietly declines Chad's invitation, telling the king that he'll stay in the palace, working on official matters. The king, busy with the details, concedes Daniel's decision. The other cousins, along with the influential, proceed to the plain, finding a centrally located position.

> *We need not be suave. Our God has the power to deliver us. Even if He chooses not to intervene, we will not worship your idol*

The envoy broadcasts the rubric to the throng. "When the music starts, all will bow in worship to the arumic image. No exceptions! Anyone who remains standing will be executed."

The cousins look at each other and, without speaking, they know they will not obeise, they only genuflect to Michael.

The music starts.

All fall down.

All faces hit the dirt.

All, except the cousins.

They remain in a standing-at-attention demeanor.

Satan smiles beatifically. Sotai yodels with pleasure.

Chad hears of their defiance and is livid with rage. *Who is this who dares defy me? I'll show them.* "Fetch them, he rages. He recognizes them and his anger abates. He knows them and remembers they are good and loyal men.

"Is it true, Hananiah, Azariah and Mishael, that you stand, flouting my orders? I'll give you one more chance. If you continue to scorn my statue, my orders, my authority ... well, over there is the kiln used to fabricate this idol. I'll hurl you into it. There is no god anywhere who can rescue you!"

"With all respect, our liege, we need not be suave in our answer to you. Our God, if He so chooses, has the power to deliver us from your verdict. If He chooses not to prevent our destruction, even so we will not worship your arumic idol." The cousins stand humbly before Chad, awaiting their fate.

Chad's fury rages again, "I am THE king. These Jews will do as I command. Even their god cannot countermand my orders."

Satan whispers in his ear, "Heat the kiln. Use seven times as much fuel as normal. Make it hotter than hot. Heave these insubordinates into it." Chad echoes Satan's words. Compliance is instant.

The searing kiln destroys the guards as they fling the cousins into the conflagration. Chad is watching intently. He likes the cousins, not really wishing their destruction—yet defiance must be broken.

He sees the lifeless guards lying before the kiln. He sees the snarling flames. He sees the roaring inferno. He sees the cousins promenading through the blaze. He starts. He stands. He trembles. "Wait! It was t-t-t-three insurrectionists we p-p-p-pitched into the kiln, wasn't it?"

"Absolutely, my king."

"B-b-b-but I see four! T-t-t-the ropes are gone. T-t-t-they're strolling within the f-f-f-fire. It's not h-h-h-harming them. And the f-f-f-fourth looks like a g-g-g-god!" He staggers towards the kiln. It is hot. "Hananiah, Azariah and Mishael, obligees of the supreme G-G-G-God, come here!"

They comply, standing in front of the king, just as if nothing has changed. The horde on the plain gathers round. They touch, feel, smell the cousins. There is no damage to their apparel. There is no odor of fire lingering on their garments. Not even their coiffures are scorched.

Satan skulks away, totally defeated. Sotai's exuberance quelled as he creeps after Satan. I wonder if they will ever be able to best Michael. I doubt it.

The scene looks unchanged, yet something is changed. Chad is different. Michael's allies allow Him to quietly chide Chad for his arrogance. Chad accepts the remonstrance and proclaims the cousins' God as the God of gods that all shall worship. Chad still doesn't understand Deity's absolute lack of coercion, so his decree attempts to compel devotion as it threatens destruction on all who do not worship Michael.

* * * *

Chad is so proud, so arrogant. Michael is having a difficult time teaching him to be meek. He yearns for Chad to cease rebellion and follow His example of using persuasion instead of compulsion.

He gives Chad another dream. None of his counselors and advisors are able to interpret this new dream. Daniel appears later. Chad retells the dream for Daniel's ears.

Daniel understands the meaning of the dream and it disturbs him immensely. Michael is attempting to pierce Chad's haughtiness. The dream warns Chad to curb his conceit or a huge consequence will come.

The thought appalls Daniel. He hesitates to relay Michael's message to Chad. "I'd rather the dream applied to the king's enemies, yet it does not. Michael says, 'you became great and strong. The God of Shalem gave you power and prestige. But you allow it to feed your ego.'

> *Your God, whom you always serve— He will protect you*

"I plead with you to break your rebellion by doing righteousness and by showing mercy to the destitute. Perhaps Michael will relent His punishment."

It happens. A few months later, Chad is looking out over his capital and his ego blurts, "Look at this beautiful Babylon. I built it by MYSELF, with MY vigor and for MY exaltation."

At this instant, Chad goes insane, the words, "Your domain is removed from you. You will live in the pasture and eat grass like the cattle," echoing in his ears.

His sanity is gone. At the end of seven years, he regains his sound mind and becomes lucid once more. Again, he issues a proclamation extolling the cousins' God as the most powerful God in the entire Universe. He humbles his heart and ceases his rebellion.

* * * *

Chad ceases living. Babylon is attacked and falls. The Medes and Persians are the next kingdom, shown in Chad's dream about the metal idol as the silver. The Babylonian monarchy ceases. The new king is Darius. The other three cousins are already destroyed. Only Daniel outlives the Babylonian kingdom. His excellent character impresses Darius, who appoints him as one of his chief sages. The rest of Darius' advisors hate Daniel because he is honest and truthful and perceives their mischief and greed.

Your God, whom you always serve—He will protect you.

The advisors are talking one day; no one is listening!

"How can we solve the Daniel problem?"

"I don't know. I've been wondering, too."

"I hear Darius is planning to put him over all of us."

"That would be a nightmare, wouldn't it?"

Sotai hisses, "Trap him. Use his Michael worship."

"Hey guys, perhaps we could set up a trap for him."

"I've thought of that. He's pretty canny. Would avoid any trap."

"Hmmm, how can we rid ourselves of his smugness?"

"He would see through anything we could set up."

"Perhaps an 'accident?'"

"Too dangerous. If the king learns, we'll all be destroyed."

"Well, there is one 'trap' we could set."

"Oh, what's that?"

"It's about his God. He worships the Jewish God, you know."

"Three times a day, even."

Sotai interposes, "Make Darius the only worshipee."

"Yeah, so?"

"Daniel only worships his God and always will."

"Of course! That's critical to the trap!"

"The critical part of what?"

"Maybe we can persuade Darius that he's the greatest king."

"He already thinks that."

"Sure. Maybe he'll sign a decree that all must worship him!"

"Yes, yes, yes!"

"Make the decree last for thirty days only."

"Yes, and the lion cave makes a great punishment."

"Darius would love having all worship him."

"Darius is so vain; he should go for such adoration."

"And a law, stamped with the royal signet, can't be changed!"

"That's it! We've got Daniel now."

Sotai speeds away—to tell Satan of his success.

They induce Darius to seal the decree. He is so pleased with the idea of all worshipping him. The decree is posted. All know the requirements and the consequences.

Daniel's enemies gather around his house, watching. Daniel is home for the midday meal. As always, he opens the second-story window, the one facing Jerusalem and seeks Michael's presence.

They dash to the throne room, babbling excitedly. It worked!

"Oh, king, do you remember that edict you just sealed?"

"The one about worshipping only me?"

"Yes! For the next thirty days."

"Because you are so beloved by all."

"Those who disobey are to be cast into the lions' cave?"

"The decree which cannot be changed?"

"Yes, I remember, why?" Darius looks at them, puzzled at their exuberance.

"Well, we found your first scoff-law."

"How dare he flaunt my decree! And who would that be?"

"Daniel, your majesty, ignores you and scoffs at your laws. He still prays three times a day toward Jerusalem."

Darius' face pales. Now, he sees the trap. He's been used to accomplish the destruction of his best administrator. He paces. The trap has been set perfectly. He roars. There is no alternative. He growls. He waits 'til dusk then yields to the inevitable and orders Daniel into the lions' cave. Anguished, he cries out, "Your God, whom you always serve, He will protect you."

Darius staggers back to the palace, spending a long, restless, worrisome night. His brave advice to Daniel seems more like bravado. He torments himself that he missed the trap. Why hadn't he noticed Daniel wasn't in the crowd that inveigled his acquiescence?

Dawn is faint in the eastern sky as Darius rushes to the lions' cave. "Daniel, Daniel, did He do it? Did Michael protect you? Are you there?"

"I hope you slept as well as I did!" Daniel chuckles. "Michael sent His angel to close the lions' mouths! I am guiltless in His eyes. Neither have I offended against your majesty."

"Release him! Now! At once! Immediately! ... . Go get those confounded advisors and their families. Those lions are hungry and need feeding."

* * * *

Daniel is old. He's been Michael's ally for many years now. He knows the seventy years of the prophecy is nearly complete. He also knows at his advanced age, he will not return to Jerusalem. Yet, he's been Michael's ally for so long, Michael will give him a signal honor by revealing to him the exact time Michael will come to Earth as a baby and when the beginning of the end of time would start.

Both Michael and Gabriel come to explain the import of the tidings given to him. I listen eagerly. I, too, want to know what will happen. There is still much I don't understand about this rebellion and Deity's response to it. Satan has mostly alienated my heart. Sotai is not the same friend I had known.

As I listen to Gabriel's explanations, a newer, clearer understanding of Deity's plans about and responses to the rebellion come to me. Just five centuries and Michael will become a human. That is pretty near. It will pass like a flash. I'm beginning to apprehend that Deity's plans are much, much more profound than I'd ever recognized before.

Slowly, thoughtfully, I wing my way back to Shalem.

New duties await! Gabriel's mansion needs a thorough spiff up.

Five centuries is not a long time to wait!

Metamorphosis

I am animated in a solemn sense. All Shalem is diffused with the same spirited sense of awe. It is ubiquitous and the momentous mood spills out to all orbs, planets, stars, except Earth. Right now, I can no more sweep Gabriel's floors than I can create a baby.

Shalem's mood as we await Michael's metamorphosis is intense and solemn. Earth's mood is blasé.

This is the last Assembly. Michael is saying good-bye. He is leaving Shalem to become a human. Things on Earth are worse than awful. In a way, we would be relieved for Eli-Mehlek to destroy every human being. I remember when nearly every humanoid was destroyed during the flood. It didn't help much. This time, instead of destroying mankind, Deity sent Itself to show Earth, Shalem, the watching Universe what Deity is like. The eyes of all of us angels and Sons of Eli-Mehlek are riveted on Earth. There arc things we want to know, answers we want to find.

> **Shalem's mood as we await Michael's metamorphosis is intense and solemn. Earth's mood is blasé**

We are still dumbfounded at The Plan. By now, Satan's mantra, "Michael is selfish, wanting all the homage for Himself," is familiar. Yet, here is Michael leaving all of the honor, all of the glory, all of the adoration in Shalem to become a human. And just like every other human, He will be born as a baby. And just like every other person, He will be able to rebel, if He so choses.

Mixed with the solemnity is sadness. Michael's empty throne will not be occupied for many orbits. At the beginning, Michael told us we will be assigned a part in The Plan. So far, our part has mostly been people protection and a check on Satan's power—as well as watching and learning.

He reminds us Satan will do anything to destroy The Plan. He will exert maximum efforts to cause Michael Himself to rebel. He will struggle to kill Michael before He can show mankind the character Deity possesses. Now our part in The Plan includes protecting Michael's life from some of the attacks of Satan. Every cherub and seraph volunteers to be a part of that shield.

Michael reminds us there will be times when we can't interfere nor can we help Him. Satan's accusations are directed primarily against Michael. Michael must meet those accusations—Himself. He must personally face Satan and He must prove Deity's case—Himself—alone, with no help or interference.

My contemplations go deep as I leave the Assembly. When Michael described the battles ahead, I could hardly believe my ears. This doesn't sound like the Lucifer I knew and loved. Will he really attempt to kill Michael while He is a little baby? Surely, Satan will not try to destroy Michael. I remember the anger Satan displayed. Will that anger really be directed against Deity? Yes, I suppose it will be.

As I enter the Archangel's mansion, Gabriel is there.

"Hi, Zuriel. You look deep in thought."

"I am. Michael's predictions seem incredible. The Lucifer I know won't do what Michael says he will do. But then he wouldn't have treated Job so abysmally either. I must admit I am not enamored with what Earth has become, but I still have a hard time believing Satan is totally at fault, totally blamable."

"Yes, Zuriel, that is why Michael, Himself, must answer those charges. Satan will be given a fair chance to prove his accusations. Only Michael can disprove them, only Michael can show Deity's character. That is why Michael is going to Earth. After this demonstration, every being in the Universe will understand who is being truthful and who is lying. All questions will be answered, no one will be puzzled."

"That will be wonderful. I'm still torn between them. Sotai has no more a soft spot in my heart, but Satan … oooooh, I'm so tired of arguing with myself!"

"By the way, Michael wants you to assist me as His guardian while He is on Earth."

"Gabriel!" I gasp. "I'm just a mansionkeeper!"

"Yes, but you did guard the Tree of Life and the flood's Boat. And Michael asks for you."

"That's true, but I still have a mansion-keeper's heart. However, I am honored. I'll do anything Michael asks me to do."

"Good! And now I must be on my way."

"Where to this time?"

"Earth. Zechariah is praying for the people of Israel. I have a message for him. He will have a son."

"He's old. But so was Abraham."

"Yes, Eli-Mehlek intends that many things be done to call attention to Michael's birth. One of them is that two people who are too old to have children will have a baby. The baby's name will be John and he will be the one to introduce Michael to Earth."

With that, Gabriel's off. It isn't long before he is back with a bemused air about him.

"Zuriel, it is so difficult for humans to believe—even when they believe! Zechariah believes Eli-Mehlek, yet he couldn't believe Eli-Mehlek will give him a son. He stammered on a bit about being old and wanting a sign."

"What sign did you use?"

"I obliged him by making him mute. He won't be able to talk until the baby is born!"

"Oh, Gabriel! That is comical!" I chuckle.

As I finish the mansion, Gabriel sweeps by.

"I'm going to visit a young girl named Mary. She lives in Nazareth."

"I've seen her. Why do you need to visit her?"

"Eli-Mehlek chose her to be Michael's mother."

"Oooh." It's a gasp of surprise. "But she is poor, so very poor. Isn't she engaged to be married? To Joseph?"

"Yes, she's in the poorest class, as is Joseph. That's part of The Plan. Satan claims Michael wants honor and glory. Yet this poor family has no honor and no glory. Michael, Himself, said He did not want people to come to Him because of His wealth or power or charisma, so He will have no wealth and no power and no charisma, other than the attractiveness of the truth about Deity."

And with that, Gabriel is off—winging his way across the Universe to an unremarkable house in a nondescript village, visiting an unsuspecting girl, telling her that Eli-Mehlek chose her to be the mother of the Promised One. I stand there looking after him, thinking deep thoughts about the accusations Satan made and Michael's response to those accusations.

It is nearly time for Michael's birth as a baby. All Shalem is waiting with expectancy. Mary and Joseph have to pay the taxes and are on their way to Bethlehem, just as The Plan indicates. So are a lot of other people. The taxes are inflexible and unavoidable.

A band of us angels go to Earth to share in the celebration. We envisage the news to be on everyone's lips. We go to Jerusalem, expecting to find everyone looking for Michael's birth. Daniel's prophecy is well known; many are perceptive enough to realize that the predicted time is now.

We find no one in Jerusalem who cares the biggest event in the Universe's history is occurring. Deity becomes a human! Deity somehow wraps Its infinity in a baby!

We find a small group of shepherds, huddling around their fire, who seem to appreciate the importance of the day's events. Their intense conversation is about the promise made to Adam and Eve. They are reading the prophecies as we approach.

Gabriel leads the way and gently increases his brilliance so as not to startle them. He tells them about the Baby and where they can find Him. We are so impatient we can hardly wait to burst into song. Gabriel is so very bright; the night is so very dark; it takes them awhile to absorb the idea that we are there. Gabriel gives the signal and we all sing the Anthem we have been practicing. Those shepherds race into Bethlehem, rejoicing. We go along, just to get another look at this Unique Baby.

We travel on and search through Shechem, Jericho, Capernaum, Samaria. We fly on to the surrounding nations—to Damascus, Alexandria, Philistia, Athens, Rome. We can't find another person anywhere who cares about this Baby, much less anyone who wants to revel in the birth along with us.

A scout angel comes winging back. Away off in Babylon, there is another group interested in finding the Baby. They are reading about the star, which will come out of Jacob. Gabriel's commands us to form the shape of a star and we lead them to the Baby. Great is our rejoicing as they worship Michael.

It is such a small celebration. The people of Earth don't seem to care about Michael. But we are fascinated, intensely engrossed. Will Deity's character emerge unscathed or will Satan's accusations be proven true? I hope Michael will win. I still love Lucifer—even while my doubts about him are growing.

* * * *

Satan was ecstatic. Michael became a human. He was in their power. Sotai'd never seen Satan so upbeat before. They all hated Michael. That hatred kept them together. Otherwise, the fighting and bickering between his angels would have driven them apart. They were smart enough to put aside their differences and concentrate on defeating Michael. Of course, Satan was the general, yet they all had their parts.

* * * *

"Mary, how are you doing?"

"Just fine, Joseph. A little uncomfortable, but I'm okay. Are we there yet? I'm feeling an occasional twinge."

"Bethlehem is just over the next little hill. It will be rocky for a while. I'll hold the burro's reins and help him step gently. We need to hurry before those twinges become contractions!"

"Thank you, Joseph. This baby is really kicking me."

"That is a good sign. He is alive!" Joseph chuckles.

"Augh," Mary groans. "That's for sure. He'll be born soon."

"Hope He waits until we get to Bethlehem. Here is not a good place for a birth. In Bethlehem, I'll find a place where we can stay."

"I see what you mean. These rocks are difficult, even for you. This little burro is having trouble keeping her footing."

Just then, Sotai flashes by. I am there, but he races by—behind my back. On his way by, Sotai nudges the burro. Down he goes! The place chosen was particularly rugged. A great place for a bad accident! Just exactly what Sotai wants.

Mary gasps as she falls.

"Are you all right, Mary?"

"I-I-I think so. I banged my head on the rock, but I don't think I'm hurt."

"How is the baby?"

"He's quiet right now. I hope He's okay."

* * * *

Sotai thought he'd been really sneaky, but just as he nudged the burro, Zuriel saw him and caught Mary as she fell. Gabriel protected the burro's leg from damage when his hoof slipped into the crack between two boulders. Sotai was livid, thinking *I am so much smarter than that imbecile—Zuriel. Sooner or later, I will catch Zuriel sleeping and destroy Michael.*

Satan had some impressive plans for Michael. The Rebel angels had learned how to induce people to rebel. They'd gotten very good at it since the first success in The Garden. Not one human had ever been able to resist them. If one of the lower Rebel angels could not influence them to rebel, they'd call on Satan. His cunning always worked. There was no way

Michael, as a human, could remain loyal. They could hardly wait to see Michael rebel. That would be the ultimate proof that Eli-Mehlek's law was impossible to keep.

Ministry

Gabriel and I are busy. Satan knows Michael comes to challenge his rulership of Earth. With a new intensity, he works to turn human hearts away from Michael and toward himself. I hadn't realized how fierce the conflict would be. There are so many attacks on Baby Michael. We are constantly alert for whatever might happen. Some of them are Sotai's work. Other times, it is another of Satan's angels. Some are random. The most notorious incident was Herod's destruction of all the babies in Bethlehem. Sotai worked with Herod for that one and helped Herod to adopt Sotai's attitude towards Michael. Gabriel directed Mary and Joseph and the Baby to safety in Egypt for a while.

Michael grows taller and stronger. He is different from all other people on Earth. Never once does He rebel against Eli-Mehlek. You might think that is easy, yet He faces the same pressures and urges as all other humans face. Every time He wins a victory, Shalem cheers and Satan stomps off in sullen anger. One other difference is the amount of time He spends communing with Eli-Mehlek. He studies the synagogue scrolls, pondering them intently.

Sometimes I see the Rebel angels urging the children of Nazareth to torment Michael in some manner. Gabriel and I work just as purposefully, urging them to be kind, but their teasing is often particularly cruel. Often, I see Michael seek out one of the children who is hungry or discouraged. He gives the child a small bite of food or puts His arm around his shoulders. He listens to a girl who is disappointed from some dashed hope. Then Sotai works on the child's heart and the next day, the next week, he or she becomes so cruel to Michael.

In the carpenter's shop, Michael plies the mallet, chisel, gimlet at the sawbench. I watch the furniture take shape beneath His careful hands. It is beautiful. His work is always done correctly. He doesn't hurry and He doesn't dither, just works at a steady pace. As He works, He often hums and sings quietly to Himself. As I watch, I ponder the scene. Michael, the beloved of Shalem, the Creator of Earth, using the implements of the poorest of the poor. I think about Satan and remember his boast that he will become like Eli-Mehlek. Would he be content here, like this—with nothing? And not just content, but joyful, as Michael is joyful?

* * * *

Michael continues on in the carpenter's workroom with his brothers. Joseph has been buried, leaving Mary as the only human who knows all the secrets of Michael's birth.

We are in preparation for Michael to move on to His mission. The Rebel angels are marshaling, too. Zechariah's miraculous son, John, baptizes in the Jordan River. Thousands respond to his call to become Loyalists. The crowds grow bigger every day. Even the authorities begin to notice, particularly when he talks about the coming Messiah.

"Mother, the time has come. I must be about My Father's business. The shop is in the hands of My brothers. Eli-Mehlek will be with you. John is preparing the way for My mission."

Mary answers sadly, "Go, my son. You are a special Child, announced by the angels and wiser than Solomon. May Eli-Mehlek be with You."

"Tomorrow morning, I depart for the Jordan."

And with that, Michael hugs Mary and retires.

* * * *

He fades into the crowds making their way to the Jordan, seeking no recognition, mingling with the throng as one of them. At the Jordan, the throng's eyes see a man, dressed in camel hair and their ears hear a message calling them to repentance. John's message is clear:

Feed the fatherless
Care for the poor
Reject rebellion
Be baptized as a Loyalist
Michael is coming!

Many in the multitude weep, as Ruash touches their hearts. They do choose loyalty and John baptizes them.

Finally, Michael steps forward. Puzzled, I glance between Gabriel, John, Michael.

In all of the thousands of people whom John baptized, he hasn't seen anyone as noble and virtuous and loyal as Michael. John hesitates, "I need to be baptized by You."

"It's all right. This is part of The Plan." And John accedes to His request.

Not many notice the conversation between John and Michael. Yet, as Michael arises from the water, every eye is riveted on Him. The gates of Shalem are thrown open, Ruash forms a brilliant white dove settling on Michael; Eli-Mehlek's marvelous voice speaks, "This is My cherished Son. He delights Me."

I tingle from head to toe! Surely now everyone knows this is Michael. THE Michael, OUR Michael, Who comes to show the Universe that Eli-Mehlek's way is the way of truth and rightness by saving Earth's Rebels from destruction,

I look across the Jordan—there is Satan watching. My love for the old Lucifer still wells up occasionally. Today it startles me. I remember Michael's victory means Satan's defeat. Do I want Satan to lose? Is he perhaps right about Deity? I don't think so—even though my dwindling love for Satan allows me to wonder. Gabriel says that soon all will be clear. As I watch Michael walk out of the water—I hope so.

Ruash takes Michael by the hand and leads Him out into the desert. Gabriel and I provide escort. Satan comes along, too.

* * * *

After Michael went to the wilderness, Satan came back and had a big council with his cohorts. Satan kept muttering, "'My beloved Son' and 'I am delighted,'" angrily, sarcastically mimicking Eli-Mehlek. His angels all chimed in with various ideas. Satan kept insisting that the only way to win would be to make Michael disbelieve the voice of Eli-Mehlek. After a while, they all saw the wisdom of this strategy. As long as Michael believed the words from Shalem, He would be impregnable.

"I've got it!" Sotai squawked.

Satan looked at him. "How could you ever think of something I have not already thought about?" he sneered. Sotai winced. Satan didn't sneer at him too much, but when he did, Sotai was crushed. "So, what is it?"

Hesitantly, Sotai said, "Could you pretend you are Michael? Or Gabriel?"

"Why would I … . Wait, that has some possibilities … .Yeah, right! … . I could pretend that I am Gabriel and tell Michael that Eli-Mehlek sent me. Yes, yes, yes! Thank you, Sotai. That is an excellent idea! With Michael being weak and hungry, that will work."

Satan turned on his throne, closed his eyes and all could tell he was thinking. No one dared interrupt him. He could be really vitriolic at times.

After a while, he said, "Yes, that will do," and he outlined his basic plan. "I'll return with Michael's capitulation in hand. Trust me; I've gotten every other human. I'll get this One, too."

* * * *

Michael stays in deep communion with Ruash and Eli-Mehlek. Night and day, they talk and plan and laugh with each other. Never before have I seen any human being so close to the Deity. Not even Enoch nor Moses nor Elijah have been this close. Day after day and night after night go by. Forty days and forty nights pass. Slowly, Ruash and Eli-Mehlek withdraw from the wilderness, leaving Michael alone.

Gabriel touches my arm and points over towards the ravine, where Satan watches Michael intently. He sees us and glides over to where we are. We occasionally talked with him while Michael was having enraptured communion with Deity. I haven't seen him for a few days now. There is a different air about him.

"You really trust Deity, don't you?" he asks.

Gabriel just looks at Satan, but I answer, "Your subjects are nothing wonderful. Why should I follow you with them being such lousy advertisements? Enoch, Noah, Job, Moses, Elijah, Daniel make compelling billboards for Eli-Mehlek and His way."

Satan's face flushes as he retorts, "Well, get ready to follow me. When I win, you will be my subjects, as will Michael. You watch! Michael will show His real colors now."

He strides off towards Michael.

After forty days and forty nights without food, Michael is weak. Eli-Mehlek and Ruash are gone. I tremble that perhaps Satan is right. Perhaps Michael will be found to be as evil as Satan claims He is. Perhaps it is true that all of this trouble is because of Eli-Mehlek. I look at Gabriel with worried questions in my eyes. "Should we interfere?"

"No, this is one battle Michael must win Himself and we cannot help Him. Satan must be given the chance to prove that he is right. If we interfere, Satan will claim he was cheated of the chance to prove his case and some will believe him."

I scrutinize Satan, who still gives the impression of being the old Lucifer I love. He taps Michael on the shoulder. Michael looks up at him, squinting His eyes, shielding Satan's brightness. Satan speaks his voice full of melody. "Pretty hungry, aren't you?"

Something in his voice makes me think of Job. I tremble.

"I've just come from Eli-Mehlek's throne and He doesn't want you to be so hungry. He's concerned about your well-being. If you really are Eli-Mehlek's Son, why don't you make these stones into bread? Eli-Mehlek will be pleased when you are not hungry anymore."

If you really are Eli-Mehlek's son? What implication is Satan making? He heard Eli-Mehlek's voice at the Jordan. Ah, yes, he is inviting Michael to disbelieve Eli-Mehlek. I remember some of his words in Shalem. Subtle words, subtle enchanting words, words which lured so many of my friends.

Michael answers with words taken from the scrolls, "The roeh says man doesn't live by bread alone. Eli-Mehlek's word gives life."

"Well, yes, of course, Eli-Mehlek's word gives life," Satan answers smoothly.

Smoothly, yes, but I see Satan's startlement. Both Adam and Eve had eaten what Eli-Mehlek forbade. Most hungry humans would do as Satan suggests—if they possessed Michael's power to do so. He fully expected Michael to disbelieve Eli-Mehlek's word and make the bread. But Michael lives only to obey Eli-Mehlek. And He remembers the words of Eli-Mehlek about His "beloved Son." Michael's answer cheers my heart.

"That certainly is true," Satan continues smoothly. "Say, here's an idea. Come along with me." Gabriel and I shadow them.

With that, Satan picks up Michael and flies over to Jerusalem, right to the temple, right up on the roof of the temple, right where you could look down into the courtyard. From there, it is many spans to the courtyard below. I have seen humans destroyed in shorter falls. Satan gently positions Michael on the apex.

"It's treacherous up here, isn't it? You know You don't need to be scared, don't you?" Satan comments amiably. "Why You could actually jump off and You know You won't get hurt. Remember what the poet says, 'Eli-Mehlek will send His angels to protect You. They will keep You from even hurting your foot on a stone.' With that promise, my fellow angels will catch You before You stub your toe on the courtyard rocks. Go ahead. If You are the Son of Eli-Mehlek, jump."

Without hesitation, Michael answers, "The roeh says, 'Do not have the audacity to test Eli-Mehlek's goodness.'"

"Ah, yes," Satan softly answers. "We wouldn't want to be so bold. That would indeed be presumptuous. We know He is all-powerful and full of virtue. But, say, come along, I'd like to show You something."

Again, Satan picks up Michael—this time, carrying Him to the top of a high mountain. We tag along at a distance. As they land, Satan puts his arm around Michael and points with his other hand. "Look, here is Jerusalem. Over to our right is Athens. Just beyond is Rome. Off to our left is Alexandria. All this is part of my kingdom. Look at the beautiful Acropolis. See the glorious Temple … . Alexandria's library is full of learning. This is all mine!" Satan takes his arm from around Michael and turns to face Him. "I give all of this beauty and glory to whomever I choose to give it. I'd like to give it to You. All You have to do is worship me." I gasp in shock. "And I'll give it all to You. Wouldn't You like that? It would be so much easier than torture, humiliation, destruction."

Michael looks Satan in the eye as He answers, "Depart, Satan! The book says, 'You must revere Eli-Mehlek and serve only Him.'"

The tension has been great. I let out my breath as Satan flees. He is visibly angry. Michael falls exhausted. Gabriel and I fly to His side and, as we did for Elijah, we feed Him and cradle Him in our laps. Slowly, He begins to revive. Soon He sits up and walks around. We take Him back to His wilderness location.

* * * *

As He leaves the wilderness, I think about what just happened. Satan asked Deity to worship him. I think about the words, "I will make myself like Eli-Mehlek." I could never really believe Satan's words, until I saw it with my own eyes. Imagine an angel asking Deity to worship him! I am aghast at his audacity! Satan has just done the most presumptuous thing I have ever seen. How brazen he is! I remember what Michael said before He came to Earth. I couldn't believe my ears then and can hardly believe my eyes now. Yet, how little I know. As shocking as this is, I suspect a plethora of awful news awaits Earth, Shalem, the Universe.

* * * *

Satan returned as irate as he'd ever been. He berated Sotai for offering the Gabriel-impersonation idea. Woe to any angel who irked him in the slightest. He turned on them with withering scorn. Finally, he called a board meeting of his cabinet.

"Michael is still loyal." Satan growled and looked at each member. "He did not rebel. I was certain He would agree to my suggestions. All humans rebel sooner or later. But Michael has been here for thirty years now and has yet to rebel. Any ideas?"

A few timidly offered some ideas—each met with a sneer. "That will never work," and "Michael will see right through that."

Finally, it was quiet. Satan began to speak again. "There is only one way we can prevail. We must work through The People, Michael's own

People. We need to turn them against Him. If they do not believe Michael is Eli-Mehlek's Son, He will become discouraged and we can conquer.

"Now, listen up! Here is how we proceed. First, Michael's people are expecting a mighty king to free them from their enemies. Michael does not look like a mighty king. Tell them this cannot be the One they are looking for.

"Second, point them to the fact that Michael has no wealth. Thus, He cannot help them in their poverty. The One they seek will give them wealth.

"Third, Michael says His kingdom is not of this world. Remind them about that and emphasize what they really want is someone who has a kingdom here and right now.

"Anything we can advocate that will turn them against Michael is exactly what we want. There may be other things that will come up. So keep thinking how to divert Michael's people from the message He brings."

The rebellious demons dispersed over all of Judea. They concentrated on the rulers and leaders, telling them that Michael's way would take away their power, their riches, their good life. Whenever one of them began to believe Michael, they'd crowd around and point toward another idea, any idea, they didn't care which one—as long as it was one the Rebels liked. The plan worked well. Only two of the leaders ever believed Michael and they didn't say anything for a long time.

Mission

Things on Earth slowly begin to change. People are beginning to know who Michael is. It starts simply and quietly. Michael goes to a wedding with His mother. It's a big, happy time, lasting several days, with numerous guests. They run out of drink. Mary asks Michael to help. Knowing Michael, I know He can do something—and He does. From some well water, He creates more drink. As at creation, it is pronounced very good. Wherever Michael goes, He spreads health and happiness.

In the synagogue, Michael reads from the roeh. Listen:

> The Spirit of Eli-Mehlek is upon me
> Because He chose me
> He sent me
> To encourage the poor
> To help the brokenhearted
> To release the captives
> To free the prisoners.

Michael's demonstration of Eli-Mehlek's character is winning hearts. His refutation of Satan's depiction of Deity's nature is telling. Satan is frustrated at losing men's loyalty

Satan and his angels are always around. I see Satan urging Michael to rebel against Eli-Mehlek. I see Satan deep in thought, his brows furrowed as he tries to puzzle out what he can do to induce Michael to rebel. But Michael never even thinks about rebelling. He just continues with His work, ignoring Satan's suggestions.

Michael gathers a small Squad of men around Himself. This Squad is constantly with Michael. He teaches them things that He cannot teach the crowds. But they are so slow to understand. A great deal of Michael's work is to teach them Eli-Mehlek's way.

Another part of Michael's work is healing those who are diseased. A man who has been sick for thirty-eight years is healed with just a word. A man who was born blind receives his sight as Michael touches his eyes. A paralyzed man has four good friends who carry him to see Michael. The crowd is so great they cannot get through. I am touched as they come up with a unique solution. They climb up on the roof, remove the roofing and let the paralyzed man down—right in front of Michael! Michael not only heals him, but also forgives him of his rebellion. And always, Michael is talking about Eli-Mehlek. "I love you and so does Eli-Mehlek. Eli-Mehlek and I are alike."

I watch as Michael defeats a Legion of Satan's Rebels with a simple command. Michael and His Squad sail across the sea. Satan fabricates a major storm. Michael calms the waters with just a word.

As they land at Gadara, two pitiful men rush down to the beach, intent on attacking Michael and His Squad. The victims are possessed by a Legion of Rebel angels who moved into the wretches and took over their lives and bodies. No human can control them. The Legion makes certain of that, breaking their chains and tormenting them day and night. It is impossible for the contrast between the Legion and Michael to be greater.

The Squad panics back to the beach, over the gunwales, into the boat. Michael simply looks at these two men. They stop—screaming vile epithets inspired by the Legion. I recognize some of those voices.

"What is your name?" Michael asks.

"Legion—because there are many of us," they answer in chorus. "Why are you here? We know who you are, Michael. Have you come to distress us now, instead of waiting for the proper time? Please don't hurl us into the abyss."

Michael doesn't answer—He just continues to look at the men. That Legion of demons cannot stand His look. "If you compel us to leave, could we go over into that herd of pigs?" they whine.

"Go," is all Michael says and they retreat in chaotic disorder. Each chooses a pig and occupies it. The Legion is so agitated they drive the entire herd over the cliff and into the lake. The pigs all drown.

As the Legion leaves the pigs, I hear the demons laughing, thinking they have ruined Michael's plan for the Gadarenes. They chortle because the Gadarene people are even more under their power, hating Michael for destroying their hogs.

Michael and the Squad find a few extra pieces of clothing for the two men. They sit at Michael's feet, listening as Michael teaches them for a few moments.

The Gadarenes rush up. The swinekeepers are so angry they order Michael to leave. Calmly, He and the Squad board the craft and depart— leaving behind two ambassadors who tell the story of how Michael expelled the Legion, how Michael restored their manhood, how Michael stood like a rock before the Legion, how Michael—with one word—dismissed the Legion, how Michael returned their sanity.

They want to go with Michael; oh, they long to be with Michael. Yet He knows they will tell the Gadarenes about Him and so it happens, over and over and over again. After hearing the men's story repeatedly, watching the continual change in their lives, the Gadarenes welcome Him back with open arms the next time He comes. Many believe and become Loyalists.

It finally registers in my mind. Michael designated the two healed men as emissaries to tell the Gadarenes about Him, just as He is an envoy telling the world about Eli-Mehlek.

* * * *

Neither the Legion nor the other Rebel angels know what to do with Michael. Satan, himself, doesn't know what to do with Michael. After all, he convinced most of humanity that Eli-Mehlek is harsh and severe. But Michael simply tells humanity, "I don't condemn you. Go and don't rebel anymore."

The stark contrast between Satan's description of Eli-Mehlek and Michael's description of Eli-Mehlek is plain to anyone willing to observe. Satan understands he is losing the hearts and minds of man. He recognizes Michael will attract a large number of his adherents if He is allowed to continue teaching people about Eli-Mehlek. He based his entire rebellion on the idea that Deity has a flawed character and an imperfect government. Here is his chance to prove it. But what can he possibly do? He cannot stop Michael nor can he interest Him in any form of rebellion. His infuriation's intensity is obvious. He becomes more and more enraged as Michael stays in constant conversation with Eli-Mehlek and Ruash and continues to repudiate the charges Satan continuously repeats to seraphim, cherubim, human beings and all the other inhabitants of the Universe ever since his rebellion started.

As Satan becomes more furious, I know something must happen. The simmering volcano of his emotions will eventually erupt. I ponder when that will transpire.

Majesty

Michael's little Squad is amazing in the way its men do not understand Him and what He is trying to teach them. There are only twelve of them. After three years, they still do not understand. One night, Michael calls the three most promising of these men and goes up the mountain to pray. Poor Peter, James and John! They don't know the storm blowing about them. They do not know what Michael knows and how soon He will be destroyed. They are asleep as Michael pours out His heart to Eli-Mehlek. He knows how fierce the battle will be. Michael knows Satan will unleash every lethal device in his armory. Since Michael knows the difficulty ahead, He pleads with Eli-Mehlek for strength, for support, for endurance.

An intense light shines on Michael as Moses and Elijah chat with Him

Gabriel and I flank Michael, one on each side; but a short distance away, Satan is trembling with rage as he dashes about trying to get Michael's attention. Satan knows he must get Michael to rebel or his kingdom will ultimately fail. His intensity increases each day Michael doesn't rebel. Satan has several of his angels with him, equally agitated.

Suddenly the gates of Shalem open and out fly several angels along with Moses and Elijah. Across the Universe they flash, right to Michael. They are sent as bearers of light and glory from Eli-Mehlek to Michael. Eli-Mehlek knows the explosion erupting around Michael as the climax of His mission approaches. These new angels and Gabriel and I form a circle around Michael as we watch in awe. Satan and his angels try to break through, to interrupt. They cannot.

I hear Michael, Moses and Elijah conversing. These two understand the crisis He is facing better than any other beings in the Universe, as they each faced similar crises.

"Michael, we are with you." Moses speaks first. "The time is fast approaching."

"I know."

"It will be rough." Elijah's voice holds a deeply compassionate resonance. "Satan is planning to destroy You. When that time comes, You will be all alone. There will be no one to help You."

"Remember all You have endured," Moses gravely adds. "Satan is defeatable. Remember, he fled in the wilderness. Remember, his angels flee when You send them out of their captives. Satan is using his most powerful weapons. He is holding nothing back. You are the center of his attack. He realizes if he fails to defeat You, he loses the war. Every weapon he possesses, he will use against You."

Michael answers quietly, "We have truth on Our side. Satan is a liar and is the father of lies."

> *Michael, the Creator, is being encouraged by two men He created*

Satan continues to try to break into the middle of their conversation. We loyal angels prevent any interference. I miss a portion of the conversation while contending with Sotai.

Elijah continues, "We know how bitterly Satan will attack. He has nothing to lose and everything to gain. He will be unmasked as the liar he is. All of creation will see the falsity of his charges against Deity. After he reveals his character, the victory will be won. The entire Universe will acknowledge Your rule."

It is quiet for a few moments. Satan intrudes repeatedly. We prevail.

Moses speaks, "Remember all of the people—Adam and Eve, Seth, Noah, Abraham and Sarah, Ruth, David and all of the other people who sided with You—they will be with You for eternity."

Michael smiles.

I sense something happening. Suddenly Satan and all of his angels flee. I look around, knowing why. There is only one reason Satan bolts like that. Eli-Mehlek and Ruash come. Once again all of Deity is united on Earth. Eli-Mehlek's voice peals out of the night sky, "Michael is My Son. I am more than enchanted with Him. Listen to Him." We bow in love and adoration.

Moses and Elijah, the other loyal angels, Eli-Mehlek, Ruash—all leave for Shalem.

I look over at Peter, James and John. The glory awakes them and Eli-

Mehlek's voice intimidates them. They are face down on the ground with their hands over their heads.

Michael gently touches them saying, "It's okay. You can get up. There is nothing of which you need to be afraid."

With Satan and his angels gone, I have awhile to ponder what I just saw. Here is Michael—the same Michael who created the entire Universe—being encouraged by two of the men He created. Here is the Creator, talking with the created—as if they are peers.

In contrast, Satan always attempts to get mankind to worship him. Somehow, from my experience, I can't see him talking to any human on a friend-to-friend basis.

I am glad I remained loyal. I'm even more convinced—all of this trouble really is Satan's fault.

Following the visit of Moses and Elijah, Satan redoubles his already intense efforts. I no longer wonder about Sotai—he is right beside Satan, as Satan is everywhere. He constantly tries to persuade people that Michael is their enemy. He finds great success among members of the Sanhedrin. The rulers of the nation do not want the change of heart Michael offers. Instead, they become willing allies of Satan, doing his bidding.

The two political parties, who always violently disagree on everything, both actively attempt to cause Michael to rebel. Constantly, they keep looking for a reason to destroy Michael. They send spies to test Michael. They dream up wily tricks to catch Michael in His words. And behind the scenes, Satan guides them, leading them to reject Michael and join his rebellion. It breaks Michael's heart. It breaks my heart as well.

* * * *

It's Passover time. On the afternoon of first day of the Passover celebration, Michael calls two of His Squad, sending them on a strange mission:

"Go into that hamlet. Immediately, you will find a donkey and her colt. Untie the colt and bring it to Me. If anyone asks what you are doing, tell him, 'The Lord needs to borrow it' and he will agree at once."

The entire Squad is curious, agog with excitement. Never before have they seen Michael riding. He always walks. They wonder if now is when Michael will announce He is Israel's king. Excitedly, they tell those around their thoughts. As the two return with the colt, onlookers gather around. Some of the Squad throw their coats on the colt as a saddle. Michael mounts as I gently pat the colt's mane, keeping him calm, quieting his terror. He gentles as Michael's weight descends on his back, calmly obedient. With the crowd surging around, Michael begins to ride towards Jerusalem.

The farther they progress, the bigger the crowd becomes. Children run to get their parents. Friends call friends. The resurrected Lazarus is there, as is the formerly blind Bartimaeus and Jairus' daughter, older and prettier. Lepers Michael restored are part of the crowd. Lame legs Michael strengthened dance through the crowd. Mute tongues Michael released are singing praises about Michael. Blind eyes opened by Michael drink in the wonderful scene. Children who sat on Michael's lap recount all Michael has done. The twelve of Michael's Squad lead the way as the crowd cuts down palm boughs, waving the fronds over Michael's head as if He is King, laying the branches and their cloaks in the street as a carpet for Royalty.

It is a long time since Jerusalem has seen such a happy celebration. The people swarm the colt, calling Michael the "Son of David," singing praises to Eli-Mehlek. People from the entire world are there for the Passover. These strangers ask what is happening. The celebrants all joyously answer, "This is the roeh, Michael, from Nazareth. He's restored the destroyed. See, He's given lepers their health! Look, He's made the deaf to hear and the blind to see! Behold, the lame people are dancing! He cured their lameness, too! And He's fed our souls with His gracious words."

> *A shriek is heard ... a heart-breaking, soul-wrenching shriek*

Not all of the mob is rejoicing. Some of the rulers of Jerusalem storm up to Michael, snarling, "Get control of your disciples. This unseemly tumult will aggravate the Romans. Do you want our blood on Your head?"

Michael answers with a smile, "I'll tell you something. If these people were to be still, the rocks under your feet would cry out." The happy, joyous crowd surges on. Jerusalem is just beyond the corner.

As the gates come into sight, the evening sun is shining on the city. Jerusalem's walls shimmer whitely and the temple gold sparkles in the spotlight. The king's palace gleams with grandeur; the governor's mansion is aglow with a rosy hue. The crowd's ovation grows louder at the sight.

Abruptly, a strange sound is heard ... a heart-breaking, soul-wrenching shriek. The celebration stops in the middle of a cheer. All eyes focus on Michael. A nameless grief surges over Him. "Oh, Jerusalem, Jerusalem. You've killed the roehs of old. You've rejected Me. Oh, how can I let you go? I must let you go, because you will not come to Me. If only you had known the peace that only I can give you." Michael pauses—groaning with an enormous grief. He sways back and forth on the colt, nearly falling. "Now your enemies will surround you and destroy you. The destruction will be complete—not even one stone will be left on top of another. Oh, Jerusalem, if only you had come to Me."

The crowd is caught up in the passion of Michael's grief. They weep along with Him. The jubilation is simply a memory, as Michael dismounts and walks through the gate into the city. The subdued crowd follows quietly, some drifting off in various directions. Michael makes His way into the temple.

The hubbub inside the temple is a startling contrast to the parade's joyous revelry and the solemn deportment of Michael. All eyes turn to see Him standing there, surveying the scene. With thrilling power and a royal dignity, He gives an uncontestable reproach to those buying and selling in the temple. "The Scriptures say, 'My sanctuary shall be called a haven of prayer,' but you make it a swindler's shelter."

A regal aura surrounds Him as He approaches the sheep vendors. They flee in fear as He reaches their tables. With a firm dignity, He dumps their money boxes on the floor and sets the tables aside. The dove sellers don't wait for Him to arrive. The money changers abandon their illicit profits and join the other dealers in their flight. He placidly takes the animals outside, turns them loose, sweeps the floor. The sanctuary has not been this tidy in a long time.

As He works, some children look in and He beckons them. They race in to join their Friend. He sits; two tots snuggle in His lap. The more exuberant dance, as they excitedly jabber about the big parade in which they marched. The adults, always more timid, peek around the corner. Seeing the children, they ignore their trepidation and slip inside. Those who are ill, sick, broken seek Michael. Michael welcomes them all into Eli-Mehlek's sanctuary.

* * * *

Night darkens. Michael and His little Squad leave Jerusalem and walk out to Bethany. As He sleeps, I ponder the scenes of the day. I know the crisis is coming. Never before has Michael done anything to attract a crowd. Oh, certainly the crowds gathered, but He'd never sought to receive their praise or their adoration.

But now, He is within days of whatever is going to happen and Earthlings as well as the rest of the Universe need their attention drawn to both Michael and to Satan.

I think about His heartbroken, shrieking grief over Jerusalem. Never, since the days of Moses and Elijah, have I seen any man as heartbroken as Michael. Moses, in his grief, said, "Alas, this people has rebelled greatly. But please forgive their rebellion. If You cannot, please erase my name from Your book."

Elijah in his anguish cried out, "The Israelites abandoned you, tore down your altars, killed your roehs. I am the last Loyalist left and now they want to kill me." Their heartache is nothing compared to Michael's.

Today, Michael is in the temple, with the children sitting on His lap. Across the Universe, from galaxy to nebulae, from giant red star to asteroid, Satan accuses Deity of being unloving. Deity never argues. Instead, Michael invites some children to sit on His lap. Satan's accusation disproved by children snuggling on Deity's lap. Sometimes the smallest events are the most telling.

Magnificence

Speaking of small, telling events, Michael pulls another lesson out of His repertoire. It is Thursday night, the night for the Passover meal. Michael sends two of His Squad on a mission. This time it is to secure a room for the Seder.

The thirteen walk into the room. Twelve of them are arguing about who will be the greatest in Michael's kingdom. I wonder if they will ever learn the lessons Michael wishes to teach.

Satan looks over at Gabriel and me, as he sneers, "I've got them right where I want them." Sotai chuckles with a contemptuous attitude. "We're winning," he avers.

"Hey, Peter, you think you are so good. Michael always chooses you to go with Him. But I've got the treasury position all sewn up."

"Judas, if you don't stop bragging about the treasury, I'll stuff that money bag down your throat and follow it with my sword," Peter answers.

Thaddeus chimes in, "No, you won't. Michael won't allow it. Besides, I'm going to be the vice-regent. I won't allow it."

"You? The vice-regent? How conceited can you be? You couldn't be the vice-footwasher, even if you wanted to be," Judas responds. "Hey, Andrew, do you think Thaddeus could be the vice-footwasher?" He laughs with merriment at his witticism. "Thaddeus, there is the towel. Maybe you could be the only footwasher."

"No, it takes brains to be the vice-regent and I'm the only one with that type of brains," Thaddeus snaps back. "At least, I've got the brains not to be a footwasher. You do it, John, you're the youngest."

> *The Squad is bickering over who Michael will promote. Satan urges each to wrangle for his own interests*

And the conversation goes on, the Squad disputing about who is going to be the greatest in Michael's kingdom. To be fair to some of them, they are still smarting over James and John getting their mother to ask Michael if they could sit beside Him, one on His left and one on His right. But even with that, this argument seems especially ugly. Every one of Michael's Squad keeps insisting he will be Michael's right-hand man and that someone less important should wash their feet. Satan is in their midst urging them to fight for their rights.

Michael waits until their frustrations are close to an explosion. Quietly, He rises. The arguing ceases. He takes off His tunic, wraps the towel around His waist and proceeds to wash Judas' feet. The myriad looks on the faces of the Squad are fascinating. Shock, disbelief, guilt, shame are all registered there. It is absolutely quiet in the room. Even Satan pauses with his mouth agape. The only sound is the dripping of the water and Michael's footsteps. Michael stands in front of Peter.

With amazement and sorrow and shame, Peter exclaims, "Michael, are You washing my feet?"

"Peter, right now you do not understand what I am doing. But after this, you will know."

With genuine pain, Peter cries, "Not You, Lord, not You. I can't let You wash my feet."

"If I do not wash you, you cannot be with Me."

Michael's reply breaks Peter's heart, causing him to answer brokenly, "Lord, not only my feet but my head and my hands, too."

"If one has a bath, one only needs to wash one's feet."

Michael pauses as he dries Peter's feet. He looks Peter in the eye, "You are clean." He looks over at Judas and continues, "But not all of you."

He finishes washing the feet of the rest of the Squad, empties the water, refolds the towel, sits down. The Squad speechless with amazement, waits. I, too, cannot believe my eyes. Michael, the Creator ... Michael, the co-equal with Eli-Mehlek ... Michael, the one we angels worship ... this very same Michael, on His knees washing the feet of the one who, just yesterday, sold Him for thirty silver scraps. After Judas and Satan leave together, the atmosphere changes noticeably. It almost seems as if the Squad members actually love each other. After eating, they sing a hymn and leave for the Mount of Olives.

* * * *

I wish I could adequately describe to you the events of Michael's struggle in Gethsemane (geth-SEM-an-ee). Michael knows what awaits Him. He knows the absolute ferocity of the attack that is coming. It makes

Job's, Moses' and Elijah's suffering look like puppy play in comparison. Michael's humanity shrinks from the conflict. Gabriel and I watch intently as He converses with Eli-Mehlek. He keeps pleading for another way, if there is one. Satan is right there telling Him there is an easier way. He keeps trying to get Michael to join his rebellion. There are a few Legions of Satan's angels right there with him. They keep after Michael, too, crowding around, tormenting Michael. Sotai is right in the middle of the front row. The Rebels' attacks are ferocious.

Michael's humanity shrinks from the ordeal ahead. He implores, begs, pleads with Eli-Mehlek to find another way. There is none

I am in tears as I look at Gabriel. Gabriel is deeply affected also. But still he keeps his hand up. Our legions of loyal angels all want to fly to Michael's defense, but Gabriel's raised hand prevents our interference. Gabriel reminds us this is THE battle that will decide the fate of the Universe. Michael has to fight this battle for Himself.

The struggle is so great, so intense. I thought the temptations in the wilderness fierce, yet they were nothing like this night. Michael looks little like His normal self. The emotional tension is so great that Michael's blood actually oozes through His skin and His face bears the marks of the vicious struggle.

After three times of begging Eli-Mehlek for another way, Michael accepts Eli-Mehlek's decision and falls, almost dying. Gabriel flashes to His side. He cradles Michael's head on his heart and points towards Shalem, speaking words of comfort and hope. He wipes the bloody sweat off Michael's forehead and Michael is revived, prepared, calm.

The mob, led by Judas, appears right on schedule. Judas kisses Michael. Gabriel's hand stops me. Michael asks Judas, "Friend, do you betray with a kiss?" Judas doesn't even blush. I startle at Michael's use of *friend*.

"Whom are you seeking?" Michael turns to the crowd, speaking just as if it is an ordinary day and they are looking for a friend.

"The Nazarene!" the mob shouts back.

"I am He," Michael answers. The leaders tie His hands.

Gabriel looks pityingly on the bloodthirsty crowd. Do they not know what they are doing? He lets out a flash of light. The mob falls down. It is one last warning to the rabble, one last reminder of Michael's identity, one last sign of Michael's divinity.

"If I am the One you want, let these others go." He gestures to the Squad.

Peter draws his sword and begins to fight. The ropes around Michael's wrists loosen as Michael restrains Peter. "You know, I could call more than a dozen legions of angels." We tense in anticipation. Every nerve taut, we eagerly await the call. "Yet, if I did, how could The Plan be fulfilled?" At that Peter, along with the rest of the Squad, flees. Most of them return to the Seder room. Satan looks at us with a knowing sneer. "I won that round," he jeers.

We angels watch in disbelief as Michael permits Himself to be led away, hands rebound tightly. His fingers turn ashen. The mob looks like a pack of mad dogs, circling for the kill. Michael is the only calm person in the crowd. I watch intently—my amazement knows no bounds, my horror knows no limit. Right there, in the middle of the crowd, I see him again. It is Sotai, posing as a human. I watch as he picks up a stick and whacks Michael on the back. The others in the crowd follow Sotai's example.

I fly to Gabriel. "What can we do, Gabriel? You see what they are doing to Michael. We've got to do something!" My voice is indignant, my wings atwitter.

"Yes, Zuriel, it is appalling, is it not?" The pain in Gabriel's voice is clear.

"And Sotai is down there in the crowd. He's leading the pack in abusing Michael. We've got to do something, Gabriel. Could I go talk to Sotai?"

Gabriel's voice is strained almost beyond recognition, "No, this is the one battle Michael must fight alone. Satan's charges accuse Michael. Michael alone must disprove those charges. No one else can interfere. Sotai cannot do anything to Michael—without Eli-Mehlek's permission. And Zuriel … ," Gabriel pauses.

"Yes, Gabriel?"

"This will only get uglier. We have not yet seen the worst of it." I shudder.

All along the line, we angels are anxious to go to the relief of our Commander. I can see and hear little knots of angels as upset as I am. It is almost more than Gabriel can do to keep us from swooping down to rescue Michael. It is only the Archangel's constant assurance that this mockery, this viciousness, must be permitted, which restrains us. I want to shut my eyes and block out the whole hideous scene, but I can't.

I cringe as I see the priests and rulers themselves revile Michael with foul epithets befitting only the basest of people. The most dissolute men engage in the vilest abuse of Michael. I flinch as one poor wretch spits in His face. Even the hardened Roman soldiers are angry at the brutal treatment Michael receives. My head droops as Annas and Caiaphas, the high priests, both condemn Michael to be crucified.

Pilate is called from his bed. Only he can order a crucifixion.

Michael stands before Pilate. My hopes rise. Perhaps Pilate will stop the assault on Michael. "Listen," he reports, "I find no fault in this man." At this, Satan rages around uncontrollably. Sotai and other demons encourage the crowd in their violence. I wonder what happened to my friend. My heart sinks as I hear Pilate say, "So I will scourge Him and release Him." Scourging is hideous. Some people never recover from a scourging. The rabble, urged on by Satan, becomes even more uncontrollable. I can't watch the scourging. I have seen enough.

I hear Pilate ask if they want Barabbas or Michael. Like the bellowing of wild beasts comes the answer of demons and humans, "Liberate Barabbas!" Louder and louder swells the cry, finally becoming a deafening, hysterical chant— "Barabbas! Barabbas! We want Barabbas! We want Barabbas! We want Barabbas!"

Satan, Sotai and some other demons are in the crowd. "What about this man?" Pilate asks. The surging multitude roars with the demons, "Execute Him! Execute Him! Execute Him!"

Gabriel is right; it is more revolting, much, much more repugnant. Finally, Pilate washes his hands—as if that could remove his guilt—and turns Michael over to the crowd. They tie Barabbas' cross on Michael's shoulders and lead Him towards the crucifixion site. Each step Michael takes up Golgotha Hill is a knife in my heart. It is my difficult task to stand by and watch. Much rather would I have been beside Michael, defending Him.

Michael reaches the top of Golgotha Hill to find Satan there, awaiting Him. He taunts Michael. "Think you're better than me, now? I'll show you. Hey, look; there is an easier way than this. All you have to do is to worship me." I cannot believe I ever loved Satan. Whatever sympathies I had for him are gone now.

Michael, stripped naked, is nailed to that cross, I feel every blow of the hammer. My indignation fully roused, I would have destroyed every one of those humans, had Gabriel permitted. I bolt out of my station, but Gabriel holds up a stopping hand and I reluctantly return. Finally, I cover my face with my wings. I can't bear the sight. Gradually, I peek out again, my tears disfocusing my eyes.

We witness something we never thought we'd see. Eli-Mehlek turns His back on Michael. The bright light beams between Eli-Mehlek and Michael retract. "Michael, Michael," my heart cries, "How can you bear all this. It feels like everyone, including Eli-Mehlek, is against You. But, Michael, Michael, I'm not! I'm on your side!" Through my tears, I notice that Michael cannot hear my cries; Michael cannot hear anything. Michael is destroyed.

I, with the rest of the angels, weep. Most of them return to Shalem. Gabriel goes back and confers with Eli-Mehlek. I stay behind and ponder what I have seen.

My emotions churn and roil. My thoughts swirl and chase themselves round my head. I remember how Michael, in the middle of the most intense agony of mind, body and soul, thought only of others. He warned the weeping women to mourn for Jerusalem; He encouraged the thief to believe and He forgave his rebellion; He pled for the forgiveness of His murderers; He placed His mother into the keeping of one who would care for her. Through it all, He continued to love everyone, even those who were killing Him.

My turbulent thoughts turn to Satan. Never before have I really understood what Satan's character has become. Those mockers of Michael as He hung upon the cross are permeated with the spirit of Satan, the great Rebel. He imbues them with vile and loathsome speech. He inspires their taunts. He joins them in their foul work. Yet today, he lost. He did not win our hearts nor did he cause Michael to rebel.

Yes, Michael told us what would happen. Yes, Gabriel tried to explain it to me, but I kept remembering Lucifer and what he had been like before his rebellion. Now, Satan's new character reveals itself to me, to all of us angels and to every intelligent being on all the other spheres. Only mankind is still deceived.

It is not improvement of Eli-Mehlek's government that Satan seeks. He desires to dethrone Eli-Mehlek and set himself up as supreme. He will do anything to achieve that goal—destroying anyone and everything that interferes with that goal. With loathing and disgust, I think, *Satan, you will never be able to tempt me again. Now all is plain to me. Were you once the glorious angel who ministered in Shalem's courts? It is hard to imagine you were once loved by all of Shalem.*

Through my tears, I watch as Satan exults in his victory. He and Sotai and all the rest of Satan's devils are boasting about what they have done to Michael. Satan boldly claims Michael's body. He marshals his strongest devils in battle array around the mouth of that cavern. We do not dispute with them. We don't even talk to them. We just dazedly watch, in shock, as they brazenly and openly, yes, jubilantly celebrate their victory. Their malevolent party lasts for several hours. Satan quiets his angels and reminds them Eli-Mehlek will attempt to raise Michael to life again. He speaks with great power about how they must fight once more with Michael's angels if they are to keep Michael as their prisoner.

Whoosh … !

With an aura of glory, Gabriel blazes across the sky. Never has he been brighter. Never has he been whiter. Never has he been faster. Satan's warrior devils flee as he approaches. Satan is furious at their desertion. He stands there by the stone cavern door, trying to prevent what is going to happen.

Gabriel does not pause or say anything. He just touches the stone and it rolls aside as if a pebble. The rumble of his footsteps on the ground shakes the guards awake. Stupefied, they stumble to their feet. Awestricken, they watch as Gabriel calls with a tender, trumpet-like voice, "Michael, Son of Eli-Mehlek, get up! Eli-Mehlek is calling You!"

Gabriel blazes across the sky. Never has he been brighter. Never has he been whiter. Demons flee

Michael rises! I fly to Gabriel's side. Together, we unwrap His shroud. Gabriel hands Him new clothes and Michael dresses.

Outside, I hear a roar of anger as Satan follows his henchmen. As he retreats, I hear him growl, "It's over. I have lost. But I'll not be destroyed easily, nor alone. Every man, woman and child on Earth will also … ." I can't hear the rest of his threat, but I shudder.

Michael steps to the door of the cavern. His glory fills the skies with brilliance. His voice, such a melodious voice compared to Satan's growl, peals through the morning air, "I AM the Resurrection and the Life."

The guards stare, paralyzed.

Gabriel stands beside Michael and proclaims in a heraldic voice, "Here is the Majesty of Shalem. Here is the King of Glory." I, along with all of Shalem's angels, bow before Him.

The troopers bolt, racing back to town, carrying a story of a bright whiteness and an earthquake and a living dead man and an empty cavern.

We see Michael, our Commander, is human, yet retains the full glory and the total resplendence of Deity. We sing, like we have never sung before:

"Conquered! You conquered Satan!
Darkness, darkness' power's overthrown!
Evil's mastery's ended!
Michael is our King!
Michael is our Monarch!
Michael is our God!"

Other voices join the chorus. Voices we haven't heard in many orbits. Noah, Jeremiah, Isaiah and Amos. Miriam and Deborah are there—and others too numerous to mention. They, too, have been resurrected. They, too, are bowing low at the feet of Michael. They, too, rejoice at Michael's victory.

Slowly, the joyful celebration ends. Gabriel goes back to Shalem, but I can't take my eyes off of Michael. I wait until a quiet moment and hesitantly fly over to Michael. I don't dare put my arms around Him, but I cover my face and my feet in His presence. He looks over at me and says, "Thank you, Zuriel. I could not have won without your help." Michael puts His arm around my shoulder and squeezes tightly. I burst into tears of joy for my heart overflows with happiness.

* * * *

The great day is here! We all throng about for the victory parade. We know right where it will start. Right here on the Mount of Olives. Right where Michael prayed and wept over Jerusalem. Right where the Garden of Gethsemane witnessed His titanic struggle. This is the starting point for the greatest parade the endless cosmos has ever seen. We can hardly wait! Our excitement intense. Some of us flutter back and forth. Others chatter with uncontrollable joy.

I wonder what His last minutes on Earth will be like. Will He hurry to be away from Earth? Will He be anxious to be away from the place of His humiliation? Will He flee from those ingrates who abandoned Him in Gethsemane? Will He be anxious to be back with us after thirty-three years of misery? Will He now withdraw from them His love and center it on the rest of His creation? After all, Michael has the entire host of Shalem waiting for Him, ready to do His bidding. Will He abandon his Squad? Somehow, I think not.

Suddenly the word sweeps through the cherubs and seraphs like a whirlwind, "Here He comes!" I wait with a deep interest. I see Him leading His Squad. I catch the sound of His voice.

"I will not leave you comfortless. I am with you always. I go to prepare a place for you, so that you may come and be with Me. Peace I leave with you; my peace I give to you. I will be with you, even till the end of the world." Other words of loving assurance fall from His lips, reminding that little Squad of His tender care for them.

I watch Him raise His hands, almost as if He is protecting them from an unseen danger. Beams of light radiate from His form, as He slowly rises from Earth. Thomas, Philip, Thaddeus, Matthew—all of them stare up at Him as He rises higher into the air.

Michael looks at Gabriel and motions towards the watching men. Gabriel nods, catches my eye, beckoning me. We dive straight at the center of the Squad. Sure, we are in a hurry, but we have an eternity to praise Michael and Eli-Mehlek. Pausing just above them, Gabriel says, "Oh, little Squad, don't be troubled. Michael is not gone forever. He will return, just as certainly as He is leaving." I see them relax and big smiles come over their faces. Mission accomplished! We hustle upwards to join the cavalcade.

The singing is already started. We are so exhilarated we can't wait. If you aren't here, you're missing the most magnificent pageant! Everyone is welcoming our King, the One who—by sacrificing Himself—unmasked Satan's lies once and for all. I look back at Earth. I can tell the Squad is hearing our music by the look on their faces. When they go back to Jerusalem, their joy astonishes the people of the city. The citizenry doesn't understand that their King is alive. The residents don't know that their Friend is in Shalem. How can they be sad?

All of Shalem is waiting to welcome Michael home. Those who waited behind decorated the city with festive flowers and palm branches. Rifs and radecs delightedly donate their boughs to decorate walls and windows, gates and gables. Rosahedrons and parynippers rapturously release their flowering fragrance to welcome Michael home again.

It isn't just Michael. He brings the resurrected people with Him. The first ressurectees from Earth join us in the parade. Their voices are heard throughout the company as they sing praises to Him who redeems them from Satan's captivity.

As we near the gates of Shalem, Gabriel signals for quiet. In tones of thrilling jubilation he calls out the challenge:

> "Lift up your heads, O gates
> And be lifted up, O everlasting doors
> The King of Glory shall come in."

The waiting sentinels respond jubilantly:

"Who is this King of Glory?"

They know! They know! They don't have to ask. They just want to hear His name one more time. We love to say it, so we reply:

"Michael! Michael, strong and mighty!
Michael, mighty in battle!"

And Gabriel finishes with:

"Lift up your heads, O gates
Even lift them up, O everlasting doors
And the King of Glory shall come in!"
Again the thrilling challenge,
"Who is this King of glory?"
We answer with exultation!
"Lord Michael
He is the King of Glory!"

The sentinels fling open the gates of Shalem and the parade sweeps into the city amid a burst of ecstatic music. Angelic warrior formations line the streets, their spears form an arch for Michael's honor, their swords glitter a sparkling welcome. The parade's pomp is beyond ecstatic!

We make our way to the Assembly Grounds for an Assembly like no other. There is the Throne, around it the rainbow of promise. All loyal cherubim and seraphim are there. The commanders of the angelic hosts, the Sons of Eli-Mehlek—from across the far-flung cosmos—are all there to welcome Michael, the Reuniter. All are eager to celebrate His triumph and to glorify their King.

But first, Michael raises His hands for silence. He turns to Eli-Mehlek and points to the scars on His head, His hands, His feet, His shredded back, His punctured side. He presents to Eli-Mehlek the first fruits of His sacrifice—the people He is bringing back with Him. In melodious tones that peal across the vast expanses of the stars, He says, "It is finished. I have done your will, Eli-Mehlek. If justice is satisfied, I crave these to be with Me here in Shalem."

The voice of Eli-Mehlek proclaims—in resonating diction—the words that thrill our hearts. "Justice is satisfied! All people, all humans who choose Michael's way are accepted by Me. These resurrectees, these cherubs, these seraphs, these Sons of Eli-Mehlek are witnesses of My acceptance. This handful of people is the promise, the earnest that multitudes more will reunite with Us."

As Eli-Mehlek's arms encircle Michael, Ruash surrounds them and Gabriel signals, "Let all worship Him!"

With joy unutterable, rulers and principalities and powers acknowledge the supremacy of Michael. Trillions of angels bow before Him. From one side of the Assembly Bowl to the other comes echoing and reechoing:

"Michael, Michael, Michael!
To You we give power and adoration
To our King we give honor and glory!"

More songs of triumph mingle with the music from angel harps. Shalem overflows with joy and praise. Love conquers. The contrite Rebels reunite with the Universe. Shalem rings with voices in lofty strains proclaiming:

"Blessing
And honor
And glory
And power
Be unto Him
Forever and ever!"

* * * *

The Assembly lasts a long time. Finally, I make my way back to the mansion. I sit and ponder the events of the last little while.

Another of Satan's charges against Deity is disproved. Satan said that Deity cannot save Rebel humans and still be a just Deity. Yet, Deity found a way to save the Rebels without sacrificing Its justice. Deity sacrificed Itself instead. Deity, in the person of Michael, took the punishment that justice demanded, the punishment that humans could not survive.

Michael's love broke the rebellion. Satan's destruction is assured and, along with him, Sotai will be destroyed. For the first time, I think of both Satan and Sotai without a pang in my heart. They had both been there—destroying Michael. They had both been there jubilantly gloating over Michael's destruction.

This is neither the Lucifer nor the Sotai I had known and loved. Satan's charges against Michael are shown to be false. His lies are exposed. His own choices changed him so much that he could destroy Michael and delight in so doing. He lost Shalem; he lost his friends; he lost everything, including my love for him. I only hope that his destruction won't be too painful.

Soon, and none too soon, the rebellion will be gone and peace will return to the Universe.

* * * *

A minor, but significant, change ensues after Michael's destruction. Prior to that time, the Rebel angels would occasionally come and visit in Shalem. Satan would occasionally attend the meetings of the Sons of Eli-Mehlek. Now, we loyal angels decide their visitations will end. Deity concurs. To that end, gold cards are issued to all residents of Shalem. We post guards at the gates to check the credentials of any entering angel. Those without are turned away. At first, the Rebels screech, yowl, caterwaul as they are turned away, but eventually the demons quit attempting to gain entrance.

No longer can they annoy us in our own homes. No longer can they pester us on the streets. No longer can Satan accuse a Loyalist in the meetings. While the battle for Earth rages even more fiercely than ever, tranquility reigns in Shalem.

Results

Gabriel is extremely busy. I join him and together we fly to Earth. We revisit the rooftop room where Michael ate with His little Squad. The entire group is there, along with many more. Never have I seen any group pray as that Squad is praying. Others loved Deity, but this little Squad walked and talked with Michael. They know Michael and remember His promises to them. I know something wonderful is going to happen. This little Squad will tell the entire world about Michael.

Nathaniel walks up to James. "James, I have something on my heart."

"What's that Nathaniel?"

"James, I … I … I was so angry at you and John. Remember when your mother asked if you could sit on Michael's right and left hands? If I had been carrying a sword, I would have destroyed you. Forgive me, James for my anger."

"Nathaniel, of course I forgive you. When I think of Michael, nailed on the cross, asking Eli-Mehlek to forgive those who are killing Him … ." James pauses and wipes some tears from his eyes. Nathaniel shares a shred of cloth with James. "How, Nathaniel, could I not forgive you? And can you forgive me for trying to wangle the best positions ahead of you."

"Of course, James. Now we can forget about this. Isn't that wonderful?"

Other similar conversations are occurring all around the room. It is wonderful as they settle all the old grievances. We feel the unity of the Squad in that rooftop room. We see they are indeed following Michael's command to "Love one another as I have loved you." The more united they become, the more excited we become. We know what they can do if they are united as one heart.

On Pentecost, the Squad is praying, when suddenly a glorious light appears on each of the Squad and all the others in the Seder room. It is Ruash. Michael sent the Comforter! The Squad marches out of that rooftop room right down to the temple.

They excitedly talk to everyone they meet. They converse with each audience member in their own language. Peter stands, giving a powerful oration. It is obvious that many hearts are deeply moved. Some three thousand people instantly leave the ranks of the Rebels. This is just the beginning of great things.

Ruash invests all of the Squad, both the original members and the newcomers, with His power. Jerusalem is stirred to its very roots. Exiled Jews from all parts of the Roman Empire hear the story of Michael, believe, and become Loyalists. They leave Jerusalem singing joyfully. Along the way, they tell the story of Michael's amazing sacrifice. The good news spreads across the entire Roman Empire. Everywhere people hear the story and wonder if it is true.

The unity of heart remains for a long time, several orbits. Daily, hundreds, if not thousands, join the Squad. And among them, not a quarrel is heard. Oh, yes, there are things that need to be solved, but when hearts are united, solutions are easy to find.

Often, I visit this person or guide one of the Squad to a seeker for truth. Other angels are also engaged in this Ruash-led work. Gabriel and I often compare notes about what we have been doing. I am surprised to find our work is almost identical. Gabriel tells me my work pleases Eli-Mehlek. When I slip back to Shalem for a quick visit, Michael asks me about His friends and tells me He appreciates my work.

As time goes by, the unity fades. People begin to seek their own will, instead of Eli-Mehlek's will. Persecution begins to happen to the enlarged Squad. Some turn their backs on Michael and return to the Rebel cause. Those who killed Michael begin a general slaughter of the Squad. Finally, most Squad members leave Jerusalem and flee to other parts of the Roman Empire.

Reckoning

Now that Satan's lies are unmasked, I see many things I haven't seen before. His government is not based on a better idea, but is based on worshiping Satan himself. Those who do not venerate him are targeted for much misery.

Satan, as he promised, works tirelessly to tangle mankind in his rebellion. Earth falls into an era when men are little better than animals.

We work just as tirelessly as Satan and his minions, but mankind seems bent on turning away from Eli-Mehlek, away from Michael, away from Ruash. Millions of Loyalists are killed in wars and persecutions. Some who claim to be Loyalists deceive the people and promulgate Satan's lies about Deity. Wars are fought about who is more pious. Threats, coercions, persecutions attempt to compel people to follow Satan's way.

Finally, in Eli-Mehlek's own time, things begin to change. Slowly, slowly, some of the hearts of mankind begin to turn toward Deity. Some of the old truths that Michael taught are rediscovered. Ruash works mightily on Earth.

Thousands, perhaps millions, of mankind turn their hearts toward Michael. It isn't easy. Many of them pay for their belief with their lives. The blood of the exterminated becomes seed sprouting and growing more believers than there had been before.

Science and the arts bloom. Medical discoveries cascade one after the other. There is a renaissance of music, sculpture, art work of every manner, literature. Remarkable scientific discoveries open doors closed for many orbits—some of them hidden since Noah's flood.

Mankind regains a lost dignity, Freedoms are won that mankind has not enjoyed since Michael's time.

Gabriel is busier than ever; I am often pressed into service as his assistant. When we have a chance to talk, he tells me things I'd never thought about. Even before Decision Day, he understood many things. So it is an exciting day for me when I mention something that causes Gabriel to pause and say, "Zuriel, that is really a wonderful observation. I've never thought about that before."

* * * *

Gabriel calls Jokim and me to go with him for a conference with Michael.

"Jokim, Zuriel, Gabriel, there are three important messages to deliver to Earthlings. Jokim, I want you to take the first one. Zuriel, I want you to take the second one. Gabriel, I want you to take the third one."

We all agree.

"Jokim, your message is the foundation for the other two. The time is coming to end the rebellion. The time is come to go over the records of every human being. As Eli-Mehlek always requires, the decision about each human must be openly and fairly decided.

Three vital messages are to be given to Earth before Michael returns

---

"Soon, I will begin to open the books and make the decision about every human being who ever lived. Mankind must be warned about this coming investigation adjudicating everyone's behavior, actions, motives.

"Jokim, that is your message. 'The hour of adjudication is come.'"

"Okay," Jokim answers, "Here is how I think we can proceed."

Michael and Jokim make a plan about how the warning could be given. With that, Jokim is off, winging his way to Earth. His message is given with power. Hundreds of human messengers begin echoing his warning.

Within just a couple of years, the entire world is aroused. Millions of people begin to believe and turn their hearts to Michael.

"Zuriel, your message will follow Jokim's. It is a solemn warning. Tell them that if any man worships Satan or adopts his ways or even acts as if he believes Satan, Eli-Mehlek will be forced to annihilate him. Go, Zuriel, warn the world. Use a similar plan to Jokim's."

I leave as Michael turns to Gabriel. I follow Jokim's pattern and soon the world is hearing the warning about worshipping Satan.

After I gave my warning to the world, Gabriel sounds his warning. His message is simple. "Loyalists who love Michael, separate yourselves from the Rebels."

During these warning messages, Satan works harder than ever to blind people's minds to the messages from Eli-Mehlek. Each message is received and believed by a smaller number of people. In the meantime, Michael is in the Temple in Shalem. He works before Eli-Mehlek's throne, weighing each human being's record, judging each man, woman and child to see who is safe to bring to Shalem. It is a sobering time. Earth's Decision Day lasts for several orbits. I think of the humans whom I guarded. I wonder if any of them will be judged worthy. I am glad I don't have to make those decisions. Michael is the perfect One. He knows what it is like to be a human because He is a human. He also knows what Deity knows because He is Deity. And I know, from watching Him, Michael is perfectly fair to all.

Rescue

As Michael nears the end of His investigation, the whole Earth is in turmoil. I am reminded of three other times of intense agitation. One was just before Noah's flood. All of humanity, except Noah and his family, were dissolute, rebellious, steeped in evil, vile beyond belief. There was the night of wild abandon, just before Sodom was destroyed. There was the day Michael was crucified. Now the entire population of Earth is acting like that bloodthirsty mob.

Eli-Mehlek sends six angels to deliver increasingly potent blights to Earth. They are reminiscent of the ten scourges of Egypt and are Eli-Mehlek's last plea to the rebellious humans of Earth. A pandemic of sores attacks all Rebels. The entire ocean turns to something appearing to be blood. All marine life is destroyed. Next, all fresh water, lakes, rivers, wells also turn to the same bloody substance as the sea. The sun scorches Earth, blackening all things living. I think this would awaken some of the Rebels, but they unanimously curse profanely. Not one of them changes loyalties. Darkness reigns in various places, a darkness so dark it is painful, causing the Rebels to gnash their teeth, gnawing their tongues as they do. The pain incenses Mankind, causing war—a global war, far more devastating than any of the previous world wars. I am resigned that none of the Rebels will change loyalties. They continue to choose rebellion.

Throughout these epidemics, there remains a small band of Loyalists, people who are true to Eli-Mehlek. They exhibit the same calmness Michael displayed during His trial. They struggle in a similar manner to Michael's struggle in the Garden. They wrestle with Eli-Mehlek with the same intensity as Michael wrestled.

Slowly, regretfully, Ruash begins leaving Earth. Eli-Mehlek is permitting Satan to demonstrate, one last time, his character and the principles of his government—this time without any restrictions from Eli-Mehlek.

With this freedom, I expect Satan will do something dramatic. It's happening. He gathers his devils around him and with great pomposity and much rejoicing, he appears on Earth. Gently, graciously, he steps off his cloud and walks the streets of Earth. His voice is the same sweet voice I've always known. He still appears as the lovely angel he once was. If I didn't know him—and Michael—better, I might believe his words.

"Hello, people of Earth. I am your Lord. I've come to alleviate all the blights. I've come to resolve all the conflicts you've been having. I've come to bring peace to all. Come, worship me—there will be peace, safety, health, wealth. Eli-Mehlek is using these epidemics to punish Earth because of your rebellion. Come to me and repent of your rebellion."

Satan walks on Earth, promising peace, garnering praises from almost all

Almost all of mankind welcomes Satan and shouts his praises. From Asia to Africa, through the Americas, Europe, Australia— his promises of peace, relief, safety are welcomed and cheered. Nations and colonies, continents and islands proclaim him their king and their lord. Prince and president, commoner and counselor, pope and preacher bow low before him. The rebellion is nearly worldwide.

The only challenge to his global adoration is the small band of Loyalists. They stoutly resist, flatly stating that this is not their king—they worship Michael. Instead of bowing at Satan's feet, they use scripture to show that this is an imposter. Unmitigated execration is hurled at them. They waver not.

Satan's maledictions thunder worldwide, "It is this group of dissidents who are preventing the amity I promised. All must make me first in their hearts. These nonconformists must be removed, if they will not accept me as their lord. I am greatly displeased with them. My blessings cannot come until all worship me."

The response is swift and unambiguous. All the governments of the world enact laws enforcing unity. All must comply. Those who refuse will have their homes, vehicles, clothes, furniture, food confiscated. In addition, deniers are blocked from buying or selling anything. At first, it is believed these economic sanctions will persuade them. Great is the test these Loyalists are given. Ragged, homeless, destitute they cling to Eli-Mehlek's promise that their bread and water are certain.

As the world realizes these economic sanctions will not persuade Michael's Loyalists, further laws are enacted specifying a day when they should be destroyed. Sweetly, Satan urges the world on with its demonic work. In the various Houses of Government, his vibrant voice rings as he declaims, "We must have unity. They are destroying that unity. Without harmony, peace is impossible. Unanimity of all mankind is the only way we can have the peace I long to bring to Earth. Without their concurrence, we must eliminate them from Earth."

Michael's Loyalists echo the centuries-old words of the three cousins standing in front of Chad many centuries before. "Michael is able to deliver us, if He chooses to. And if He doesn't deliver us, we would rather be destroyed than rebel against Him." As the Loyalists petition Deity, all of their faces distort with strain. Their test is nearly as intense as was Michael's in Gethsemane.

Just before the appointed day, Michael stands up in the Temple. All Shalem hears His words. "He that is repentant, let him be repentant still. He that is rebellious, let him be rebellious still." His investigation finished, Earth's final Decision Day passes. Michael examined each life. He made the decision about each person. He knows which ones chose loyalty and which ones chose rebellion.

As Michael leaves the Temple, we begin to gather for the trip. Michael promised to return to Earth and we will go along with Him. Every angel in Shalem is a part of Michael's retinue. With us all away, it is totally silent in Shalem. We are solemn, yet intense. We know the consequences of this trip. Every humanoid will either be destroyed or return with us.

On Earth, trouble doubles and redoubles. Some of the Loyalists languish in prison cells. Others hide in the forested mountains. A few are secreted in the deserts. A handful melted into the jungle. All plead for Eli-Mehlek's protection.

It is the worst trouble ever seen anywhere in the Universe. How can it be any other way with Satan as Earth's acknowledged king, with every government yielding control to Satan? Earth appears to be falling apart. Satan is still promising eternal peace and happiness forever, but only if his wishes are carried out and the Loyalist's extermination is complete.

As Michael rises, His voice trumpets, "It is done." His words reverberate throughout the Universe as the seventh angel delivers the last blight. No one is safe anywhere. Murderous rioters roam without restraint. When two mobs meet, they fight like opposing armies. Earthquakes, fires, floods, tornadoes, hurricanes batter the proud cities of Earth. Huge hailstones fall from clear skies, obliterating great swaths of civilization.

In all parts of Earth, bands of heavily armed men prepare to slaughter the Loyalists. Sotai and all the rest of the Rebel angels are everywhere, goading them to complete their evil work. With mocking jeers, derisive shouts, hissing expletives accompanying them, they start to charge. Sotai and his cohorts cheer every plan, every curse.

Suddenly darkness falls upon Earth. Eli-Mehlek's rainbow wraps the Loyalists. The armed mobs stop, fear entering their hearts. The sun bursts through the darkness. There is a violent earthquake; the welkin snaps open and closed.

Eli-Mehlek speaks! His voice rumbles throughout the Universe. It cuts through the turmoil on Earth. The Loyalists hear it, "Be faithful, Michael is coming, be faithful." We depart for Earth.

It is none too soon. Without us, the Loyalists will be killed by Satan's Rebels. The trip is one of those solemn, yet happy times. We sorrow over the billions and billions of humans who will be left behind, destroyed. Yet we are more than ready to see the end of Earth's rebellion.

I remember Michael's words to Caiaphas, *Someday, you will see Me coming in the clouds of heaven.* As we flash to Earth, I look to see if they are there. They are, all of them, resurrected—Caiaphas, Annas, Pilate, Herod, all of their lackeys. There is the one who spit on Him. There is the one who wove the thorny crown. There is the one who spiked Him to the cross. Almost in unison, they cry, "He is Deity! He is Michael! We are lost!"

Michael reveals His glory. Every being on Earth sees Him as He sits on His cloud. Murderous hands drop. Cursing lips still. Anger turns to fear. The Rebels take one look at Michael and know the truth. As they realize they chose the wrong king, their agony knows no bounds. They made their choice, just as Satan made his choice so many eons ago. Seeking to hide from Michael's glory, they find any hole into which they can crawl, begging the rocks to cover them. Nature complies as Earth seethes with a terrible ferocity. Mountains collapse, burying cities built among them. Islands sink with their inhabitants. Tsunamis rage, flooding coastal cities. The massive destruction leaves not one Rebel human alive.

In the midst of this chaos and upheaval, Michael speaks, "Awake, all of My friends. Rise and come to be with Me where I am." Instantly, the graves of all of Michael's sleeping Loyalists open! From stately Adam and Eve to Abraham and Isaac, James and John, Peter and Paul,—all of the martyrs—destroyed in Michael's service—many children and infants, all sleeping Loyalists respond to the call of their King. They are no longer feeble and emaciated, but are changed into a freshness that is more than youth, vigor that will never fade. We angels swoop to greet them and escort them to Michael. We tenderly, with tears of joy, deliver the babies to their mothers and fathers, as they rise to join Michael.

Michael speaks again, "Come, My loyal followers. Come and join us!" With that, we present the emancipated Loyalists to Michael, immortal humans who will never be destroyed and who will live with us forever!

After everyone is settled, we head back to Shalem. We aren't in any hurry. This is Michael's victory parade, with all of His trophies, the plunder and spoils of war. We visit some of the other worlds who welcome Michael's people with open arms. It is a thrilling trip, one that will never be equaled.

As Shalem comes into view, the parade stops while Michael presents each with his crown, his new name, his royal regalia. This is appropriate. Michael, The King, is their Brother. As Gabriel raises his hands, the angelic choir joins with human voices and sings a song defying description. Each heart is rapturous with unutterable thrills, an eagerness giving the music a distinctly unique quality as they sing Michael's praises.

Michael leads us to the gates of pearl and we all enter Shalem. Michael moves in front of the throne, welcoming each person to their new home. "The war is over … .This is your inheritance … .Welcome to Shalem!"

A delighted cry peals over the throng.

"Adam!" Michael exclaims, "Come! Eve! Come!"

"Michael!" Adam, so tall and noble, nearly as tall as Michael, hastens to where Michael is standing. Eve follows, just slightly behind. The jubilant throng parts to watch. It is Adam—the father of all humans. It is

The Loyalists receive their royal regalia—a crown, white clothing, a new regal name

Eve—she whose rebellion started Earth on its perilous course. It is Adam; it is Eve—who, before their rebellion, had talked face to face with Michael. It is this very Adam and Eve, welcomed back into Deity's arms.

As Michael holds out His arms to welcome him, Adam takes one look at the scars in Michael's hands and falls at His feet, crying, "Where I failed, You conquered. Michael! Worthy is Michael! You were destroyed for me." Tenderly, Michael lifts him to his feet and with His arm around his shoulders, points to all the people who quit being rebellious and became Loyalists. He shows them some things he and Eve have not seen for ages and eons. There is the Tree of Life and their son Abel.

Adam can bear no more. He takes his regal crown and hurls it at Michael's feet. "Oh, Michael," he cries again, "Oh, Michael, how could

You suffer for us?" With awe and adoration and with tears streaming down his face, he wraps his arms around Michael.

* * * *

I weep, too. But this time, they are tears of happiness. I remember my grief when Adam and Eve rebelled. But Michael! Michael restored all things better than they had been. It has neither been cheap nor easy. Always, always there will be with us the reminders of what the restoration cost. Every time anyone sees the scars—in Michael's hands, in Michael's feet, in Michael's side, on Michael's head—we will be reminded of the unfathomable cost of the restoration. Oh, all glory to Michael!

As Eli-Mehlek looks over the restored throng, He is satisfied with the price He paid. And Michael, observing all of His brothers and sisters, is satisfied with the results of His suffering.

* * * *

Many interesting things happen while we are in Shalem. Oh, don't get me wrong, all the people Michael chose to restore are Loyal people, who love Michael with all their hearts. But they have so much to learn or should I say, unlearn. The words of the roeh keep coming to my mind; they are growing up like calves in a barn—not only physically, but mentally, socially and spiritually.

As I fly around Shalem doing my assigned duties, I watch Michael visiting the former Rebels in their homes, often with an angel or two.

I'm cleaning Gabriel's mansion as Michael comes in. "Hi Michael! It's good to see you."

"Hi Zuriel, you always keep Gabriel's mansion looking pleasant. I love to visit here."

"Thank you, Michael. I'm glad to be a simple mansionkeeper again!"

"Would you be willing to go visit Uriah with me?"

"Of course. What do we need to do there?"

"Well, as you saw, Uriah was a warrior—a very good warrior, proficient in the art of destroying the enemies of The People. On Earth, those abilities were needed and were within My will. Up here, those talents are obsolete and he needs to learn some new skills.

"As a warrior, he died in battle, with combat blood lust surging through his veins. It will take some work to help him unlearn his warrior mentality and learn the gentler outlook he needs here in Shalem.

"I'd like you to help with tutoring him in Shalem's style. He has so much to learn in order to adapt to Our way."

Jokim and I began spending much time with Uriah. We enjoyed working with him, teaching him how to soften his heart and how to love everyone. He made an almost complete adjustment in his thinking. Ruash assisted us as Uriah learned new skills.

We are there when David comes to visit. It is the first time he's met Uriah since arriving in Shalem. Gabriel is with David.

After the initial greetings, David asks if he may sit.

"Sure David. You look nervous."

"Uh, Uriah, I've got to talk to you."

"Sure David, what about?"

"Well, Uriah, there's … there's … uh … there's something I need to tell you," David stammers.

"David, what's the matter? I've never seen you like this before."

"Oh, Uriah, I would do anything to be able to ignore it, but I cannot. I must confess. I need to admit my evil. I need to tell you … ."

Slowly, the story reveals itself. Bathsheba … the rooftop … the fatal order … all the wretched details. As it dawns on Uriah what David is telling him, the old warrior mentality rises to the surface. He sits there; his eyes, blazing with anger, are fixed on David.

Jokim, Gabriel and I worry. *Is Uriah ready for this?*

"Do I understand you correctly? You stole my wife and had me killed?" Uriah snaps.

"Yes," David's voice is almost inaudible; he knows his guilt.

Uriah sits there staring at David; the tension in the room is palpable. Slowly, Uriah relaxes, his eyes gradually become calm, though the pain of the betrayal still shows, his words deliberate. "On Earth, David, I would have destroyed you for such an offense. I would have cut you to pieces for your crime. You know the culture would have sanctioned your destruction."

David nods, miserable, guilty.

"Yet, here in Shalem, I have learned much I never knew on Earth. David, I am also a great Rebel. I should not be here in Shalem. The only reason I'm here is because Michael's destruction covers my evil.

"It occurs to me that Michael's destruction can cover your evil as well as it can cover my evil.

"David, I forgive you because Michael has forgiven me."

Jokim, Gabriel and I exchange glances of relief. David is forgiven. The mess he made is cleaned up. We want to happily throw our arms around Uriah, but the old warrior is not quite ready for such a demonstration, yet.

Michael slips into the room, gently going directly to Uriah and David. He wraps an arm around each of them; *somehow He can do so.* "How about we take a walk?"

They exit, Michael still in the middle.

Uriah and David are all right. They resume their interrupted friendship, making it even stronger than before.

I don't know how many times this little scene is repeated between two people, husbands and wives, brothers, sisters, friends, who, on Earth, hurt each other so deeply and the damage remains unrepaired, the wrong unforgiven. Michael never loses His patience with them, even those, like Uriah, who have a hard time yielding to His way. Eventually, each of them forgives the other and the reconciliation is complete. Slowly, slowly, the rough spots smooth out, the former Rebels indeed become Sons of Eli-Mehlek and brothers of Michael.

* * * *

After a few orbits, Eli-Mehlek and Michael have an Assembly of the Loyalists. We angels attend also. At this Assembly, Michael outlines some of the work the Loyalists are to do while in Shalem. I am not surprised; Deity is still being fair to the Rebels.

"My brothers and sisters, there is important work we must do. Sadly, there are Rebels who chose to remain Rebels. They stand condemned of treason against the Deity. However, their punishment must be determined by the sentencing jury. This will not be a pleasant task. All members of the sentencing jury will be close to the Rebel being sentenced. The person may be your father, your mother, your husband, your wife, your child, your best friend. The sentencing jury's task is to determine the appropriate punishment for that person's rebellion. We will grieve together—we'll have as many wipes as needed—as we decide what is a just and fair sentence and record it in the books."

Michael outlines the process. As each Rebel is discussed, those who knew that Rebel will sit on the sentencing jury. After comparing the Rebel's life record with Eli-Mehlek's law, Michael and the rest of the jury will determine a unanimous sentence.

The first one is Cain. Michael, along with Adam and Eve, Abel and all the rest of those who knew Cain personally comprise the jury to decide his punishment. The angels who guarded Cain and those who recorded his history also sit on his jury.

On and on it continues. It takes many orbits, because the process is painstakingly thorough and exact. Finally, each human's sentence is recorded. The process moves on to the Rebel angels. We angels comprise a larger portion of these juries, because we know them better than the humans did.

As this work went on, I thought about how Eli-Mehlek handled the rebellion from the very first. He was always totally fair. He gave Satan a chance to prove his accusations. He gave each angel a chance to decide for himself. He gave each human the freedom to make his own choices. He did not arbitrarily choose a punishment for anyone, but allowed each of us to participate. No one could ever think Eli-Mehlek has been unfair, even in the sentencing process.

When Sotai's name comes up, I am there. As we read his history, I begin to see what he is. Satan indeed made him a vice-regent of his kingdom. No other Rebel angel is as vitriolic as Sotai. His excitable nature takes him to extremes where other Rebels venture not. We read for a long time. After a long deliberation, we sentence him to a punishment greater than any other Rebel angel.

The last Rebel to be sentenced is Satan. Everyone in Shalem, angelic and human, sits on his jury. During the reading, Job exclaims, "So, that's what happened!" He hadn't known the cause of his troubles until then. Not only do we consider Satan's rebellion, but we also include all the rebellious acts he caused Michael's repentant brothers and sisters to perpetrate. At the end of the deliberation, Satan's punishment is far greater even than Sotai's punishment.

* * * *

We are so busy in Shalem that I haven't gone near Earth for a long time. When I do, I am shocked by what I see. The entire planet is obliterated. Nothing is growing anymore. The cities are destroyed. Uprooted trees and broken rocks are strewn in an ugly mishmash. Where there had been great mountains, now there are chasms. Some buildings are upside down and others shattered to bits. Earth is so totally ruined it almost reminds me of how Earth was before Ruash brought light to it.

This is Satan's kingdom—or what is left of it. He lives there along with his Rebel angels. Michael said Satan will be here for a thousand years. I watch from afar. Since Satan can't leave Earth, he cannot annoy the Loyalists and the Rebels are all destroyed. With no one to harass, he can do nothing, except think about his part in the rebellion, what he's done to his kingdom, his future. I overhear him talking to Sotai.

"So this is your better way, huh, Satan?" Sotai snarls.

"Quiet, you insignificant piece of refuse," Satan roars back. "No one made you follow me. Stupidity is not allowed. You're free to go now."

"Perfect freedom and liberty is what angels deserve!" Sotai snaps back.

"Quiet! Quiet, gnashgab, quiet, I say." Satan is as angry as he could be. "You're just as useless as rubber lips on a woodpecker. Some are 'has-beens'—you're a 'never-was.' You're beneath my contempt."

Satan approaches Sotai, threatening vociferously. I fear for Sotai's life. Yet he seems to know just how far he can push Satan and get away with it. Perhaps he's pushed like this many times before.

Other Rebel angels join Sotai, quoting Satan's words back to him. He is most miserable. He calls them all lubberworts. I feel sorry for him, yet he chose his own way and now is reaping the consequences.

For many millennia, he made Earth tremble. He killed indiscriminately and destroyed anything good. Now, with nothing left to do, he thinks about what will come, what will happen. His agony knows no bounds. His terror causes him to tremble.

I quietly wing my way back to Shalem, my mind ruminating over what I had seen on Earth. I shudder, thinking I could be one of the Rebel angels, stuck in the midst of the destruction, hatred, formlessness, anger.

Back in Shalem, Michael's brothers and sisters are singing a song about being free of Satan's molestations. It is so good to be rid of the Archrebel and his insurgent minions. The rejoicing of the restored Rebels—forever Loyalists—is a distinct contrast to Satan's misery.

I might have been the last one to choose Michael's side, but I made the right choice on Decision Day.

Rebellion Annihilated

A short time after Satan's sentence is recorded, Michael calls me and asks me to find Gabriel. He has a message for Gabriel. I turn to leave. Michael speaks "No, Zuriel, I'll have you do this task. Please organize My People and the angels with their commanders. It is time to move Eli-Mehlek's capital to Earth. Contact Jokim and he will help you choose the legions and their commanders."

My head is spinning. I, a simple mansionkeeper, am in charge of organizing the biggest move in the history of the Universe! I seek Jokim and together we coordinate the entire relocation.

Michael is first. The city, with all the Loyalists in it, follows. We angels, in full battle gear, surround the city. Satan and his evil followers will challenge our intrusion.

As we near Earth, Michael's majesty blazes with a terrible glory. His voice calls with trumpet-like clarity, "Awake, Rebels, awake! The final judgment day is here."

Billions and billions of Rebels come from their graves. The contrast between them and Michael's people is harsh. The Rebels come out of their graves just as they went into their graves, including the blind, the deaf, the lame. The Rebels take one look at Michael and exclaim, "It is He, Divinity in humanity." It is not a loving acknowledgment. Their rebellion is unabated. I see some of my protégées in the crowd.

Michael descends upon the Mount of Olives, the very spot where He ascended some three millennia before. As His feet touch the peak, it splits wide open, making a gigantic expanse which becomes the resting place for the city. Michael leads the angelic legions into the city.

Satan looks over the billions and billions of his people with growing excitement. Here are his subjects—his army! Quickly, he organizes his angels and they organize his troops. He stands in front of them and the deceptive words that come from his mouth don't surprise me.

"I am the prince of this world ... My inheritance snatched from me! I am your king and the one who brought you out of your graves. Follow me and we will defeat this cruel tyrant." He walks among his people and makes the lame to walk and the weak strong. He inspires each with his own demonic passion.

"Look! See the vast numbers on our side. They haven't nearly as many on Their side. We can take the city, destroy the inhabitants and live in peace and happiness forever."

Among his subjects are antediluvian giants, great generals who never lost a battle, experienced engineers who designed some of the most powerful weapons of all time, cruel kings whose approach caused vast cities to tremble. Together, these wily wicked warriors make their plans to take the city. They build their weaponry. They organize themselves into companies and divisions. When all is ready, Satan gives the signal to advance. His army clambers over Earth's broken and crumbled surface, appearing as army ants as far as the eye can see. Their war engines grind over ruins and rubble heaps. He leads the way as they approach the city, his rebellion unabated.

Michael commands, "Close the gates."

Satan's hordes surround the city.

Michael appears above the city, sitting on His throne. The majesty of Michael is indescribable. The power of Michael is beyond depiction. The glory of Eli-Mehlek encircles Him, filling the city, spilling beyond the city, flooding Earth with unbelievable brilliance. In the presence of all assembled humanity and with the rest of creation watching, Michael is crowned as The King of the Universe. Eli-Mehlek performs the coronation, investing Michael with infinite power. All living creatures, other than the Rebels outside the gates, acknowledge Michael as The King.

Michael's people sing:

> Announce Angels, who wing the cosmos
> Proclaim Messengers, who ply the Universe
> Let cherub shout it from the apogee
> And seraph call out from the perigee

> Let trumpets sound
> Let cymbals echo
> Let supernovae observe
> Let galaxies watch

For Michael shall go forth
For Eli-Mehlek shall rise up
Witness, O waiting heavens
Behold, O expectant cosmos

The judgment is set
The books are opened
The verdict is decided
The sentence is declared

Now Deity will perform its strange act
Now Majesty will execute its strange deed
For rebellion shall end
And defiance shall cease.

After His investiture as King, Michael conducts the Rebel's trial. Without saying a word, He opens the record books and looks at the Rebels. His look burns into each Rebel's soul, causing each to become acutely aware of the nature of his or her rebellion. Each Rebel understands how they rebelled and where their rebellion led them. Each Rebel recognizes the enormous price Deity paid—and which they rejected—to regain their loyalty. Each Rebel grasps that he or she is personally unfit for eternity and that an endless life with Michael—in His presence always—would only be torture, not happiness, for him or her.

In the welkin over Michael's head appears a breathtaking view of Michael's cross, and the scenes —from the beginning of the rebellion to the end—slowly move across the backdrop of the welkin. The scenes start with Lucifer's initial rebellion ... Decision Day in Shalem ... the day Adam and Eve rebelled ... Michael's birth in a filthy cow shanty ... His baptism ... the life He lived, full of love and mercy ... that awful night in Gethsemane ... His mercy as they mock Him ... beat Him ... crucified Him ... His resurrection and return to Shalem ... Satan murdering the Loyalists ... the day Satan impersonated Michael ... and finally, the rescue of the Loyalists!

Neither Rebel nor Loyalist, cherub nor seraph, demon nor devil can turn their eyes away from the scene. The Loyalists in the city, with deep awe and solemnity, remove their crowns and throw them at Michael's feet as they cry out, "He was destroyed for me." Satan stands mesmerized at the sight. Sotai is, for once, speechless, no longer rodomont. Each Rebel sees his place in the scenes.

The evidence is complete. The Rebels stand convicted of treason against Deity. Admitting that no excuse can be found for their rebellion, they plead guilty. The sentence of eternal destruction is confirmed. All living creatures in the Universe, including the Rebels themselves, acknowledge the justness of their sentences. The weight of the evidence compels the Rebels to acknowledge Michael as the rightful King of the Universe. There is no more brashness in Sotai as he kneels and concedes his surrender.

> *The evidence is complete— Satan, Sotai and the Rebels all acknowledge Deity's supremacy. They acknowledge how Deity's unbounded love and justice dictate the Rebel's destruction is fairer than continued living in misery. All confess their sentence is deserved. Satan's character remains unchanged*

I watch the myriad of emotions on Satan's face as he remembers how he had once been a Covering Cherub. How he had been peaceful and content until he instigated the rebellion. He sees how his choices exclude him from the City, from eternity. He recognizes that the purity of Shalem would be cruelty to his very soul. He comprehends Eli-Mehlek's love and compassion dictate his destruction. Finally, compelled by the evidence, Satan does what he vowed he would never do. He, too, kneels in surrender, confessing that Michael is King and his sentence is just.

With all the sordid details of Satan's rebellion revealed, the entire Universe—Loyalists and Rebels, angels and demons, humans and Sons of Eli-Mehlek—acknowledges, "Deity is just and merciful. Deity is vindicated of all charges against It. Deity is the rightful Sovereign of the Universe."

Suddenly, Satan leaps to his feet, in a wild frenzy, bellowing, "No, do not surrender! We can still overcome." He attempts to rally his troops around him, but they cease to acknowledge his kingship. The rest of the Rebels all see that further defiance is useless. They recognize the deceptions with which Satan lured them; their fury is roused. They attack Satan with ferocity unequaled.

At last, no one acknowledges his dominion, not even Sotai.

At last, Satan's power is totally broken.

At last, The Rebellion is over.

At last, the cleansing fire falls.

I watch the conflagration with tears welling up in my eyes. I think one last time about the Lucifer and the Sotai I had once known. I wonder what might have been had they made different choices. I am not the only one weeping for the last time. Michael visits each weeping one and with gentle tenderness wipes away the tears.

Through my tears, I hear Eli-Mehlek groaning a dirgeful song. Michael wept over Jerusalem with a lament beyond understanding. I hear that same lament as the cleansing inferno consumes the rebellious.

> O Lucifer, Lucifer, Star-of-the-morning
> How can I let you go?
> You were perfect in all your ways
> Until rebellion was found in you
> You were the highest of My creation
> But you desired to be like Deity
> O Lucifer, Lucifer, Star-of-the-morning
> How can I let you go?

As established by the jury's sentence, Satan is the last one to finish burning. He is the Archrebel, the instigator of all rebellion, the one with the most guilt. But as I hear Eli-Mehlek's lament, I see again how hard it is for Deity to destroy Satan. I marvel once more at the infinite love of Deity. I am astonished that the Archrebel—the cause of all the troubles of the rebellion—should be one for whom Deity unabashedly grieves.

Rebellion—and all who embrace it—are gone. Our rejoicing fills Shalem. Never again will rebellion return

The fire purifies Earth and purges the Universe. Rebellion is gone. The demands of justice are met. The sentence for treason against Deity is executed.

After the ground cools, Michael opens the gates of the city. With a solemn joy, we all go out and walk on the surface of Earth. Our joy is not in the destruction of the Rebels, but in the destruction of rebellion and all of its vile results.

We rejoice that at last—at long last—the great insurrection is over! We rejoice that once again the entire Universe is loyal to Deity. We rejoice at the unity of heart displaying itself throughout creation. We rejoice because love and joy pulse through Eli-Mehlek's creation as if from one heart. We rejoice that from Michael flows vitality and exhilaration to all His creation throughout all regions of deepest space. We rejoice that the entirety of creation acknowledges the obvious: Deity's infinite love stands unmatched, anywhere in the entire Universe!

So it is with a delight beyond all measure that we sing:

Awake, O Cherub
Arise, O Seraph
To Our God, we will sing
To Eli-Mehlek, we will praise

For He is mighty
For He is strong
For His right arm upholds the heavens
And His left hand restrains the Universe

In His strength, He holds the flower
And in His might, He carries the babe
For His strength is His mercy
And His might is His grace

Our God is merciful
Our God is gracious
Our God is faithful
Our God is Eli-Mehlek

Merciful
Gracious
Faithful
Honorable
Eli-Mehlek is our God

Hear, O Seraph
Give ear, O Cherub
Go, search it in the heavens
Go, seek it in the cosmos
To right column

From left column

No Seraph can see another god
No Cherub can find another deus
None can observe another creator
There is none other like Him

In His strength He holds the flower
And in His might He carries the babe
For His strength is His mercy
And His might is His grace

Our God is merciful
Our God is gracious
Our God is faithful
Our God is Eli-Mehlek

Tell it in the heavens
Speak it past the quasars
Proclaim it among the stars
Voice it through the galaxies

Spread it abroad, you who sail the Universe
Fling it abroad, you who cruise the cosmos

Tell it
Say it
Sing it
Shout it

Shout it
Our God is Eli-Mehlek

Glossary

A note about the vocabulary used in this book…

The prepublication reviewer's most consistent comments were about this book's vocabulary. The vocabulary used is the result of much consideration and careful thought. This vocabulary was chosen because the angels are much more intelligent than we are and so the vocabulary they use is more advanced. Also, they use the language of heaven and an attempt was made to portray that by using uncommon words or creating names of things in Shalem.

Since many of these words are uncommon or author-created, this Glossary is included to help the reader understand how a word is used in this book. As with many English words, a word may also have other meanings.

These word meanings hold the key to understanding the nuances of actions and emotions portrayed in this book.

The Author

Note: Author created words are in **bold italics.**

Word	Meaning
abase	voluntarily lower in rank or prestige
abate	reduce in intensity or amount
abdicate	to relinquish power
abhor	to hate
abi	my father, more like daddy
abode	dwelling, home
abutting	adjoining, bordering
accede	agree, approve or give consent
acerbic	caustic in temper or mood
acquiescence	passive submission or compliance

adherent	supporter of a particular cause or leader
agape	with an open mouth, in a state of shock or wonder
agog	full of intense excitement
akimbo	disheveled, haphazard looking
Alexandria	a city in Egypt
allay	calm or relieve
alleviate	relieve
amethyst	purple quartz gemstone
amity	friendliness and peaceful relations
animant	any animal in general
annihilate	to destroy completely
antagonist	an adversary or opponent
antediluvian	pre-flood person
antiphony	responsive alternation in singing
apogee	highest, greatest, furthest from center
apostasy	act of abandoning the faith
appall	to shock or disgust
appraise	to evaluate the work of
apprehend	to arrest or seize; to understand
aquians	fish or sea animals
arborant	a plant used to make an arbor
Arcturus	a giant star
armaments	weapons
arrogate	seize without having a claim to
arum	gold
ashen	deathly pale, grayish
atwitter	nervous and excited
atwizzle	spinning, whirling
auklet	small northern bird
auricle	ear
aver	verify and prove to be true
avians	birds
awestricken	filled with awe
azure	blue color like a clear sky

beatifically	with a blissful appearance
bedlam	uproar, confusion
befuddled	confused, perplexed
beguiled	deceived
beleaguer	to trouble or harass
berm	sloping mound
Betelgeuse	a red supergiant star
bevy	group
blanch	remove the color from
blasé	not caring about
bombast	pompous, pretentious speech
braggadocio	arrogant, empty boasting
canny	clever, shrewd
capitulate	surrender, yield
captor	one who captured something
caterwaul	yowl loudly
cavalcade	procession
celebrant	one who celebrates
chalice	large drinking cup with a stem and a base
charioteer	one who drives a chariot
charlatan	one who makes showy but fake claims of ability
chasten	to discipline by punishment or suffering
chastise	to inflict punishment on
chide	to voice disapproval
choleric	having unreasonable, excessive anger
chrysolite	a green jewel
clamber	to climb awkwardly
coercion	act of dominating by force
cogitate	ponder, think deeply
coiffure	hair style
conclave	private gathering to discuss issues
concurrence	cooperation, agreement
confections	sweet foods
confederate	united and banded together

confiscate	seize with authority
conflagration	large destructive fire
confound	to frustrate or put to shame
conic	having the form of a cone
consign	transfer to another's care
contrite	showing sorrow and remorse
coronate	crown as king
countermand	an order cancelling a previous order
courtiers	persons in a royal court
covet	to desire what belongs to another
crag	steep, rugged rock
culpable	deserving guilt for a wrong
debauchery	unrestrained self-indulgent behavior
declaim	speak formally and dramatically
defection	to reject or abandon a loyalty
defile	contaminate, make unclean
dehydrate	to lose body water and fluids
deific	pertaining to Deity
demesne	territory
denunciate	accuse publicly, betray
deportment	outward behavior
depravity	state of moral corruption
derisive	ridiculing, showing contempt
desertion	act of abandoning
Deus	God
discomfiture	state of embarrassment and perplexity
dishevel	disarrange, mess up
dispirit	deprive of enthusiasm
disquiet	without peace and tranquility
dissolute	lacking restraint
dither	to be nervous or indecisive
dousing	a drenching with water
dwindle	decrease in size or number
earnest	a pledge

egotist	one with an exaggerated sense of self importance
elation	state of feeling joy or pride
emancipated	freed
emissary	a governmental agent or representative
enamor	to captivate or charm
encrust	decorate richly, embellish
engulf	overwhelm, surround
ennui	boredom, dissatisfaction
enraptured	filled with delight and wonder
ensue	take place afterwards
envisage	imagine, make mental picture
eon	immeasurably long period of time
epithet	insulting statement
equanimity	emotional calmness
equivocate	be deliberately unclear
espy	to catch sight of
evict	expel
exasperate	frustrate, anger by repeated annoyance
execrate	curse someone, call someone vile, loathsome
executioner	one who puts another to death
expiation	freedom from guilt
fabricate	invent, create
feign	to pretend
festoon	decorate with a garland, lei, or hanging ribbon
flabbergast	amaze or astonish someone totally
flagitious	extremely wicked, cruel, vicious
fliod	a flower in Shalem
flout	to treat with contempt
fractious	irritable, unruly
frond	palm leaf
fructi	fruits
furlong	a measure of distance
furrowed	grooved
gape	to be open-mouthed

garble	jumble speech unintentionally
genuflect	to bend at the knee as a sign of respect
gesticulate	use arms or hands to make gestures
gimlet	small tool for boring holes
gnashgab	someone always complaining
goad	to force to act
gopher wood	the pre-flood wood used to construct the ark
gossamer	light and delicate substance
grovel	plead, beg, cower
gunwale	the upper edge of the sides of a boat
haughty	conspicuously proud and scornful
henchmen	trusted followers
heraldry	royal regalia, usually quite beautiful
hesed	great mercy
hillock	small hill
histrionic	reacting in an overdramatic, theatrical way
hominoid	a human being
humanoid	a human being
hyaline	a sea
imbecilic	weak minded, foolish
imbue	to permeate and influence
impersonation	act of taking the identity of someone else
imperturbable	not easily excited
implements	tools or utensils
imprecation	curse, swearing, blasphemy
impregnable	cannot be captured or opened by force
inaugurate	to bring into an office with a ceremony
incantation	repeated chant, often used in religious rituals
incinerate	burn to ashes
inferno	raging fire
ingrate	ungrateful person
instigate	action to provoke or incite
insubordinate	person who disobeys authority
interpose	to put one's self between

intoxicant	an alcoholic beverage
intuit	know or understand by insight
inveigle	charm or entice to do something
investiture	act of being inaugurated, sworn-in
irked	annoyed and irritated
jabber	to chatter
jeer	to mock or taunt
jubilation	expression of great joy
lackey	servant
languorous	slow, unhurried
largesse	generosity
liege	a superior to whom loyalty is due
lilian	a flower in Shalem
lintel	horizontal beam above door or window
livid	very angry, enraged
loathsome	disgusting, painful
lubberwort	a lethargic, fuzzy-minded person
magnificence	quality of being noble in character
malcontent	one who bears a grudge
malediction	a curse or slander
malevolence	intense hatred
matriculate	enroll in a school
melzar	a steward
mesmerize	hypnotize
millennium	one thousand years
minion	a servile follower, devotee
morose	sullen, gloomy
naught	nothingness
Nepherlim	someplace out in the Universe
Neptorium	someplace out in the Universe
nonplused	baffled, perplexed
obeisance	a bow of deference or respect
obeise	to bow to someone of importance
obligee	someone obligated to another

obliterate	to remove from existence or memory
ochre	earthy, red color
opulence	great wealth and abundance
orb	star, planet, moon, etc.
Orion	a real constellation in a galaxy
oscillate	move rhythmically, like a wave
page	attendant to a person of rank
Pargoland	some place out in the Universe
parynipper	a flower in Shalem
pauper	very poor person
penitence	regret, sorrow for sin or wrongdoing
perigee	the opposite of apogee
permeate	to penetrate and spread throughout
persimple	a flower in Shalem
perturbation	a disturbed or troubled state
perversion	action that is corrupt or morally wrong
phalanx	a moving group in tight formation
pique	a fit of resentment
pithoi	ancient pottery storage jar
plies	continuously offers and supplies
pomposity	self-important behavior
ponderously	clumsily because of size and weight
presumptuous	taking liberties without asking
privation	hardship, deprivation, poverty
promulgate	proclaim
protuberance	something that sticks out
provender	food
purported	alleged, not proven
quasar	an astronomical body emitting huge energies
quaver	speak with a trembling voice
rabble	a disorderly crowd of people
radec	a tree in Shalem
rankle	to irritate, anger, or make bitter
rapturous	ecstatic

recompense	to give compensation for
recount	to relate in detail
refurbish	make like new
regalia	emblems of royalty
relent	to let up or give in
remonstrance	forceful protest, often by a superior
renascence	rebirth or revival of lost skills, culture, a renaissance
repast	a wonderful meal, food
repentant	sorrowful for misdeeds
reproof	criticism, rebuke
repudiate	to reject as being untrue
repugnant	disgusting, revolting, nauseating
rescind	to make void an order or command
resplendence	the quality of splendor
resurrectees	people who have been resurrected
retinue	traveling attendants of an important person
retrocede	to go back
revelry	noisy partying
revile	to abuse verbally
rif	a tree in Shalem
riffle	go through quickly or snappily
rill	channel made by a small stream
rivulet	small stream
rodomont	be boasting, pretentious
roeh	a prophet
roil	stir up or agitate, to move turbulently
rosahedron	a flower in Shalem
rovings	random, aimless wanderings
ruminate	go over and over again in the mind
rumormongering	spreading rumors
sage	a wise person
sagely	wisely
salver	a tray for serving food
sarsen	rock

scabbard	sheath for a sword
scintillate	sparkle, flash
scoff	to show contempt
scoff-law	one who disrespects and breaks the law
sear	burn, scorch, or mark
secrete	to hide
seder	the Passover meal
seethe	move violently
sepia	deep reddish brown
sere	dry, withered
shanty	poorly built shelter, hovel
Sheol	the Hebrew word for *a grave*.
signet	official ring for sealing documents
skulk	to move in a secretive way
smidgen	a small amount
smugness	condition of being very satisfied with oneself
sonorous	resonant with deep, clear, loud tones
startlement	action of suddenly being alarmed
strod	a measure of distance in Shalem
stupefied	dazed, nearly unconsciousness
stylus	instrument used to write or mark
suave	superficially smooth and sophisticated
supersede	replace with something newer
supplant	take the place of, substitute for, replace
swindler	one who obtains things by fraud or deceit
taunt	to challenge in an insulting way
totter	move unsteadily, about to fall
trenchant	severe, caustic
trice	an instant of time
trounce	to punish severely or defeat
twit	to taunt or ridicule
umbrage	resentment at an imagined insult
unabated	at full force or strength
unanimity	agreement

uncontestable	cannot be argued against
underling	a subordinate
unfathomable	impossible to understand
unfetter	release, free
unmitigated	unrelieved, continuing
unrepentant	not feeling sorrow or regret
untainted	not bad or spoiled, without blemish
vacuous	lacking content or intelligence
vegetali	vegetation
vehemence	intensity, fervor, passion
venerate	to honor and show respect
vertex	the highest point
vertices	plural of *vertex*
vex	to irritate and annoy
virtuous	pure, morally good
vitriolic	expressing bitter hatred
voluble	characterized by rapid speech
wadi	occasional water runoff channel
waffle	continually changing one's mind
waft	move lightly as on the wind
waggle	sway from side to side
wangle	a devious method of accomplishing something
welkin	the sky, upper air
wend	to twist or travel
winsome	pleasing, lighthearted
witticism	clever remark
worshipee	one who is worshiped
wrangle	argue noisily, obtain by loud argument
wretch	miserably unhappy person
yodel	alternate the natural and falsetto voices
zephyr	gentle breeze

TEACH Services, Inc.

P U B L I S H I N G

We invite you to view the complete
selection of titles we publish at:
www.TEACHServices.com

We encourage you to write us
with your thoughts about this,
or any other book we publish at:
info@TEACHServices.com

TEACH Services' titles may be purchased in
bulk quantities for educational, fund-raising,
business, or promotional use.
bulksales@TEACHServices.com

Finally, if you are interested in seeing
your own book in print, please contact us at:
publishing@TEACHServices.com

We are happy to review your manuscript at no charge.